'I am afraid we shall have to act a little,' said Patience.

'Far be it from me to cast a blight on your happy dream, but since Florence is known to be engaged to me, it is hardly likely that any gentleman, who can call himself such, will make advances to her.'

'No, I know.'

Charles groaned.

'Do not tell me, I am cast for the villain of the piece. I can feel it in my bones.'

'Well, yes. You must be very stern, very possessive and strict. You will make everyone pity Florence for being tied to someone so much...so much older, she must appear to be frightened of you.' Patience paused as Charles buried his face in his hands. 'You will not mind too much, will you?'

Deverham raised a face suffused with suppressed laughter. 'Mind? Why should I mind? You do not think, perhaps, that people might find this change of character rather sudden?'

LORD DEVERHAM'S CHOICE

Petra Nash

MILLS & BOON LIMITED
ETON HOUSE   18-24 PARADISE ROAD
RICHMOND   SURREY   TW9 1SR

*First published in Great Britain 1989
by Mills & Boon Limited*

© Petra Nash 1989

*Australian copyright 1989
Philippine copyright 1989
This edition 1989*

ISBN 0 263 76644 6

*Set in Times Roman 10½ on 12 pt.
04-8911-70994 C*

Made and printed in Great Britain

CHAPTER ONE

'AND what I have suffered since then, nobody can possibly know!' Lady Winterbourne's voice, though plaintive and, indeed, gentle, carried remarkably well. Her daughter Patience, at that moment engaged in bringing to her mother her daily glass of water, reflected for perhaps the thousandth time, as she crossed the Pump Room, that it would not be her mother's fault if people remained in ignorance of her trials. She also thought that if there was still anyone in Bath or its environs who did not know exactly how much Lady Winterbourne had suffered, and the minutest detail of what had caused her to suffer, that person must be either profoundly deaf or a hermit.

Lady Winterbourne took the glass with her usual sweet, sad smile, and sipped at it distastefully.

'Thank you, dearest. Now you may sit here with me, or go and amuse yourself, just as you wish!'

Since there was no one in the room much under the age of seventy, and the few people who were present were none of them more than mere acquaintances, such gracious permission could afford her little pleasure, and as usual Patience sat near her mother, and attempted to divert herself with her own thoughts. This was no great hardship to her, for she had had plenty of practice, and was accustomed to finding amusement in the minutiae of everyday existence. It was now nearly ninety years since the death of Beau Nash in 1761. The glories of Bath were but a distant memory, and in this year of 1849 even the usual invalids were beginning to forsake it for the more fashionable seaside resorts.

Lady Winterbourne's companion, whom Patience hardly knew, was an elderly lady, correctly if somewhat shabbily dressed, who was obviously enthralled to hear the saga of her ladyship's troubled life. Patience knew the story so well, had heard it told so many times, that she could almost have saved her mother the trouble of repeating it, since she had it word for word by heart. Lost in her thoughts, she would find a phrase here or there seeping its way into her consciousness, and without wishing for it she would find herself repeating the next few sentences. In the expected places the voice dropped to a murmur, as details of an intimate nature were given. Such details were supposed to be unfit for her maidenly ear, although Patience sometimes thought that if she was not old enough, at twenty-six, to hear them, when would she be?

In a moment of irritation she had once asked her mother that very question, to be indignantly informed that she had no delicacy of mind, and that an unmarried woman, of any age, had no business to be thinking of such things.

It was not often that Patience set herself up in opposition to her mother's wishes. It was not that she feared her, nor, it must be regretted, that she felt any great respect for her. Lady Winterbourne was the widow, or, as she preferred to put it, the relict, of a well-to-do baronet, having married him at eighteen, encouraged thereto by her own family, who saw an alliance with a gentleman in possession of a tidy estate and five thousand pounds a year as too good to be passed over. They had been happy enough, and in time she had presented him with a daughter and then, in due course, an heir. A third child and a fourth having died in infancy, Lady Winterbourne was happy to settle on the Winterbourne estate. She was content that the overseeing of house and nursery should provide as much interest and occupation as her not very agile mind needed.

These were, as she often told everyone, the happiest years of her life. Her two children survived their childish ailments with robust ease, and gave her, she said, not a moment's anxiety. Julia, the elder, was taken to London for the Season at the age of seventeen, and dutifully accepted a dull but eminently suitable offer for her hand. Even better, a few years later, Julia's brother Augustus, his mother's darling and heir to his father's estate and title, fell in love with and married the only daughter of a certain Henry Westerham. This gentleman, though a younger son of an impoverished parson, had taken himself to India at an early age and had succeeded in making himself a fortune, all of which would descend to his daughter Florence.

The Winterbournes were naturally delighted for, although the family was not short of money, nobody could fail to view with pleasure the acquisition of so much gold to swell the family coffers. Also, by this time, what Lady Winterbourne insisted on referring to as 'The Trouble' had come upon her.

It had been the year of Augustus's wedding. He had met his Florence when he was only nineteen, two years earlier, and since both he and she were so young it was agreed by their families that they should wait for a year or two before the marriage should take

place. Henry Westerham doted on his only child, and
was not willing to part with her too soon. At length
the date was fixed, and all was set in train for the
great event. Lady Winterbourne had been so much
occupied, so full of happy bustle, that she had dismissed a feeling of unusual lassitude as merely the
result of too much work, and failed to notice other,
more intimate, signs that might have told her what
fate had in store for her. As it was, it was not until
she was well into her fourth month that the awful—
to her—truth dawned on her—that after a lapse of
sixteen years she was again with child.

'You may imagine my feelings!' she was wont to
expostulate to anyone who would listen. The request
was unnecessary: she would leave nothing to her
hearer's imagination. 'There I was, actually in my
forties, with my daughter Julia a mother already, and
finding myself in such a condition! It was positively
shaming! It was as much as I could do to get through
the wedding, and scarcely possible to hide my state,
for skirts, you know, were so very much narrower
then! Naturally, as soon as the festivities were over,
I fled to the country, and hid myself at Winterbourne.'

Long years had accustomed Patience to hear these
words without a pang of sorrow. There had been a
time, when she had been much younger, when she
had realised wistfully that her chief fault among many,
in her mother's eyes, was that her unwelcome presence
had spoiled those wedding celebrations, which should
have been the highlight of Lady Winterbourne's
career, and had cast a shadow of embarrassment and
discomfort over her mother's pleasure. Used as she
was to bearing the blame for so many things, it said
much for her strength of character that she had put

aside the feelings of guilt and shame that her early upbringing had fostered in her. It was of no use, she knew, to tell Mama that she had not asked to be born at all, and that it was hardly her fault that she had made so untimely an appearance in the world. In time, she had taught herself to pity her mother, and even to laugh with some affection at her foibles.

Lady Winterbourne's voice had once again dropped to a murmur. Patience's memory supplied the unheard words. The difficulties and discomforts of the last few months—the concern of the doctors, the worry of Sir John Winterbourne—the confinement, two days, my dear, and the doctors in despair—and finally the appearance, not even of a second son to secure the continuation of the family, but a tiny, weak, sickly daughter. Herself.

'Of course, they never expected her to survive. So very tiny, and so difficult to rear! And her crying, such a little, piercing sound, and going on day and night!' Lady Winterbourne's tone was peevish. Patience thought wryly that her mother made it only too obvious that the best thing that the useless infant could have done would have been to fade tactfully out of life, and allow herself to pass into a merciful oblivion. A kindly and sensible nurse, however, had not only succeeded in rearing her and seeing her through the usual succession of childhood diseases, but had encouraged good health by a sensible regimen of good food and fresh air, with the result that Patience, though slight, was now perfectly strong.

Lady Winterbourne's ill health, however, had dominated the house. Cosseted throughout her pregnancy, and encouraged to think of herself as delicate, she had discovered the joys of an invalid life. A difficult confinement and the fear it engendered in her husband had made it easy for her to continue in the habits she had acquired, and she had only to sigh and complain of mysterious aches and pains to have the entire household in an uproar, and her every wish gratified. What had begun as reasonable care for a comparatively elderly woman undergoing a late pregnancy ended in self-indulgence and hypochondria of the worst sort. The slightest opposition to her wishes led to palpitations and faintness, and a reiteration that she was sure she was not long for the world, and would soon be at rest.

In the event, of course, it had been not she but her husband who had died. Engrossed in her own health, she had not noticed that *his* was failing, and it had come, therefore, as a great shock when he had succumbed to a cold, which turned to pneumonia and carried him off within a week. Her grief was genuine, for she had been fond of him in her way, and he had spared nothing to please her, but she was also angry with him for dying so suddenly, and leaving her alone with a child of two to bring up. Her own income was secured to her by her marriage settlement, and she would have at least fifteen hundred pounds a year for her own use, but so unexpected had Patience's birth been, and so sudden her father's death, that he had not thought to provide for his youngest child. Augustus would inherit both the title and the estate, which was entailed, and Julia had received her own generous settlement when she had married, and hardly expected anything more. Lady Winterbourne saw that, when the time should come that Patience reached a marriageable age, she would be dependent on her brother's generosity to dower her. She herself, naturally, could not be expected to provide for her youngest child out of her own money, since she had no intention of limiting her present comforts to put anything aside for this troublesome daughter.

That was, of course, far in the future, and since Lady Winterbourne did not at that time expect her latest offspring to reach adulthood she did not worry overmuch. A more pressing consideration occurred to her. Since the estate and, more important to her, the house now belonged to Augustus, would he and Florence expect her to leave it, and take up residence in the Dower House? This was a not incommodious mansion set in the grounds of the house itself, but while at the time of her own marriage she had often praised its comfort and convenience, pointing out to all and sundry how much more suitable it was for her own mother-in-law than continued residence in the house, it appeared to her now that she could scarcely be expected to live in such a style. She, who had been used to a large number of huge, lofty rooms, to shrink to a building with but two drawing-rooms, and one of them, as she told her friends, hardly larger than a cupboard!

With her usual determination she had set herself to remain as mistress of the house. Henry Westerham, her daughter-in-law's father, had been ailing for some time, for he had insisted on returning to India to oversee his many interests there. Would it not be wise, Lady Winterbourne had suggested to her son, now Sir Augustus, for him to travel out to India to spend some time helping his father-in-law, and learning how the business was run? After all, in the fullness of time he would inherit it all, through Florence, and how unfortunate if through his own ignorance this great fortune should slip through his fingers.

Augustus, who was not the most intelligent of men, though very good-hearted, listened and agreed. He had some natural curiosity to see more of the world, and the splendours of India were very attractive to him.

'I shall of course stay on here, and be company for dear little Florence while you are away. It will be painful for me, of course, to continue in this place where I was so happy with your father, but I think you know that where my duty lies, there I will be found! It is not to be expected, of course, that the dear child will be able to take over the running of such a house as this all at once, and I shall be only too happy to teach her!' Here she paused to wipe away a sentimental tear, and Augustus took the opportunity to express his gratitude. Lady Winterbourne felt quite sure that during his absence, which must in the course of things be of at least one year's duration, she would be able to establish herself in a position of ascendancy over Florence, and so arrange things that she would not be expected to leave for the Dower House.

Augustus could see no flaw in this plan, but Florence, who though young was very determined, saw quite otherwise.

'What! Stay at home with your mama while you go off to India? I should not dream of such a thing! I do not care to be parted from you for so long, and only think how disappointed poor Papa would be if he were not to see me!'

'But, dearest one, the rigours of the journey! And India, you know—so very unhealthy!'

'Nonsense!' replied Florence robustly. 'As for the rigours of the journey, I should remind you that I have already experienced them. And have you forgotten that India was my home when I was a child? I have never forgotten it, though I came home when I was seven. I should love to see it again, for I remember it as being so beautiful, and, besides, I long to see Papa again, especially now he is not well.'

Augustus continued to look dubious. Florence drew nearer to him and laid a caressing hand on his. She produced her trump card.

'There is another reason, dear. You are too kind and good to speak of it, but the fact is that we have been married nearly two years, and there is as yet no sign of . . . of a happy event.'

Augustus blushed deeply. 'I would never reproach you with that, my dear, and indeed the thought has scarcely crossed my mind. Besides, we have plenty of time.'

She stamped her foot. 'But that is just what we have not got! You will forgive my plain speaking on such a subject, but if you are in India and *I* am here, there is no chance at all that I will have a child! You must remember that you are the head of the family now, and it is important that there should be an heir. With your lands, and Papa's money, our son could become an important man.'

He was much struck by this. It was true that as the only son he owed it to his family to secure the succession. It was also true that life was uncertain. Could he really afford to wait another two years before there was the chance of a child?

The upshot of it was that Florence had her way, and the two of them left for India. Lady Winterbourne told all her acquaintances how heartbroken she was to see them leave, and settled happily back to a life of comfort as the mistress of Winterbourne House.

As it turned out, it was in some ways fortunate that they went when they did. Florence arrived in time to bid farewell to her father, and to weep over his deathbed. His affairs, though sound, were found to be in some confusion, and Augustus applied himself with a will to the task of sorting them out. He found, to his surprise, that he had some aptitude for the business and the time passed swiftly by. Life was easy and gay, the seasons of hot weather were spent in the hills, and neither of them had any great wish to return to the cold and damp of England. Their happiness was crowned, after several years, by the birth of a child. Not an heir, to be sure, but a daughter named Florence, for her mother. They both felt sure that a son would soon follow, and two years later this joyful event occurred. Their happiness was now felt to be complete, and with baby Henry to secure the succession plans were vaguely discussed as to the possibility of returning home. Though both children flourished, it was felt that little Henry was too precious to be risked in the dangerous environment of India. Still, it was the wrong time of year for travelling, and they had always been fortunate in escaping all but the most minor health problems, and somehow the years slipped away until the children were six and four, and back in England Patience had survived her childhood and reached the age of sixteen.

For ever afterwards that birthday marked the end, for Patience, of what had been a surprisingly happy childhood. Largely ignored by her mother, who was wrapped up in her own complaints, she had been fortunate in having a governess who, plain herself, had done her best to give the unprepossessing child the ability to use and enjoy the considerable intelligence that she found, to her joy, in her. Patience had just reached her sixteenth birthday when the news arrived. Augustus, his wife and his son were all dead of the cholera. Only little Florence remained, and she was to be sent back at once from India.

Fate had struck a cruel blow to Lady Winterbourne. She had been sincerely attached to her son, and she could not but remember that she herself had encouraged him to go to that dreadful place. She told herself that he should not have stayed, that she had only meant him to go for a short visit, but the fact remained that, if she had not schemed to stay at Winterbourne House, he and his family might have been alive still. The worst of it was that she had brought about her own ruin. Since the estate was entailed, it must now pass not to Florence, or even to Patience, but to a distant cousin whom she scarcely knew and for whom she had the profoundest dislike. That he would turn her from the house she had not the slightest doubt. For some days her distress made her, for once, really ill, and Patience nursed her with a devotion that won, if not her love, at least her realisation that her daughter could be of great use to her. In her weakness she turned to the strength she could discern in Patience.

The cousin arrived, and he was worse than she had feared. It was true that she would have resented anyone who came to take her son's place in his ancestral home, but the new baronet made no effort to ingratiate himself, or to sympathise. In the past he had been snubbed by Lady Winterbourne, and he had neither forgiven nor forgotten the slight. He walked round the house and the estate with an insolence and a pride that annoyed even Patience, criticising everything that he saw, and after he left sent a curt message through his lawyer that he would appreciate their leaving the house as soon as might be.

Lady Winterbourne was so angry that she forgot her grief.

'Never, never did I think I would live to see the day when I would be turned out of my own house by such a jumped-up little nobody! Cousin he may call himself, but his mother was no more than an attorney's daughter, and *her* mother, I know for a fact, was the daughter of a blacksmith!'

Patience refrained from reminding her that the house was no longer her own, and applied herself to turning her mother's mind to the vexed question of where they were to live.

'I really do not think, Mama, that you could be comfortable or happy in the Dower House.'

'No, indeed. It is not at all what I have been used to.'

'I am afraid, Mama, that wherever you go it will be less than you have been used to, but we will have to find a house somewhere else. Why not in a town? You have often told me how tired you are of living in the country.'

Lady Winterbourne was beginning to look interested.

'London is by far too expensive, unless we go to some horrid, unfashionable place, and I should not like that,' she said peevishly, for she found it hard to accept any new idea that did not come from herself.

'I was not thinking of London, but of somewhere like Bath. It is not nearly so dear, but I believe it is very pretty, and there is good society there so you would not be lonely. Besides, there is your health to consider. There are sure to be good doctors there, and it might well be that the waters would be of some benefit to you. Also, you will remember that Mrs Anstruther said that the shops were almost as good as those of London, and so convenient!'

Lady Winterbourne, who had never outgrown a love of finery and insisted that the strict mourning to which she kept be the prettiest and best of its kind, brightened still further. She was still inclined to be querulous, but so sure was Patience that this was the right thing to do that she carried all before her. A house was looked for, and found, and within a month they were comfortably installed in Gay Street, no more than a short walk from both the Pump Room and the Milsom Street shops. It was true that the hill was steep, but since Lady Winterbourne herself went nowhere on foot, and Patience was used to walking, it was not considered to be a problem. Lady Winterbourne took to her bed on her arrival, and declared that she would never be well enough to leave it again. Nevertheless, after a week, she was tempted downstairs by the very pleasing number of cards that had been left, by the most unexceptionable people, all of whom had called to welcome their distinguished new resident.

It was not long before Lady Winterbourne had established a coterie of friends and acquaintances, most of them people of her own age and inclinations. Patience could only congratulate herself on her success, for beyond complaining perhaps twice or thrice a day that the rooms were too small, and too few, and that Bath was abominably hilly and steep, her mother seemed to have recovered her former pleasure in the enjoyment of her own ill health, with the additional pleasure of recounting her troubles, as now, to every fresh ear that came her way.

Florence, when she arrived, proved to be spoilt and wilful, to a degree that made her beyond the control of her youthful aunt, or her ailing grandmother. She was packed off to a good school, and from there to several others, when her increasing naughtiness made her an unwelcome presence among other, more biddable girls. Now a young lady of striking beauty, with white skin and a cloud of dark curls, she had just been asked to leave her latest seminary, and had arrived back in Bath.

'I think you are rightly named Patience, my dear.'

The low voice startled her from her reverie.

'Mrs Anstruther! I am very pleased to see you! I did not know you were back in Bath.'

'Yes, I returned early. How do you do, Lady Winterbourne? I should like to talk to you, but I see you are occupied, so may I beg for Patience's company for a short walk?' Permission was graciously given, for Mrs Anstruther, an old friend from their days in the country, was an expert in handling her ladyship.

By common consent they forsook the pleasures and temptations of Milsom Street, turning instead towards the Royal Victoria Park. The sun was warm enough to make walking a pleasure, and the surroundings were beautiful at any time of year.

'And how do you go on, my dear? You are not looking as well as I would like to see you. Is it very wearisome?'

It was a relief for Patience to be able to speak her mind freely, and she did not scruple, with such an old friend, to be honest with her.

'It is a little wearing, sometimes. Poor Mama does hark back to the past, and who should blame her, but I sometimes think that if I hear the tale of her sorrows once more I shall scream!'

'It is not to be wondered at. I wonder if she realises how lucky she is to have you. She would have been a lonely woman indeed if she had not had your company and care for the last ten years. Does she not realise that?'

'I think maybe she does. When I have my holiday with Julia each year, she always seems glad to have me return.'

Mrs Anstruther's indignation betrayed her to an unladylike snort.

'Holiday? Where is the holiday in going to look after your sister's children for six weeks, pray?'

Patience had to smile. It was true that poor Julia, given an insufficient amount of money to keep house on and clothe her six children, was only too glad to make use of her younger sister's nimble fingers when she came to stay.

'They did once take me to London,' she offered.

'And what did you do there? Go to parties? Concerts? The theatre? No, I know what you did. You accompanied the children to the dentist, and to see the sights, and all dressed in your old dowdy clothes. How do you ever mean to find a husband that way?'

'I enjoyed myself in London, truly I did. I do not care for fine clothes—at least, not greatly,' she amended wistfully, 'and I am such an insignificant little thing, you know, that they would be quite wasted on me. As for a husband, I do not think of such things. I know Mama has said that I should be married, but I am not the kind of girl that men take notice of, and I should not wish to be married to anyone of whom I could not feel fond. I do not think I shall ever fall in love.'

Mrs Anstruther sighed in despair. Fond as she was of her friend, she had to admit that she was not the kind to make a man pursue her. Small and slender, her figure was neat, and her hands and feet tiny and delicate. Her face was not ugly. There was nothing about it that one could pick out as unfortunate. It was simply that she was unremarkable. Her skin was fine, always pale, and she lacked colour even when she was not tired. Her hair was of an ordinary mid-brown, neatly but plainly arranged. Her greatest beauty, if it might be called such, was to be found in her eyes, which were grey and well fringed with brown lashes. They were not especially large, but they had a softness and a brilliance about them that could have been captivating, had anyone bothered to notice them. Her clothes, too, did nothing to help.

Today, for instance, she wore a plain brown merino walking-dress, its bell-shaped skirt untrimmed by so much as a band of braid or ribbon, and its tightly fitting bodice plain but for a narrow frill of lace at the neck. Mrs Anstruther had been familiar with it for several years, and although it was neat, the good fabric well cared for, it was not precisely eye-catching. Nor did the mantle, an uninspiring shade of drab green, or the simple close-fitting bonnet trimmed with a neat band of matching ribbon, do much to enliven the ensemble. No, thought Mrs Anstruther. Lady Winterbourne was perfectly satisfied with things as they were, with Patience to act as something between a companion and a servant. What would happen to her daughter when she, and her income, died, she had never troubled herself to think.

'My dear,' said Mrs Anstruther, not for the first time, 'you must set your mind to marrying.'

'It is not my mind that must be set, but my future husband's!' responded Patience with a laugh.

'But if anyone should present himself, dear . . . you would not be too demanding, would you? One cannot always expect too much romance out of life, you know, and sometimes it is better to live in civilised friendship with a husband than lonely with none.'

'I hope I should be sensible, but I could not marry someone for whom I had no respect, and at least a little affection. I hope I know better than to look for romance, however. I am not at all the stuff that romances are made of! Florence, on the other hand, is determined that she is. Have you heard of her latest exploit?'

'I had heard that she was back in Bath, but no more than that.'

'She arrived quite unannounced, not two days since, having travelled from Bristol on the train with only her maid for companion. It seems she was detected in corresponding with the brother of one of her friends, and had actually arranged an assignation with him, intending to slip out of school and meet with him.'

'She did not do so?'

'I believe not, so the young man says. But the school will not keep her.'

'I am not surprised. How old is she now?'

'Almost seventeen.'

'Then I suppose she would have had to come back soon anyway. Your mama must be thinking about her come-out?'

'Thinking about it, yes! And then she cries, and says she does not know how she will manage it.'

'There is no problem with money, of course, since the child has a fortune coming to her.'

'Yes, there is no problem there, and she is so very pretty she is sure to be a success. I own I think it would be most entertaining—if only Mama were a little stronger, and Florence were not so...naughty.'

'Naughty! Is this her third, or her fourth school? She is thoroughly spoilt.'

'Yes, I know she is. I own that I sometimes wonder whether I have not failed in my duty with her. If I had been able to do more——'

'My dear Patience, do not be taking another burden on to those slender shoulders of yours! The truth is that Florence was abominably indulged in India when she was a child, and when she lost all her family at once everyone went out of their way to pet her, and caress her, and the result was that she had no discipline whatever. How old were you when she arrived back in England?'

'Sixteen.'

'Precisely, and worn out with nursing your mama, and helping her move to Bath. How could you, a mere child yourself, be expected to take charge of a wilful seven-year-old, forever throwing tantrums, and screaming the house down when she did not get her own way instantly?'

'I suppose you are right. I have certainly never managed to win either her respect or her affection.'

'I have never seen her show respect to anyone and, as for affection, I doubt whether she has any to give. She keeps it all for herself.'

'You are very severe.' Patience spoke sadly, but she could not deny the truth in what was said.

'Where is she now?'

'At home. She and Mama had a violent disagreement this morning and she is sulking in her room. Partly, I think, because she has only schoolgirl dresses to wear, and she is waiting for something much smarter to be made up before she makes her appearance!'

'She is quite beyond any control you or your mama might have. My only advice is that you find a suitable husband for her and let him try. If she were already engaged, before she went to London, you would find life a great deal more comfortable.'

'You could be right.' Patience's expression was thoughtful, and later, when she and Lady Winterbourne were alone that afternoon, she reverted to the subject, and repeated Mrs Anstruther's suggestion.

'But where are we to find such a man? We have no suitable acquaintance here.'

'She is young, and rich, and very beautiful. It should be someone older than she, of course, but not too old. What a pity we may not advertise for a husband!'

'Sometimes, Patience, your levity betrays you into the most indelicate remarks. Advertise, indeed!'

'I beg your pardon, Mama. Not advertise, exactly, but there are ways of letting it be known. A few discreet words among your wide acquaintance here, Mama, might not do any harm.'

'Well, I can think of nothing else to do with her, so I suppose we must try it. Something must be done about her, or I shall go distracted!'

CHAPTER TWO

THE March sun shone brilliantly, warming the air with the promise of approaching spring, but Lord Deverham was frowning as he walked up St James's. A more sensitive man might have let him pass by, but Mr Doublebois was not known for his tact. An inveterate gossip, he could not bear to let the opportunity of acquiring information slip, the more so as he had also some news to impart, the effect of which he wished to see.

'Deverham! I say, Deverham! Do you mean to cut a fellow dead?'

Charles Deverham paused in his swift, long-legged stride and looked round. His face was not welcoming, and while he had obviously not seen the man who hailed him, he would equally obviously have been happy to behave as Doublebois had suggested.

'Well, what is it, Doublebois? I am not much in the mood for conversation, I warn you.'

This was not encouraging, but Doublebois was not to be deterred. He was not particularly acquainted with Deverham, but they had been to the same school, and he flattered himself that he did not easily take offence.

'I have just been talking to Yoxall. D'you know Yoxall? Capital fellow. Keeps as good a stable as any man I know.'

'I do not have the pleasure, though I believe I have heard of him. Hunting man, isn't he?' Deverham's tone was bored, and Doublebois felt he could place little reliance on his continuing with the conversation. He hurried on.

'The thing is, old Yoxall has just come back from Manchester.'

Deverham's frown deepened, and Doublebois was suddenly struck by the fact that he was taller than himself by at least six inches, and considerably broader too. Deverham said nothing, however, and Doublebois continued.

'Yes, from Manchester. It seems he has an elderly aunt lives up there, from whom he has—shall we say, hopes? If not expectations. He says that everyone there is talking of you.'

Deverham looked bored.

'I am surprised that they can find no better subject of conversation.'

'My dear Deverham, you must know that the subject of you and Lady Belinda has reached even there! A beautiful young wife and an elderly husband, and you, an eligible bachelor! It is not to be wondered at.'

'But you are, my dear Doublebois, believe me, you are.' There was a warning note in the quiet voice that Doublebois chose to ignore.

'But everyone is saying——'

'Then everyone had better stop saying. Beginning with you. I do not choose to discuss any lady's name in the open street, and least of all with you.'

'You had better listen to what I have to say, Deverham. Yoxall tells me that your grandfather has heard the tale, and is very angry. He also says that he met your cousin Uffington in Manchester, and looking mighty pleased with himself,' finished

Doublebois with waspish satisfaction. He had the pleasure of seeing that he had finally pierced Lord Deverham's armour. His finely chiselled lips had tightened, and there was a white, angry look on his face.

'I am much obliged to you—and to him also—for taking such an interest in my affairs,' he grated. 'I must beg, however, that you will from now on cease to meddle in what you do not know of, and could not understand if you did. Good day!' He made no move towards Doublebois, but the look on his face was enough to send the other hurrying away, torn between the satisfaction of having scored a hit, and the fear that he might have stirred up a hornet's nest for himself. He hurried to his club, where he downed several large brandies before going off to find further stimulation for the day.

Charles Deverham continued his interrupted walk. In truth he was in no hurry, for he had no particular purpose in view. He simply walked because he had much on his mind, and he could think better while moving. Blind to his surroundings, his steps led him without conscious decision to Hanover Square, and he came to his senses realising that he was almost outside Lady Belinda's house. Damn the woman, for being so indiscreet! There had in truth been no more than a harmless flirtation, such as he had often indulged in, but she was inexperienced, and spoilt, and had thought she had tamed him. She had boasted of her conquest to a few friends, who had been happy to pass on the news that Deverham, who had for so long kept himself free of entanglements, was at last snared.

Doublebois and his detestable crony Yoxall had not, in fact, told him anything that he did not know. In his pocket, at that very moment, reposed a letter from his grandfather, ordering him in no uncertain terms to present himself, and to explain what was behind the disgraceful rumour which he, his grandfather, had heard concerning Charles and a married woman. Deverham was fond of his grandfather, and knew well that he was his heir, but while he owed him respect and duty he was not, he felt, to be ordered about like an errant schoolboy. He had half a mind to send an angry reply to his grandfather, and another half a mind to ignore the letter completely. Not wanting to act while he was still angry, he had set out that morning to walk off some of his ill humour, and to decide on his course of action.

Being honest with himself, he knew that he could not really afford to upset the old man. At the age of thirty Deverham was blessed with outstandingly good looks, and a title, but his income was only moderate. His father, before his death, had diminished the inheritance considerably by a series of ill-judged investments, and only his marriage to the daughter of a wealthy manufacturer had saved him from ruin. His father-in-law had not grudged the money, for he was deeply gratified by the fact that his only daughter had married into the nobility, but he was a shrewd man, and had kept a tight rein on his money otherwise. Charles, his only grandson, was the apple of his eye, but increasing age and infirmity had strengthened his irascible tendencies, and he did not take lightly to being crossed. Nor, brought up as he had been by strictly Nonconformist parents, did he care to make allowances for the rather different moral values obtaining in London society.

So much Charles was prepared to acknowledge, but he knew that he had been angered and hurt by the tone of his grandfather's letter. Heretofore there had always been between them a relationship of trust and respect. Mr Moreton made a generous allowance to his grandson, and would never have dreamed of asking for an accounting of how his money was spent. It had been enough to him that his grandson was a gentleman, moving in the best of society, and that through him he could enjoy vicariously the life of the great. But in this letter there had been an undertone of distrust, and more than a suggestion that he had bought his grandson with his money, and was entitled to know that he had a good bargain. In this Charles detected only too easily the fell hand of his cousin, Alfred Uffington—that Uffington of whom the detestable Doublebois had spoken.

This person—even in his own mind Deverham could not bring himself to refer to him as a gentleman—was Mr Moreton's nephew, the son of his only, and much younger, sister. She had run away at the age of seventeen with an equally young subaltern, and had thereafter been helped on numerous occasions by her brother. Alfred, her son, now worked as an attorney, and had achieved a certain notoriety, if not fame, in that field. He was always very polite to his noble cousin, but Charles knew that he both envied and hated him. When they were younger he had sought to ingratiate himself with his uncle, and had once or twice endeavoured to turn the old man against his grandson. Now Charles had been foolish enough to hand him a most useful weapon on a plate, and he had undoubtedly been using it to its utmost advantage.

Deverham's steps had slowed as he mused, and he paused for a moment to make up his mind.

'Damn it all, I'll have to go,' he said to himself, kicking at the kerb with one elegantly shod foot. 'But I'll not humble myself to him, or let him think that I feel I have done anything to be ashamed of. I'd do without the money, rather.' With that resolve, he resumed his walk.

Above him, Lady Belinda stood at the window of her drawing-room and watched him. As he paused, only a few steps from her front door, she held her breath, and her fingers tightened on the curtain she had eased to one side so as to see him better. When he walked on she bit her lip in vexation. She had lost him, she knew. He would never come back to her now. Her fingers had creased the heavy silk; hardly noticing what she did, she smoothed the folds and, lifting her chin, turned away from the window. Her friend, Mrs Finchdean, looked up at her from her seat by the fire.

'He was not coming here, then?' she asked with spurious sympathy. Lady Belinda mentally cursed herself for having been so foolish as to say that she had seen Deverham outside. On the watch for him, she had recognised him from afar. One could not mistake that tall, broad-shouldered figure, with its crop of well-cut blond hair and lithe walk. She had been so sure—so sure!—that he was coming to her. Of course, he had been very angry with her. She gave a little shiver as she remembered the cold look in his eyes at their last meeting. Of late, she had seen, or thought she had seen, much warmth in those brown eyes, when they rested upon her. She had mistaken that warmth for love and had thrilled, not so much in her own feelings of affection, as in the pleasures of conquest. He, one of the most notoriously independent bachelors, was under her sway. But in her pride she had been rash, and he had looked at her with icy fire in his eyes, and spoken words that even now burned in her memory.

'Oh, no,' she replied with affected carelessness. 'I did not really expect him. As a matter of fact, his attentions were becoming a little too pronounced for my liking, and I was forced to—speak to him about it.'

'Very wise,' said Mrs Finchdean drily. She looked at her friend, who was still biting her lip, hardly knowing that she did so.

'Nothing but misery could have come out of it,' she said with some kindness. 'It is better so.'

'Oh, yes, very much better,' said Lady Belinda with a hysterical little laugh. 'After all, he has scarcely any money of his own, but only what he gets from that odd grandfather of his. A very amusing companion for a while, of course. But there are many more fish in the sea, to be sure!'

'Very true, my dear.'

'I think, if you will excuse me, I will go and lie down. I find I have the headache this morning. London is so very tedious at this time of year, is it not? I declare I shall ask Waltham to take me abroad.' She flounced from the room, and Maria Finchdean sighed. She could only hope that her young friend had learned her lesson.

Lord Deverham wrote a civil reply to his grandfather, informing him that while it was impossible for him to leave London immediately, he would give himself the pleasure of waiting on him in three days. He expressed himself with the utmost politeness, but at the same time made it quite clear that he would not come running at a summons with his tail between his legs. He then spent two days of rising irritation, unable to settle to any occupation and doing his best to quarrel with his friends to relieve his feelings. His friends, of whom he had many, declined to give him that pleasure, for news of his affairs had been spread through London by the incorrigible Doublebois. On the third day he travelled up to Manchester, arriving in time for dinner at the opulent mansion where Simeon Moreton lived in solitary state.

He received a cordial welcome from the butler, with whom he had been on friendly terms since he was a scrubby schoolboy, in trouble for breaking a window in a glasshouse with a cricket ball on one of his visits, on which occasion Nateby had protected him valiantly from the wrath of an irate gardener.

'I'm glad you're here, Master Charles. Master's been proper put about for the last few days, waiting for you to come. I don't know what's afoot, but Mr Alfred has been here, and that means trouble, and always has done, as you know. Fretting, that's what Master's been doing. Not himself at all. I'm working out my notice again, and he's let it go on for two whole weeks! That'll show you.'

Charles frowned.

'Two weeks! You would not really go, would you, Nateby? My grandfather would be lost without you, and you know he does not mean above a quarter of what he says.'

'Bless you, Master Charles, I know that! I should do, after all these years. Why, I lose count of the number of times he's given me notice, aye, and I've given in my notice and all, more than once. It's a game, like. Keeps us on our toes. He'll come round. Like as not he's forgotten all about it.'

'What was it about this time?' Charles grinned. He had always enjoyed the sparring matches between his grandfather and the butler, which were carried on like some kind of stylised war, full of trumpets, alarms and ambushes, but with no blood shed.

'It were a dish of sweetbreads. Fond of sweetbreads, he is, but Master had a touch of a cold, and he said they didn't taste right, and that Cook was trying to give him food poisoning. I told him to try a little more salt in them, to give them more flavour, like, and he threw the dish at me. Got a powerful throw, has Master, for a man of his age. Nearly hit me, he did!' Charles laughed at the expression of admiration in his old crony's face.

'You are as bad as he is, Nateby. I believe you both enjoy yourselves over these battles like a couple of schoolboys.'

'I won't say as how you're wrong, Master Charles. There, now, there's Master's bell. You'd better hurry along and get ready for dinner, you've not too long. Cook's made one of her special apple tarts for you.'

Feeling more and more like a schoolboy, Deverham took the stairs two at a time and found his accustomed room, where his things had been laid out for him by Mrs Nateby, who acted as his grandfather's housekeeper. His toilet might be hurried, but he would make it with care. He prided himself on his smartness, and certainly nobody could have faulted the gleaming white of his linen, the shine on his boots, or the excellent cut of his coat. Though he knew that he and his grandfather would be dining alone, he dressed with as much care as if he were to visit the Palace.

As he walked down the stairs he was conscious of a feeling of—not trepidation, but a certain tension, a girding up of his mental loins. Entering the drawing-room where his grandfather awaited him, he knew that his instincts had been correct. He was vouchsafed, not a warm welcome, nor even the gruff scolding for long absence that failed to disguise a warm welcome, but a grim stare from beneath bushy eyebrows, and silence.

Simeon Moreton was a hard man. Born in poverty, he had worked hard, and thought hard, and achieved at the last a great deal of money and success. He believed in the value of honest dealing, but he expected to be dealt with honestly. Never would he deny to another what he felt was justly due, but, by the same token, he would exact to the last jot what he felt was due to him, and no appeal to kindness or generosity would abate his demands. That there was a kind heart beating beneath that craggy exterior was known to but a few, but Deverham did know it, and he both loved and respected his grandfather. Resolving that he, at least, would not show any resentment, he came forward with his hand held out for the customary handshake, and words of greeting on his lips.

His hand was ignored, and after a moment he let it fall to his side.

'Do you refuse my hand, sir?' he asked in some anger. It was the deepest of insults.

'For the moment, at least, I do.'

'I have done nothing to merit this. You sent for me, and I have come. Do you not now wish to see me?'

'I sent for you three days since.'

This was mere peevishness.

'I am not a child, Grandfather. I have duties, and commitments. I cannot drop all at a moment's notice, for a whim of yours. I have come as early as I could.' This was not precisely true, but Deverham felt that the point should be made. 'Had there been any question of your being ill, or in some such trouble, I should naturally have come with all haste.'

'So you say. You have not been next nor nigh me for three months.'

They both felt that the discussion was declining into mere squabbling. Simeon Moreton drew a deep breath.

'You have duties, you say, and commitments. Commitments to what?'

'To my friends, I suppose, and to my household. And as you know, I am not idle in your interests. I am frequently at your London offices, and you have received my report on them not two weeks since. This I take to be both a duty and a commitment.'

'And your friends?'

Deverham knew very well what was coming.

'Men, and women, of society. People of my own interests, and my own class.'

'Unlike myself.'

Deverham was astonished.

'I cannot see that you have cause to say such a thing to me. When have I ever done or said anything to make you think that I do not hold you in all the affection and esteem that any man can have for his grandparent?'

'It was not so with your father. He was happy enough to take my daughter, and my money, but he would always be looking down his nose at me.'

'My father has been dead for fifteen years. I am not my father. I am at a loss as to why you should have such ideas now. No question of rank has ever risen between us. You are a gentleman, as I am, and that is all there is to say on the subject.'

Simeon Moreton shifted uncomfortably in his seat, and grunted.

'You are in pain, Grandfather. Is it the gout again? You are not well, and that has put these foolish ideas into your head. Put them aside, and give me your hand. We shall forget this.'

He knew well that they had not yet reached the nub of the matter, and was not surprised when he was again rejected. His grandfather turned away his face, and said almost with anguish, 'There is yet another thing, worse than the other. I have been hearing that about you which I would not have expected to hear of any child of mine, or my daughter's.'

'From whom have you heard it?'

'That need not concern you. I have heard it, and that is enough.'

'I think it concerns me very deeply. If it be from my cousin Uffington, you know very well, sir, how much he would like to see me parted from you. It was always so. I will not say that he lies, but he would go far to destroy my name with you.'

'He is an attorney. He knows the laws of man, and of God. He is in London, as you are, and he hears things. Things that happen in society, things that are scandals and bywords among the people you mix with—your friends, as you call them.'

Deverham was too angry to consider his words.

'What he hears, he hears from the outside only, like a servant listening at the door. And, like that servant, he may hear only one side of the story, and a garbled version at that. Would you take his word against mine?'

Simeon's face turned back to him, flushed with anger.

'Aye, you may sneer at him, and look down your aristocratic nose at him—and at me too, for all I know or care. I know what he told me, and that the story was common knowledge in London. Will you deny that you have been—consorting—with a married woman?'

'Consorting? I deny it utterly.'

'But your name has been coupled with hers, and people have talked of it?'

'People talk of many things. It does not make them true. I have been on terms of friendship with Lady Belinda. Perhaps there has been a little flirtation between us, but nothing more. It is the way of the world, Grandfather.'

'The way of the world it may be, but it is not my way. And I would not have it your way, either. I hold myself to blame in this, also. I have given you too much, made it too easy for you. You have lived the life of a gentleman of leisure, and I have been happy to have it so. Until now.'

'You have treated me with the utmost generosity, but I am not entirely a pauper. If I were put to it, I should not be afraid to go out and earn my bread.'

'I will not withdraw my support, for the moment. But I expect you to behave as I would wish.'

'I am not your chattel, Grandfather. You do not buy me.'

The old man did not dislike the sparkle of pride in his grandson's eyes, but he was determined that in this one thing he would have his way.

'I do not speak of buying. But if I am to continue my allowance to you, I want your full assurance that you will no longer be seeing this Lady Belinda.'

'Do you trust my word in this?' Deverham's voice was bitter, and his grandfather saw that he had hurt his feelings.

'Come, boy, don't be testy with me. Will you give her up? There was talk that her husband should divorce her, so that she might come to you. This is not how I would wish you to marry.'

'The talk was lies,' said Deverham wearily. 'There was no question of a separation from Lord Waltham. It is possible that the lady, like you and your informant, read more into what was meant to be a light-hearted flirtation than was really there. If so, the fault is mine, and I have rectified it. I have already informed her that my intentions were far otherwise, and I doubt that she would receive me again, even if I were to visit her.'

'I am much relieved to hear it. And now that is put to rights, we may dine.'

Deverham was still deeply hurt.

'I will not break bread in the house of a gentleman who refuses to take my hand.'

'You are stiff-necked, Grandson,' said Moreton ruefully, but not without some pleasure. 'Comes of being a lord, I suppose. Here's my hand, that I had forgotten I had refused you. Now, may we eat? For I am famished, and I don't doubt you are too.'

Deverham was not one to bear a grudge. He shook his grandfather's hand with warmth, and grinned at him.

'I am indeed, and Nateby has already told me that Cook has made me one of her celebrated apple tarts. What else will she have for my delectation, do you think?'

'Nothing but the best, and plenty of it. Of that you may be sure! I shall suffer for this, no doubt, for as you say my gout has been troubling me again, but it will be worth it. I always say I only get a decent meal when you come down here!'

Knowing his grandfather's liberal ways, and the excellence of his cook, Deverham was inclined to doubt this, and they argued it cheerfully as they went to the dining-room. Like the rest of the house it was sumptuously appointed, and if there was perhaps a shade too much silver, and gold, and velvet, Deverham was too much used to it to cavil. They enjoyed their meal in amity, and parted for the night on good terms, but Deverham could not put from his mind the feeling that his grandfather had been quick to doubt him, and to accept the word of a nephew for whom he had never felt a great deal of affection or esteem. He was getting old, no doubt, and more credulous with age, and Deverham thought it would behove him to tread warily. He was deeply attached to the old man, and it would have been a blow to his heart, even more than to his pocket, if he were to lose his love.

Lord Deverham spent a week with his grandfather before returning to London. During that week his misdemeanours were not mentioned again, and on the surface all remained between them much as it had always been. Nevertheless, Deverham felt that there was a niggling worm of distrust in Mr Moreton's feelings. However one looked at it, Deverham could not deny that there was talk of a liaison between himself and Lady Belinda. The fact that this was not so was not altogether sufficient; he had behaved in such a way as to lay himself open to this kind of gossip. That his cousin Alfred Uffington had exaggerated the amount of the talk was certain, for he would always seek to present Deverham to his grandfather in the worst possible light, but the scandal remained.

Deverham in his pride had said to his grandfather that he did not wish to be beholden to him, and that rather than submit to what he felt to be unreasonable demands he would renounce all claim on the old man, and provide for himself. His own fortune amounted to a beautiful but dilapidated country mansion, and an amount of land that brought him in about a thousand pounds a year, all told. He was not, therefore, a pauper, but it had to be admitted that the generous allowance his grandfather had always made him, and the general expectation that had always been acknowledged that he would one day inherit his grandfather's business interests and fortune, had encouraged him to lead the life of a rich man. It had never been expected, by himself or anyone else, that he would ever have to earn his money by undertaking any kind of profession, and at the age of thirty he was unqualified to do so. The law and the Church, virtually the only professions open to a man of his birth, both required some years of study and, though he had done well at school and at Oxford, his studies had ended when he left those hallowed walls.

Deverham thought ruefully that he could scarcely afford to quarrel with his grandfather. He had no wish to, in any case. The old man had always been good to him, and Deverham was fond of him. His mother he scarcely remembered, for she had died when he was but five. His father, who had survived her by ten years, had mourned her sincerely. He admitted freely that he had been driven to marry her by acute financial need, but her gentleness and goodness had won his heart, and for her sake he had never opposed Simeon Moreton's wish to see as much as possible of his only grandchild.

Deverham had therefore spent many weeks of his childhood with his grandfather. As he grew up, he became aware that, try as he might, his father was unable to see the older man as anything but a vulgar manufacturer. He appreciated his generosity, his honesty, and the fact that he was good to his boy, but he was unable to look beyond the rough exterior to the man within. Deverham, with the eyes of a child, learned to love and to respect his grandfather for what he was, and was not offended by lapses in grammar, accent, or, occasionally and regrettably, table manners.

Back in the metropolis, Deverham resolved that he would lead a reformed life. Hitherto he, like most of his class, had lived mainly for pleasure. A good horse, shooting in the autumn and hunting in the winter, a good dinner, his club, visits to the theatre or the opera, and above all the company of pretty, witty women, had made up the parameters of his existence. Handsome, intelligent, young, with rich expectations, and single, the combination of these things had been enough to have the pick of each season's young ladies ready to abase themselves at his feet. Courted by the mamas, sighed over by the daughters, he took all this as his due. He learned early the dangers of appearing too interested in any one young woman— he was not yet ready to make his choice—and therefore in the last few years had been more inclined to pay his court to a series of complaisant young wives. None of this had ever gone beyond what any but the strictest and most possessive of husbands could have sanctioned: a dance, a murmured word, the discreet pressure of a hand, a gift of flowers. It was all very harmless, and very entertaining.

Now, all at once, these entertainments were closed to him. Since Lady Belinda's careless indiscretions, the world was likely to set a far closer watch on him. Any sign of interest in another man's wife would be liable to set the tongues wagging again, and he could not allow that to happen. What, he wondered, was he to do? This was the only life he knew. He took to spending a great deal more time at his club, and to drinking rather more than was good for him.

Within a week a letter arrived from his grandfather. Charles read it, re-read it, and smiled to himself. 'My dear grandson,' it opened, in the unformed, schoolboy hand that Simeon Moreton had never gone beyond.

> You have been much on my mind since your visit, and it comes to me that it is time that you were wed. At your age, my lad, it is time to settle down, and start raising little lads and lasses of your own.
>
> You know I would not want to interfere with your life (Charles gave a wry smile at this point)

but I have to tell you that I have heard of a young woman, by chance, and it do seem to me that she would make a good wife for you. Not that I would want you to marry money, for there's plenty here, but for all that a bride with a bit of a fortune put by is better than one with none.

The girl I would tell you of is the granddaughter of old Sir John Winterbourne. You wouldn't remember him, and I never knew him. He died more than twenty years ago. His son's dead too, poor fellow, but he was married to the daughter of Henry Westerham, the nabob, and this girl has inherited all that fortune. She lives with her grandmother in Bath, and I heard of her from the General— you know he lives there now. It seems she's just left school, and pretty as a picture. Somehow, when I read that, I thought all at once of you, and how happy I would be to see you settled with such a bride. Not that I would wish to bring any pressure on you, but I think if I knew you were married to her I would not worry about you any more. At any rate, there's nothing to stop you running down to Bath and casting an eye over her.

That's all I have to say, then. Hoping this finds you, as it leaves me, well,

Your affect. grandfather, Simeon Moreton.

CHAPTER THREE

IN BATH, Patience was wondering why she had ever complained of finding her existence boring. Calm and boredom suddenly seemed the most desirable states on earth. Lady Winterbourne had reacted to stress in her most predictable way, and had retired to bed, declaring herself so unwell as to be unable to lift her head from her pillow. She had enough energy, however, to demand that Patience visit her several times a day, to listen to her complaints and her fears. It was, perhaps, fortunate that the task of spreading the news of Florence's availability, as it were, was left to Patience, for Lady Winterbourne might well have undone them all by appearing unnaturally eager to be rid of her beautiful charge. As it was, Patience contented herself with whispering to a few well-connected, garrulous acquaintances that Florence would soon be making her début in polite society, and that with her looks and her fortune she could be expected to be besieged by suitors.

Florence herself was, for the moment at least, behaving remarkably well. Patience had tried appealing to her better nature, pointing out that she owed a duty to her grandmother, who was elderly and infirm, and that she could not always have things just as she wished them. Florence simply stared at her blankly, and reiterated her demand to be taken to London as soon as possible. Sighing, Patience used the wiles that she had learned in dealing with her mother's ways.

She pointed out to Florence that if Lady Winterbourne should become seriously ill, it was quite possible that she might die, and then she, Florence, would be doomed to wearing black for some time, and it would be completely ineligible for her to be presented to society. Since Lady Winterbourne herself was always prophesying her imminent demise, Florence became thoughtful at this. She knew well that black did not become her, though it made her skin look very white. Patience then assured her somewhat mendaciously that she thought it would soon be possible to go to London, but that Florence must show them all that she was capable of behaving suitably. Florence looked thoughtful again.

The upshot was that Florence, who was no mean actress, took on the role of the ladylike schoolgirl and, in public at least, almost revelled in it. Patience would not have been surprised if people had recognised the act for what it was, but on the contrary the sight of her beautiful young niece, eyes modestly downcast, obediently following her aunt around, and replying when spoken to in a soft, shy voice, seemed to drive all memory of her previous behaviour from people's minds. In private she continued to be demanding and inclined to tantrums, but Patience was thankful that at least she need not blush in public. Only she wondered how long the act would continue to entertain her niece. Long enough, she hoped.

It was now more than a week since she had first put her careful word out as to her niece. Already, she was happy to see, an unusual number of grandsons, nephews, godsons and cousins were displaying an unusual solicitude for their elderly relatives, and paying them long-deferred visits. This was in itself a help, for it distracted Florence's mind from the pleasures of London, and made her more willing to stay in Bath. One flaw in her plan had occurred to Patience, however, and she made shift to warn her niece of possible dangers.

'You should be aware, my dear Florence,' she said carefully one afternoon, as they sat over their luncheon, 'that girls like you, fortunate enough to be blessed with a great deal of money, are likely to attract the attention of gentlemen who are only interested in getting their hands on that money.'

'Fortune-hunters, you mean?' said Florence with her mouth full. Patience reflected how unfair it was that such behaviour, which in anyone else would have revolted her, in Florence merely seemed rather charming and childish. 'Oh, yes, I know all about them.'

'I am sure you do, but now that you are in my charge—and that of your grandmama, of course—I would not wish to be lacking in care for you. I am sure you are far too wise to be taken in by such a man,' she continued earnestly and untruthfully, 'but you should be a little on your guard.'

'I think you may leave me alone for that, Aunt Patience. I am not such a fool as to be taken in. Of course, it might be that I should wish to marry a man of little fortune, but I do not think so. Unless he had a very grand title, of course. I will not sell myself so cheap, you may be sure.'

Patience winced at the lack of delicacy in her niece's language, but knew that it would be pointless, and indeed harmful, to remonstrate. She had noticed that Florence was wise enough to moderate the way that she spoke when she was in company, and that at least was something to be thankful for.

'I am thankful for that,' she said, struggling successfully to keep an acid tone from her voice. 'All I would warn you against is such clandestine behaviour as you were nearly betrayed into in Bristol. In general, you know, a gentleman whose intentions towards you are good will never ask you to go anywhere with him without the permission of your friends.'

'Oh, I know that! I told him I had!'

Patience blinked at her.

'You did what, Flo?'

'Told him that I had permission. Captain Curbridge was really quite stuffy, you know. He even wanted to come here to ask Grandmama's permission to speak to me!'

'I think the better of him for that, at any rate.'

'Yes, and so you should, for he is a very fine gentleman. Of course, he loved me to distraction, but I did not dislike him. Only,' she said wistfully, 'I should like to see a bit more of the world, first. I cannot throw myself away on the first man who asks me.'

Patience had a pang of conscience at what she was aiming to do, which she rigorously suppressed.

'If he does indeed love you, he will not mind waiting for you.'

'No, but I am not sure that I can wait for him. His ship has sailed now, you know, for I had a letter from Lavinia, his sister, only yesterday. I told him that, if I married him, he must leave the sea, for I could not endure to have my husband absent from me for so much of the year.'

Patience regarded her with fascination.

'And what did he say?'

'Oh, he agreed, of course,' said her niece blithely.

'You were asking a great deal, for a man to give up a profession that is dear to him, as I suppose it is.'

'Yes, he dearly loves the sea. But then, you see, he would have *me*,' remarked Florence sublimely.

'That, of course, would make up for all, Flo, dear.' Again Patience was careful to keep her tone bland, but her niece looked at her crossly.

'I know you mean to be disagreeable. Let me tell you, he said that if he had me, nothing else on earth would matter to him. So there!'

The childish note made Patience laugh.

'My dear Flo! The things you say!'

'I wish you would not keep calling me Flo,' said Florence pettishly. 'I cannot bear it. Indeed, I am not so very satisfied with the name Florence, now.'

'It was your dear mama's name, and your papa particularly wished you to have it.'

'Yes, I know, but I hardly remember her, or him either. Besides, it reminds me of that dreary book that Mr Dickens brought out last year. I read it at school, because all the girls were reading it, and I thought it perfectly horrid!'

'I cannot say I agree with you,' said Patience mildly. 'I thought it a very fine book.'

'Well, some of it was all right, I suppose. I am sure I cried for half an hour when little Paul died. But as for that Florence Dombey, so wonderfully good, and so feeble! How she could have brought herself, coming from the sort of home that she did, to marry that— that nobody!'

Patience suggested mildly that it was a case of true love.

'But how can any young lady bring herself to love such a man—or boy, I suppose one could call him? It is past my comprehension. And living with that dreadful old sea captain, or whatever he was. Ugh!' She shuddered, and Patience reflected with resignation that the finer points of Mr Dickens's work were likely to pass her niece by. All the same, there was some consolation in the thought that Florence was not likely to abandon all for some mad freak of love, in a whirl of romantic passion brought about by the reading of too many novels.

The following morning Lady Winterbourne decided that she was well enough to leave her room, and make a small foray to the Pump Room. Patience had assured her that, whatever might be Florence's behaviour when she was at home, in public, at least, she conducted herself with propriety. Bolstered by this, and secretly longing to have a gossip with her friends and assess what they thought of Florence, she consented to be conveyed thither. Patience saw her comfortably settled in her usual place, with a group of cronies, and invited Florence to take a turn round the room with her. This was agreed to with becoming modesty, and they made the circuit of the room, greeting acquaintances.

On their return they found Lady Winterbourne in close conversation with two gentlemen. The elder was General Thorpe, the younger had his back to them and nothing was to be seen of him except his remarkable blond hair.

Both gentlemen rose as they approached. Patience looked up at the younger man, and a pang shot through her. She hardly heard the General's introduction through the pounding of her heart. Her immediate thought was that in this tall, handsome figure she beheld an ideal of masculine beauty. Unaware of what she did, she studied his face more closely. It was not just that he was handsome, though he undoubtedly was. She did not know how to own it to herself, she only knew that she was lost. No other man could ever be, to her, what this man was. If she never saw him again, never even heard his name, the irrevocable had happened. She, the plain, unromantic, no longer young woman who had declared that she would never be in love, had lost her heart in one look.

She realised that she was staring, and dropped her eyes with a blush. She need not have worried. He had not even noticed her. He held Florence's hand in his, and in a pretty display of modest confusion she lowered her head, then raised it again and opened her violet eyes wide in a shy glance. His eyes were riveted on her face, and it seemed that he would never leave go of her hand.

'Miss Florence,' he said. 'I am...delighted to make your acquaintance.'

After an endless moment Deverham recollected himself, and let go of Florence's hand. He made a small bow to Patience, who returned the salutation with an awkward inclination of her own, and there was a small bustle as seats were procured and arranged. General Thorpe excused himself after a few minutes, having seen another friend with whom he was anxious to speak, and Deverham was left to ingratiate himself as well as he might with the three ladies. The bench seat would barely accommodate them, for the spreading skirts of the ladies, particularly those of Florence, who wore no less than seven petticoats and a horsehair crinoline to hold out the folds of silk, took up a great deal of space. It was with some relief, therefore, that Patience was able to take a small chair to herself, which she edged backwards so that she was almost invisible to the other three.

'You have just arrived in Bath, Lord Deverham?' enquired Lady Winterbourne, who naturally took the lead in the conversation.

'Yes, only last night, Lady Winterbourne. I had recently received a letter from my grandfather, who asked me to visit his old friend for a few days. He himself is unable to travel a great deal, for he is much afflicted by the gout, and at times he uses me as his eyes and ears.'

'He is fortunate in his grandson,' Lady Winterbourne approved graciously. 'In these modern times there is, I think, a sad falling off in the kind of duty that young people pay to their elders.' This was meant merely as a general observation, and was in fact a common plaint from Lady Winterbourne's lips, but Florence shifted a little in her seat.

'I hope you do not mean me, Grandmama!' she remarked, with a pretty look of distress. 'I am sure, since I returned from school, that I have done my best to please you!'

Lady Winterbourne was a little flurried by the direct attack. Not for worlds would she have admitted to this elegant and, presumably, eligible stranger that her granddaughter, in private, was barely civil to her. Deverham unwittingly saved her from replying.

'I am sure that Miss Florence is everything that is dutiful and good,' he said with warmth. Lady Winterbourne smiled, and Florence lowered her lids until her thick, dark lashes lay softly against the delicate flush of her cheeks. Patience found to her dismay that her neatly gloved hands were forming into claws, and she relaxed them and folded them in her lap, shocked to find that she could so easily revert to savagery.

Lady Winterbourne again took charge of the conversation and, with the licence that her age and rank allowed her, interrogated Deverham as to his antecedents, status and prospects. The result was highly satisfactory. Since General Thorpe vouched for him, and had known him for most of his life, he was quite obviously not a fortune-hunter, but everything that his appearance proclaimed him to be.

After half an hour Deverham, who was experienced in the arts of courtship and knew well enough the wisdom of not overstaying his welcome, took his leave, first begging permission to call upon them in the near future, which permission was soon given. He left the Pump Room, and almost at once Lady Winterbourne looked round for Patience.

'My dear, I have been thinking that I am sadly in want of a new pair of gloves. These ones are my best, and I believe there is already a little hole coming in the fingertip. Perhaps you would like to go to Milsom Street, and buy me a pair? And for yourself, too, for I can clearly see the mend in the thumb.'

This generous offer was not to be ignored, and Patience, who saw quite easily that her mother wished to be rid of them both so that she could ask General Thorpe a few more details of his protégé, rose at once.

'Certainly, Mama. Will you come with me, Florence?'

'Yes, for I should like some gloves, and I am sadly in want of some stockings also.' Patience had been fairly sure that the little walk to Milsom Street would not be passed up—Florence liked nothing better than to dawdle down its length, and buy such items as struck her fancy. Patience, who preferred to walk briskly and be done with the shopping as soon as might be, never ceased to be amazed at the amount of effort her indolent niece was prepared to put in when comparing the relative merits of bonnets, or silk flowers, or ostrich-plume trimmings. While Patience would have preferred to have the time to herself, she knew that such a luxury was for the moment impossible, and she determined that as far as possible she would not permit herself to think of their new acquaintance.

It was fortunate for her peace of mind that Florence was easily distracted. She remarked, on leaving the Pump Room, that he was certainly the most elegant gentleman she had seen in Bath, but when Patience asked her if she had found him handsome she was less enthusiastic.

'He is tall, and well made, certainly, but I cannot say that I found him so very good-looking,' she said carelessly. 'To be sure, I am very exacting in my tastes, and I am afraid that I can never bring myself to like fair hair.'

'Do you call it fair? That, to me, means that sort of sandy hue that is not, I agree, of the first style of beauty. I would have called his colour golden, and he has not that very pale skin that can make a man look so unhealthy.'

'Do but look at that bonnet, Aunt Patience! Did you ever see anything so charming?'

'It is very pretty, to be sure, but do you think that quite so many ostrich feathers are the thing? Our air here is inclined to be damp, you know, and once they have lost their first freshness and curl, ostrich tips never look quite the same again.'

'Oh, I shouldn't mind that. My maid is very good for that sort of thing, and besides, I should have become tired of them long before then! I never like to keep the same trimming to my bonnets for too long.'

Patience, who was obliged to dress within her means, was a little shocked, but saw little point in remonstrating. She was quite glad, too, that the subject of conversation had been turned, for she feared that she had betrayed some unbecoming warmth in defence of Deverham's looks. It was astonishing to her that her niece should think so little of him, but she reflected that even at school Florence had been in the habit of meeting young gentlemen, brothers and relatives of her friends, and was therefore more used to them than Patience, who mixed almost exclusively with her mother's friends.

The gloves were duly purchased and, having dissuaded Florence from buying more than three pairs of kid evening gloves, in pretty pale shades, and overseen her choice of silk stockings, Patience was able to persuade her niece that they should make their way back to Gay Street, whither Lady Winterbourne would by now have been taken. Since Florence, for all her tiny waist, had the healthy appetite of her age, it was not difficult to distract her from shopping by the mention of luncheon.

During that meal Lady Winterbourne talked incessantly of their new acquaintance. As Patience had surmised, her mama's time had not been wasted while she and Florence had been in Milsom Street. General Thorpe had been only too willing to talk of his protégé, and Lady Winterbourne was furnished with every detail of his family background and, perhaps more important, his future prospects as his grandfather's heir. She knew that he was thirty, that his grandfather had been displeased with him over some scandal with a married woman, and that it was his grandfather's wish that he settle down and marry. With this in mind, it seemed only too likely to her that he had come to Bath expressly to meet Florence, since General Thorpe had been one of those to whom Patience had whispered the news of her niece's arrival.

It was with difficulty that Patience managed to control her mother's flood of words in front of Florence. Knowing her niece as she did, Patience was sure that nothing could have been more detrimental to their hopes than to make her think that they were encouraging her into Deverham's arms. Nothing could have been more calculated to annoy her than a hint that they were attempting to settle her affairs in this way. Luckily Florence was so self-absorbed that she paid very little attention to what her grandmother said, and her mind was still full of the bonnet she had seen.

Lady Winterbourne then retired for her accustomed nap, and Patience found herself desperate for some time to herself. This was usually her favourite time of day, for she could be sure of at least an hour of solitude when she could read, or sew, or merely think, secure from interruption. Now she had Florence, needing constant distraction, and full of restless humours.

'I have some lace to wash, for myself and Mama.

Do you have any you would like me to do? One cannot be too careful with fine lace, you know, and I pride myself I am a skilled practitioner.'

Florence stared at her.

'Oh, no, I leave all that to my maid. She is very good, and if any should be spoilt, I can soon get some more.'

'Then, since I am busy, do you want to go for a walk? With your maid to accompany you, of course.'

'Oh, yes! I might have another look at that bonnet, for you rushed me so this morning, and I do think I should like to buy it.' In a fever of happy anticipation she rushed away, and at last Patience found herself alone.

Her fingers moving mechanically, she prepared the soap, and began to wind the lace round the linen-wrapped bottle that would hold it smoothly in place while it soaked. For the first time, Patience allowed herself to dwell on her memory of Deverham's face and voice. It was very wrong, she knew, to do so. That a young lady, even one so relatively advanced in years as she was, should admit even to herself that she had given her heart to any man, without having at least some indication that he was inclined to favour her, and without her parent's permission, was not proper. Hitherto her life had been so bland, so open to all scrutiny, that it had never occurred to her that such a thing could happen, and the knowledge of her own feelings was already so deep in her heart that it would not be rooted out by considerations of delicacy.

That they must remain forever secret went without saying. Even without the competition of Florence's beauty, youth and wealth, he would never have noticed her. Indeed, he had not done so that morning, and she was tolerably sure that he had not even caught her name. He probably thought of her as a governess, or paid companion to Lady Winterbourne. While he was bound to be otherwise enlightened next time they should meet, it was not likely that he would ever accord her more than the politeness due to her rank, and her position as Florence's aunt. She had seen the arrested look on his face as he looked down at Florence. No man had ever, or would ever, look at her like that.

The thought of seeing him again was both a pleasure and a pain. Already she longed for the sound of his voice, the sight of his face. At the same time, she must learn to meet him with no outward sign. She must watch him courting Florence, and show nothing but complaisance and, should the courtship flourish, welcome him as a nephew. A nephew! She could not but laugh at the thought. As such they would meet and part with a kiss. She shivered. A dutiful, chaste salute, given so lightly, and received with such a pang. She forced herself to face the probable future: after the courtship, the wedding, the honeymoon, the fashionable life of a rich society couple. There would be children, no doubt, and if she could not love him, she could love them. A pale substitute, perhaps, but one which warmed her heart a little. She vowed that she would teach herself to love him with that love which was permitted for a woman to feel for a beloved brother or cousin. For a while she was almost uplifted by the resolve, and it enabled her to carry herself through the rest of the day without flinching.

By the following day she was quite sure that she had her unruly heart well under control. Returning from the kitchen, where she had been supervising the boiling of the lace, she was surprised to find her mother loitering on the stairs. Lady Winterbourne gave a little start at seeing her, and looked almost furtively towards the drawing-room.

'What is the matter, Mama? Why are you out here?'

Lady Winterbourne put a finger to her lips, and drew Patience into the morning-room.

'Hush! He is here, with Florence!'

'You mean Deverham?'

'Yes, he arrived some ten minutes ago. I thought you had gone out.'

'No, I was merely putting the lace to dry in the sun. It is early to be calling, surely? It cannot be more than ten o'clock.'

'Yes, that is what makes it so particularly gratifying. He must be taken by her, must he not? He came to invite us to go to the concert this evening at the Assembly Rooms. We should have gone anyway, I suppose, for everyone will be there, but he asks us as his guests. So I just made an excuse, and slipped out of the room.'

She looked a little guilty at the confession.

'Was that wise, Mama? It will not do to make our hopes too obvious. Nothing will be more likely to give him a disgust of her than to feel that he is being put under pressure.'

'I am sure I do not think he would even have noticed, for he had no eyes for anyone but her. You have no business to be scolding me, when I am doing it entirely for her sake.'

Patience thought it best not to argue with this view, though she had rather thought that it was Lady Winterbourne who was wishful of settling her granddaughter in marriage, not Florence.

'Perhaps it would be as well if you were to go back, now?' she suggested diffidently.

'You are the one who minds. You go,' said her mother petulantly. Patience had no choice. With a beating heart she went to the drawing-room and, opening the door, entered the room as nonchalantly as she knew how.

She need scarcely have worried. Deverham was by far too old a hand to be betrayed into impropriety by the absence of a chaperon, and complaisant mamas had often before now left him alone with hopeful daughters. A scene of the utmost propriety met Patience's eyes. Florence, her eyes chastely fixed on a piece of delicate embroidery, sat opposite her guest, who had taken a seat on the other side of the fireplace. As Patience came in he sprang to his feet and moved forward to greet her.

'You must forgive me,' he said with a frank, friendly look. 'I am afraid that I failed to catch your name in the Pump Room yesterday. The music, you know, and then so many new names and faces! I had no idea that Bath was so lively!'

Florence looked up in some irritation, annoyed at having her tête-à-tête interrupted.

'Oh, that is only Aunt Patience,' she said carelessly. Deverham's eyebrows rose.

'Miss Winterbourne! I can only beg your pardon! May I set you a chair?' Patience just touched his extended hand with her fingers, and would have withdrawn to a seat by the window had he not, with great courtesy, been busy setting a chair so that she would be comfortably near the fire.

'I thought I had understood you to say that you had an aunt married to Sir John Skirmett, living in

Herefordshire?' he quizzed Florence. 'In that case, you know, Miss Winterbourne cannot be considered as your *only* aunt!' The mild pleasantry was balm to Patience, but Florence looked a little sulky. She did not greatly care for jokes, and though she was not over-sensitive or gifted with much intelligence she was aware that she had been corrected. She was rather in awe of her new suitor, however, who was a great deal older and more of a man of the world than any of the men she had been used to meeting, so she was quick to make a recovery.

'I beg your pardon, Aunt Patience—I did not mean that to be as rude as it sounded!' she exclaimed with a pretty deference. 'I only meant that as a member of the family you are not a visitor, come to disturb our conversation! Did you know that Lord Deverham invites us to the concert this evening? It is so charming of him. I adore to hear good music!'

She met her aunt's glance with a look of wide-eyed candour. Florence was in fact tone-deaf, unable to sing a note in tune, and even the expensive music masters at her various schools had despaired of teaching her to play even the simplest piece. To go to a concert was purgatory to her, and she had already complained several times since her arrival that this form of public entertainment was almost the only kind which Lady Winterbourne attended.

Deverham was too well-bred to limit his conversation to Florence, but civilly enquired of Patience how long she had lived in Bath, and a little general talk ensued. On hearing that this was positively his first visit to the city, Florence gave a little crow of delight.

'Oh, then we must show you all the sights! You have as yet had no time to see more than the Pump Room, and the public buildings.'

'I have not yet seen a great deal, though I was up betimes this morning, and had a walk round the principal streets and squares. I found much to admire in the architecture and layout of the city. The Royal Crescent, for instance, with that wonderful vista over the park.'

'It is very elegant, to be sure,' broke in Florence. 'How I wish Grandmama lived there! Such very fine houses, and such a good address. I do not know why Grandmama chooses to live in Gay Street.'

'She cannot afford such a house,' pointed out Patience in gentle reproof, 'and, besides, it is so much further to the Pump Room, and the centre of the city.'

'I should think it must be cold, too, and windy. You would not care to have your shawls and bonnets so blown about, Miss Florence.'

Florence gave him a coy look, and a short silence fell.

'King's Circus is generally thought to be very fine,' remarked Patience diffidently. 'Did your morning's walk take you to it?'

'Yes, and I admired the columns very much, but I do not think I would care to live there. Did someone not say it was like Vespasian's amphitheatre turned outside in?' Florence, who never looked in any book more taxing than a collection of fashion plates, if she could help it, looked blank, but Patience twinkled back at him, forgetting her shyness in the pleasure of a shared memory.

'Yes, indeed, Mr Matthew Bramble in *Humphrey Clinker*. I can never think of it without a smile!' He was surprised, and could easily have been seduced into a discussion of books he had read and enjoyed, but Florence had no idea of being left out if she could help it.

'There are so many other places to see,' she broke in with childish enthusiasm. 'Abbey Close, that is very pretty and quaint, and of course Sally Lunn's!'

'Is that where the cakes come from? I do not believe I have ever eaten one,' he confessed.

'Then you should! It was one of my treats as a child, when I came to visit Grandmama from school, to be taken to eat Sally Lunn buns in her house, with cream cheese and fruit.'

'I should not know how to go about it, unless you come and put me in the right way of it. May I crave your company, and your aunt's, if such simple amusements are not too childish for her, to feast on buns some day very soon? You see I mean to expand my knowledge of the world!' This was the kind of talk that Florence enjoyed, and she kept up a flow of badinage until, a short time later, he took his leave.

CHAPTER FOUR

DEVERHAM, as he strode rapidly down the hill towards his lodgings, thought about Florence. Hitherto he had seldom had much to do with young girls of her age, preferring the maturer charms of married ladies, with whom he could conduct an elegant flirtation without risk of embroiling himself too deeply. Now, however, his aims were different.

He remembered the conversation he had had, not many days before, with his old friend James Trewellard. It had been after his return from Manchester, and he had been drinking in his club. They had not seen one another for some months, for James had been married just over a year, and spent most of his time on his own land in Cornwall. His young wife had demanded to spend the season in London, and he could deny her nothing.

'Drinking alone, Charles? That's a bad sign, you know.'

'James! I had no idea—when did you reach town? I had not expected you for at least a week.'

'Well, you know Jenny! Once she had the idea of London in her head nothing would please her but that we come instantly. We arrived last night, and already she is out and about ordering mountains of new gowns, and writing lists of invitations for parties!' He finished with mock despondency that entirely failed to conceal his pride, and Deverham grinned.

'As lively as ever, is she? And my godson, what of him? You have not left him down in that God-forsaken, savage land of yours, have you?'

'Not a bit of it, Jenny would not be parted from him. He is come with us, and the nurse, and the nurs-erymaid—you wouldn't believe how many people it takes to look after one small baby! We know he is there, too. He's a fine pair of lungs on him, that one!'

'I must be along in the morning to pay my respects, and worship at the shrine. I am not quite sure that I know how to talk to babies, but no doubt you can put me right on that.'

They found themselves a private corner, and settled down to an exchange of news. Having been a friend since their schooldays, Trewellard knew Deverham better than almost anyone did, and he was not slow to notice that his friend was drinking a great deal more than he had ever known him to do. There was an air, too, of dissatisfaction about him that he had never seen before. Too wise to ask any direct questions, he waited patiently, pretty sure that Deverham would in the end allude to what was troubling him.

It was not long before he had heard the full story. He, too, had spent boyhood visits at Simeon Moreton's house, and alone among Deverham's friends he could fully appreciate the dilemma that he found himself in.

'I was wrong, I suppose, to lay myself open to this,' admitted Deverham. 'But I did no more than most men do, and if it had not been for the lady's loose words...however, it does not become me to blame her, and I do not do so. The fault was mine. Only, it was such a little fault. My grandfather does not know the ways of the world. And now he is suspicious of me, and only too ready to believe any other little tales that my dear cousin might carry to him. What am I to do? I must live in society. I do not want to shut myself up on my estate and live as a hermit, and yet I fear to dance with any woman in case I stir up this hornet's nest again.'

'There is only one answer, and I wonder that you have not thought of it for yourself. You must get married.'

'Oh, you are a great advocate of matrimony now that you have tied the knot yourself. Find me another Lady Jennifer, and I might be prepared to advise you.'

'Alas, there are no more—they broke the mould. Besides, she would not suit you. Surely there are scores of young ladies up for the season? You might have your pick of them.'

'I have never yet met one with whom I could pass a week, let alone the rest of my life.'

'You demand too much.'

'I do not think so. Oh, maybe you are right. I suppose I have never yet met a woman whom I could love, unreservedly. I have many times fancied myself in love, but such feelings never last.'

'What do you look for in a wife?'

'Oh, I don't know. The usual things, I suppose. I would want her to be beautiful, and elegant. I would want her to have similar interests, to like the things and the people I like. A lady, of course. Moderately intelligent, and amusing.'

'And rich?'

'I do not look for it, but of course no one could be dissatisfied if it were there.'

'Enough! You are looking for a paragon! You should be prepared to accept a little less.'

'What should I look for, then? Come, I will be guided by you. Draw a picture of my future wife for me, and tomorrow I will go out like a prince in a fairy-tale and seek her.'

He was joking, but his friend was not unwilling to oblige. He was in truth so happy in his own marriage that he could not see any other way of life so likely to please his friend.

'Situated as you are, it goes without saying that the young lady must be well born, and educated as a gentlewoman. Beauty, I think, is an essential, and you are entitled to look for some small fortune as well, though as you say that is not of prime importance for you, so long as your grandfather likes your bride! For the rest she should be agreeable, cheerful, and, I think, very young.'

'Very young? Why do you say that? I am thirty, as you well know. Should I not rather seek a bride of perhaps twenty-one or two?'

'No, knowing you as I do, I would advise you to choose a girl fresh from the schoolroom. Such a girl has yet to form her character: it will be for you to shape her, to teach her to be as you would wish her. You say you want her to share your interests, to like what you like. How better to do this?'

Deverham was thoughtful.

'You are in earnest, are you not? I had thought you were in jest. And is this really what you would advise?'

'It is.'

'Am I then so demanding that I would not be willing to accept a girl with any ideas, any character of her own?'

'By no means. I merely give you back your own words.'

'I will think it over. I am not convinced that I am cut out for matrimony, though. I do not think I can bear the idea of seeing the same face over the breakfast-table for the rest of my life.'

'That,' said his friend smugly, 'is because you have not yet met the right young woman.'

'But you have, and she will be anxious for you! Do you realise what the time is? Lady Jenny will give me a cold welcome tomorrow for this. Be off with you! I shall have one more glass, and a cigar, and enjoy my freedom while I may!'

He paid his promised visit the following morning, dutifully admired his godson, and presented him with a handsome coral. He could not but see how happy Trewellard was. For the first time he felt almost lonely, knowing that the claims of wife and family would now forever come first with his friend. At the same time, he was unable to see himself in the same role.

Only two days later, his grandfather's letter had arrived. Deverham had smiled on reading it, and half in jest had taken it round to Trewellard's house and read it to them. There was a little silence as Deverham finished reading the letter. Trewellard had, as a matter of course, discussed his friend's problems with his wife, but she felt hardly on such terms with him as to warrant her speaking first. Trewellard himself was awed.

'Dash it all, Charles, it's fate, that's what it is! Just as I was saying to you the other night—beautiful, rich, and very young! This is the girl for you!'

'What about the amiable and cheerful?'

'Oh, that is a matter of course. All girls are amiable and cheerful at that age, particularly if they are pretty and rich. Why should they be otherwise?'

'You seriously think I should make the journey to Bath?'

'Why not? You said that you were bored, and it commits you to nothing. You may soon effect an introduction by the General. Who is he, by the way?'

'General Thorpe. An old crony of my grandfather's. He's a shocking old gossip, knows all the news that's going, and sends it up to him. Lady Jenny, you have not yet given me your advice. Should I go, do you think?'

'Your grandfather certainly wishes it,' she said diffidently, 'and you should try to please him, I suppose. You need do no more than look at her, and if she does not please no harm is done.'

Still unsure whether he was serious, or merely amusing himself, he had come to Bath, and found Florence. She was very beautiful, at least, and rich, though he did not much regard that. She was certainly very young, as his friend Trewellard had counselled him, and surely any faults of temper or education could be rectified. For the rest she seemed cheerful enough, and if she was not very clever, maybe that was no bad thing in a young wife. Above all, his grandfather would be pleased, and, if he could not think of any positive reasons why he should not take this step, that one thing in its favour should be sufficient to decide him. Of her family he did not take much thought. The grandmother was all that one would expect of her age and class, and the aunt, if rather plain and insignificant, was nevertheless quite an amusing companion. He thought that if it became necessary, on the death of Lady Winterbourne, to offer his prospective aunt-in-law a home, he could easily put up with her.

*   *   *

Florence was in a high good humour, and only scolded Patience a little for coming in when she did.

'If Grandmama thought it all right to leave us alone for a few moments, I do not know why you should think otherwise,' she complained. 'Surely you can trust me to behave with propriety, can you not?'

'My dear Florence, even if I could not trust you, and I do not say that I cannot, I could certainly trust him not to go beyond the line of what is pleasing. He is most gentlemanly in his manners. No, it is merely that I did not want it to appear that we hold you cheap. Nothing is more damaging to a girl's reputation, you know. I do not like to say that Grandmama was wrong, but perhaps in her kindness to you she was a little premature. After all, this is only the second time he has met you.'

'Yes, and I think he admires me, do not you?'

'I am sure he does. Only see that your behaviour is such as will merit his admiration.'

'Oh, Aunt Patience, you are so stuffy!'

Patience thought sadly that this was only too true.

The concert that evening was judged to be a most successful outing. In Deverham's honour they all wore their finest. Lady Winterbourne's black gown was in the best of silks, trimmed with the newly cleaned lace. Florence was divinely innocent and lovely in fine white tarlatan, with white camellias set in her dark hair and at her bosom. The tightly fitting bodice came down to a V at the front, accentuating her narrow waist, and her shoulders were hardly whiter than the fall of lace that decorated the fashionable bertha that fell from the low neckline. The same lace trimmed the wide bell of her skirt. Even Patience, who as a rule studied for neatness rather than fashion, wore her newest dress of a soft, silvery mauve. She managed to procure some sweet violets, white and purple, for her hair.

For ever afterwards the smell of violets would bring back to her that evening. Lord Deverham in his evening clothes, the play of his muscles beneath the fine black cloth of his coat, and the look of his hand as it lay on his knee, the line of his jaw and the way the hair fell, just so, over his forehead—all these things burned into her memory, and as she stared up into the darkness of the tester above her bed, she saw them again. Her eyes burned hot and dry: even the luxury of tears was denied her. How could she bear it, to be with him, and to see him day after day? Grimly she turned her face into the pillow, and set herself to endure, as if it had been toothache. And yet, could she have wrenched the love from her heart as an aching tooth might be pulled from her jaw, would she, could she do it? She did not think that she would.

Patience arose heavy-eyed and tired. She splashed her face ruthlessly with cold water, trying to cool her hot forehead and soothe her eyes. Fortunately she knew that her mother and niece were unlikely to notice any slight alteration in her looks, since neither of them were interested in any appearance other than their own. The day was grey and damp, and Florence pouted as she looked out of the morning-room window.

'I don't know why it always has to rain in Bath! I never knew such a damp place.'

'We have had sunshine for a week,' pointed out Patience.

'What use is that? I particularly wanted it to be fine today, for Deverham said we should have a walk, and I should show him Bath.'

'Another day will do for that, I suppose. I own I should prefer not to walk too far today.'

Florence stared at her. 'He invited me, not you!'

Patience sighed. 'I have not the slightest wish to accompany you, but it is quite out of the question, Florence, that you should be walking out unattended. I know it seems old-fashioned, but Bath is old-fashioned, after all. You would not wish to cause talk.'

Florence looked mutinous, and quite obviously did not care how much talk it caused.

'But, Aunt Patience, it is so stuffy! Besides, it is so awkward with three! How are we to walk?'

Patience looked with wry amusement at the spread of Florence's skirts.

'It is true that you take up a great deal of room, love! Nevertheless, it must be done. I think you will find that Lord Deverham is too well aware of the proprieties governing Bath society to suggest taking you out alone.'

In this Patience was quite correct. His behaviour, when he called later in the day, made it clear that his suggested walk included both ladies. Accordingly, the next fine day, they set out, Deverham courteously offering an arm to each lady.

'We cannot walk like that!' objected Florence. 'It is much too cramped.'

'True, but what is to be done? Should I offer my arm to either of you, the other must walk alone, which is not to be thought of. Perhaps if you walked with your aunt, and I came behind you?' This reasonable suggestion was spurned by Florence, and they ended up three together. Florence, whose trustees permitted her a more than generous dress allowance, was becomingly attired in a dress of azure silk, blue as the spring sky, with a fur-trimmed pardessus in a deeper blue velvet, and matching bonnet. Patience, wanting to be self-effacing and succeeding to admiration, wore dove-grey, and tried to feel like a governess.

'How pleasant to live in such a cheerfully named place,' remarked Deverham, by way of light conversation. Florence looked blank. 'Gay Street, I mean. Why is it so called?'

'You will have to ask Aunt Patience, she is full of information.'

'Florence has lived so little in Bath, and I have been here for ten years, and have no excuse for not knowing. Do not expect anything very interesting— it was named after the ground landlord, Robert Gay.'

'A pity: I had hoped it might be for John Gay.'

'Who wrote *The Beggar's Opera*? I am afraid not.'

'Do you go much to the opera?' Florence was determined not to allow the conversation to take too literary a turn.

'Yes, I suppose so. One must, if only to see one's friends. Besides, I am fond of music, and there are some wonderful singers in London at present.'

'How lovely! Soon I shall be in London, Lord Deverham. Perhaps I shall see you there?' This was spoken in tones of innocent seduction, and Charles was suitably charmed.

'I certainly hope so, though I fear that you will have so many admirers I shall not be able to get more than two words with you!'

'Do you think so?' Florence, less sophisticated than she liked to think, blushed adorably. Patience concentrated on keeping her skirts from brushing the iron railings that separated the houses from the pavement.

For once, Florence was willing to forgo the delights of Milsom Street, where the crowds would have made walking more difficult, and they continued down Gay Street into Queen Square. The stone of the beautifully proportioned Palladian houses glowed softly in the sunshine, and Patience was pleased to find that Deverham found the place as beautiful as she herself had always done. Even Florence, seeing his admiration, was enthusiastic.

'For which Queen was it named?' He did not this time make the mistake of asking Florence.

'For Queen Caroline.' Patience kept her answer to the bare minimum.

'Well, I have heard of *her*, at any rate,' put in Florence with some satisfaction. 'She was the one they made the rhyme about, wasn't she?'

'I am not sure. Which rhyme was that?'

Florence struck an attitude, like a child reciting in class, and with a naughty twinkle in her eye enunciated her lines.

Most gracious Queen, we thee implore
To go away and sin no more;
Or if that mercy be too great,
To go away at any rate!

Patience stifled a desire to smack her niece. Of all the things to come out with, and in front of Deverham! He, however, was laughing.

'Very well, but you have the wrong Queen! I fancy the Queen Caroline of the Square was the wife of George II, not the one of George IV who inspired your little ditty!'

Florence was not a whit abashed.

'Well, they were both Georges, at any rate, and if they had to marry women of the same name, no wonder people get confused. At least I remembered it! And it did make you laugh!'

'So you did, and so I did. See what benefit you have derived from all those years at school. Why, you are quite a bluestocking.'

'Oh, no, I should not like that. Aunt Patience is the only bluestocking in our family, and I think one is quite enough, don't you?'

Patience was ready to sink with embarrassment, but was forced to rally herself when she found Deverham was asking her what other famous associations were to be found with the Square.

'Well, the obelisk in the middle was commissioned by Beau Nash himself, in honour of the Prince of Wales—that is, Prince Frederick, father of George III,' she added in haste, before Florence could get in another muddle. She might as well not have bothered.

'I never heard of him. Did we really have a King Frederick?'

Patience blushed for her ignorance, but Deverham was shaking with suppressed laughter.

'Surely you have heard of the great King Frederick?' he enquired with mock incredulity. 'He was the most wonderful monarch. Quite fabulous, indeed!'

'Completely fabulous, in fact,' added Patience, her sense of humour getting the better of her.

'No! What did he do?' Florence looked from one to the other, a little frown of doubt growing between her eyes. 'Now you are teasing me! There was no such person. Aunt Patience, how could you?'

Deverham was swift to avert the storm.

'Forgive me, my dear Miss Florence, the fault was entirely mine, and you are quite right. The unfortunate Prince Frederick died, before he ever became King. It was wrong of me to make a joke of you, and indeed we did not mean to be unkind.'

If it had been anyone else, Florence would undoubtedly have been betrayed into a tantrum, but she was still a little in awe of this suitor, man of the world that he was, and with an effort she swallowed her chagrin, and even achieved a little smile, which grew more genuine when she saw the approval in his eyes.

'Well, I never did see the point of all those history lessons, anyway. Aunt Patience will be able to give you a great long list of boring people who once lived here, but when you know that, where are you? It is not as if one could go and visit them, after all.'

'Would that we could! I must inform you, Lord Deverham, that among the bores who once stayed here you may include the man who built the square, John Wood, as well as Dr Oliver, the poet Wordsworth, and Jane Austen.'

'Ah, the wonderful Miss Austen! She was not happy here, I believe.'

'No. I sometimes think she would have liked it better as it is today, less crowded and fashionable. How I wish she were alive now! I would give anything for half an hour in her company.'

'And I! I confess that I brought a copy of *Northanger Abbey* with me, on purpose to read it again, with the sight of the Assembly Rooms and Pump Room fresh before my eyes.'

'Well, I would rather meet Dr Oliver,' put in Florence firmly, bored with this literary interchange.

'Would you? Why?'

'His biscuits, of course. You cannot deny that he was the inventor of Bath Oliver biscuits, and I am extremely partial to them, with plenty of butter! I am very hungry—may we not go to Sally Lunn's now?'

Both Deverham and Patience had to laugh at her ingenuous greed, and in a high good humour Florence encouraged them on. Patience took them down Barton Street to Sawclose, where they paid short homage before Beau Nash's house, past the Theatre Royal, which gave Florence the excuse to shudder and cling to Deverham's arm as it was supposed to be haunted.

From there they came to Cross Bath, taking its name from the cross which had stood there until some sixty years earlier. Florence hid her impatience as Deverham insisted on standing for a moment to admire the fine Ionic colonnades of Bath Street, built to shelter the bathers of a previous century as they walked, or were carried, to the King's Bath and the Pump Room. He did not miss Florence's quick sigh, however.

'I wonder what you eat here, on Good Friday?' he said whimsically to her.

'I am sure I do not know,' said Florence, rather crossly. 'Nothing at all, like us, I suppose.'

Patience was quicker-witted.

'No, child. Hot Cross Bath buns, surely?'

Florence giggled, and Deverham gave his ready smile, pleased to find his small joke taken up so quickly.

'But only when Good Friday falls on the thirteenth of the month,' Patience added seriously.

'Naturally. Now, I promise you, I shall walk with my eyes shut until we reach Sally Lunn's, and not make you wait a moment longer.' Florence was for holding him to his promise, and guiding him in and

out of the colonnades, but Patience restrained her
from making a spectacle of him, and Abbey Green
was reached without mishap.

After they had regaled themselves on teacakes,
served hot with clotted cream, cream cheese and fruit,
Florence found enough energy to saunter for a while
in Abbey Green. It was Patience's favourite part of
Bath, older than the fine squares and crescents, and
with all the charm of age and haphazard building.
Soon, however, Florence complained that the cobbles
hurt her feet, and they walked home.

This was the first of several expeditions. Deverham
was surprised to find that he was enjoying himself.
Day succeeded day, and he felt no boredom, no restless
urge to return to his accustomed pursuits in London.
Expeditions were planned and carried out into the
neighbouring countryside, and every day brought him
without fail to Gay Street. If it were fine they would
walk out, visiting the sights of the city, or merely enjoying the spring sunshine in one of the several parks.
If it rained they would stay companionably indoors,
talking, playing childish games, and otherwise
amusing themselves. In the evenings there were concerts, and small private parties in the houses of Lady
Winterbourne's friends.

Lady Winterbourne thought herself in a whirl of
activity, and though to Deverham this was a quiet life
indeed, he was perfectly content. He found it amusing
to visit the Pump Room with them, hearing all the
little details of local life that Patience was able to
impart to him, and having the pleasure of knowing
that the prettiest girl in the city was hanging on his
arm. On Sunday he attended Divine Service with them
at the Abbey. Left to herself, Patience preferred to

attend the less grand church of St Michael on the corner of Walcot Street and Broad Street. Built hardly more than ten years before, it was a great deal nearer to Gay Street, but Lady Winterbourne would not hear of it. It was beneath her dignity to attend any church but the Abbey, particularly when accompanied by such as Lord Deverham.

To Deverham the whole thing had a strange unreality. It was as if he were living in another world. He did not know why it all seemed so unreal. He had found a girl, beautiful and desirable, and moreover one whom his grandfather had positively urged him to love. He was dazzled by her beauty, enchanted by her youth. He had never had much to do with girls of such an age. In London he had been wary of them, preferring the more sophisticated charms of mature, married ladies. When he had talked with them, or danced with them, he had not found them easy company. Either they were so shy, so overawed, that they could not bring themselves to string two words together, or they went to quite the other extreme and never ceased talking and giggling. Either was equally trying.

Florence was different. She was neither bashfully silent nor disagreeably pert. She was, of course, on her best behaviour, but he was not to know that. He found her childishness, her simplicity, even her vanity, appealing and touching. She made him want to care for her, to shield her from the cold winds, and keep her forever a delightful, happy child. When, on occasions, her temper got the better of her, and she betrayed the selfish and even cruel side of her nature, he was quick to make excuses for her in his own mind, telling himself that it was merely the fault of youth, and to be expected in one who was still, to all intents and purposes, a schoolgirl.

It was, of course, unthinkable that he should be allowed to spend any time alone with Florence. Since Lady Winterbourne's state of health made it impossible for her to accompany them on any but the simplest and least taxing of their walks and excursions, it naturally fell to Patience's lot to act as chaperon. They were much together, the three of them, and, lost in his romantic dream, Deverham never noticed that it was Patience who made their conversations interesting with her quick-witted remarks, who entertained him with anecdotes and who made him laugh. She was so retiring, so much a nonentity in her drab gown and shawl, her plain bonnets and caps, that he was hardly aware of her presence. She was, as it were, in Florence's shadow, and he was scarcely aware that it was largely she who made their outings as enjoyable as they were.

CHAPTER FIVE

ALFRED UFFINGTON was not a happy man. There was
nothing unusual in this. Alfred Uffington was rarely
happy. He was moderately successful in his chosen
profession, and it brought him a moderate reward.
He could afford to live in comfort, to be fussy about
the degree of starch in his shirt-fronts, and to dine
well each day. These modest comforts, however, which
to many in his position would have been the summit
of ambition, only served to remind him that he was
unlikely ever to climb any higher, and Alfred
Uffington was a very ambitious man.

Fate had not dealt fairly with him. The only child
of impecunious parents, both of whom had died at a
young age, he would have regarded his present state
as the limit of affluence had he not been given the
chance to see something so much better, so far above
the general run of life that most people did not dream
of it.

Orphaned in his tenth year, he had at that im-
pressionable age for the first time encountered his
uncle. Hitherto there had been a rift between the two
families. That Alfred's mother, many years younger
than her brother, had eloped with a handsome subaltern would not alone have been so very terrible. Such
things had been done before, and family harmony had
been preserved, or at least patched up at a later date.

Such might have been the case for Mrs Uffington,
had she perhaps not been so foolish as to have been

taken in by a handsome face and a crafty, designing mind. Her richer brother, while he was annoyed for a time by her behaviour, would have been prepared to receive the couple and make the best of things, only that in his greed the bridegroom was unable to wait for that. He was in truth a gambler, one to whom the turn of a card, the roll of dice, mattered more in life than wife, child, or even honour. Within a few months of their marriage he was drummed out of the army. Mrs Uffington could never bring herself to believe that what they said about her husband was true—to the end of her days she saw only the handsome face and not the shallow, treacherous heart behind it.

It was not, therefore, as a repentant but happy wife that she returned to her brother's house, but almost as a beggar. He took pity on her, and from then on they lived as his pensioners. Simeon Moreton soon learned that it was worse than useless to entrust his brother-in-law with any money, for whatever he had was sure to be gone down the drain almost at once. She was almost as bad, for she could refuse her husband nothing.

The crisis point came about two years later. Alfred was then a baby of some eighteen months old, and the little family were living, as usual, in a rented house that was far beyond their actual means. Joshua Uffington's financial difficulties were about as bad as they had ever been, and he had gaming debts that were beginning to make him afraid to be out alone at night. Yet still he persisted in thinking of himself as a man with prospects, a man whose brother-in-law was rich, and who was entitled to call on his relative for unlimited help. The fact that he had had the fortune his wife had been promised more than twice over was as nothing to him. In his desperation, and his arrogance, he forged Simeon Moreton's name on a document and used it to raise money.

Simeon's anger was terrible. It was, of course, impossible that such a thing should not be discovered, particularly by him. His businesses were run by himself, overseen by himself, and, while he was in many ways an open-handed man, no money came in or went out of his hands without his knowledge of it. He had too much pride to allow the affair to become public knowledge, but from that day he had nothing to do with his sister or her husband. She, poor foolish woman, refused to believe in her Joshua's guilt, and taught by him she said things in her anger that could not be forgiven.

Even in his anger, Simeon Moreton was in some ways generous. He would not leave his sister to perish from want, and he made arrangements for a sum of money to be given to her, in small monthly amounts, on the stipulation that she was not to communicate with him in any way. In time he himself paid for his nephew, Alfred, to be sent to school. In spite of, or perhaps because of, this generosity, there was always hatred and envy in the Uffington household for the richer man. Alfred was brought up in the vague idea that they would have been a great deal better off, and happier, had his uncle not behaved so shabbily towards them.

When he was ten his father Joshua died, his handsome body weakened by drink and careless living. His mother, of whom the best that could be said was that she remained blindly loyal to her husband, followed him to the grave not long afterwards, and Alfred was alone in the world. In these circumstances his uncle was inclined to take pity on him and, as well as promising to continue to pay for his education—which Alfred had not in fact been aware was being done— he invited the boy to stay with him at his house in Manchester.

This invitation coincided with one of the many visits Charles paid his grandfather. The boys were near enough in age, though Charles was two years younger, and the old man misguidedly thought they would be company for one another. On the evening before Alfred's arrival, Simeon Moreton called his grandson to him.

'You will have a playmate here tomorrow, my boy. How shall you like that, eh?'

'A playmate, sir? I shall like that very well. Who is coming? Is it anyone I know?'

'It is your cousin, Alfred. Alfred Uffington.'

'I did not know I had a cousin of that name, sir. Who is he?'

'No, you have probably never heard him spoken of. His mother was my sister, and I am afraid we were not the best of friends. No need to go into that now. The boy is coming, and I want you to be good to him.'

'I hope I should be that, without your telling me,' said Charles, who even at that age had some pride in knowing how a young gentleman should behave. 'You said "was". Is his mama dead, then, like mine?'

'Yes, and his father too, so you see he is alone in the world.'

'Poor boy. I am very sorry for him.'

Charles was sorry for his cousin, and would have done his best to show it, but found himself repulsed at every turn. His new cousin arrived the next day, and when Charles would have welcomed him, and offered to show him round the house, and the special places in the garden, he found himself snubbed for his pains. In truth, Alfred Uffington was not suffering greatly at the loss of his parents, for he had feared and despised his father, and simply despised his mother. He saw in Charles a pampered darling, given all the things that he, Alfred, should have had, and he hated him.

That first visit was perhaps the worst service that his uncle could have paid him. It opened his eyes to a way of life which he had hitherto not seen, and from then on nothing would content him but that he, too, should live that way. He did his utmost to wheedle his way into Simeon's affections, but his uncle was no fool, and was not in any case inclined to be taken in by anyone of the name of Uffington. When he saw this, Alfred turned his hand to tormenting his cousin. Things that Charles used, or even touched, were found to be mysteriously broken or mislaid. Any small fault was reported as it were by chance, in casual conversation, and of course it ended in Charles falling on his cousin and blacking his eye. In spite of the two years' difference Charles was already as tall as his cousin, and in any case was so angry that he would have taken him on had he been twice as tall. Alfred screamed for help, declaring that Charles had gone mad, and attacked him for no reason. Simeon Moreton was annoyed, and Charles was too proud to explain why he had done what he did.

'I beg your pardon, Grandfather,' he mumbled through a bleeding and puffy lip.

'That's all very well, but have you no more to say than that? Did I not especially ask you to be kind to your cousin?'

'He just jumped on me, and took me by surprise,' snivelled Alfred, whose eye was already half closed but who had not in fact suffered a great deal. 'I am hurt bad, I am sure I am, Uncle. And for nothing, too! Vicious, that's what he is.'

Charles' eyes sparkled, but he said nothing, only looking steadily at his erstwhile opponent until his eyes dropped.

Simeon Moreton had a fair idea of what had happened, and was not too displeased with his grandson, though he would not have shown it.

'I will not have fighting in my house. You will apologise to one another, and there is an end of it.'

'My jacket is all torn, and it was my best one!'

'You shall have a new jacket. Come now, sir. Will you apologise?'

'He started it! He should ask pardon first!'

Charles lifted his chin.

'If I have hurt you, I ask your pardon. I should not have behaved so in my grandfather's house.' The words were stiffly spoken, but they had been uttered. At once Alfred saw that he would have done better to be the first to speak. The one who made the first move to reconciliation always had a moral advantage. With a display of friendliness he held out his hand.

'I forgive you,' he said grandly. 'I do not know what I did to provoke you, but I apologise nevertheless.' Charles just touched the outstretched hand, and so the quarrel was, to all outward appearances at least, made up. Nevertheless, from that moment Charles never trusted his cousin, and Alfred for his part allowed his envy and hatred to grow.

Alfred was not often asked to repeat his visit, and the cousins seldom met. As he grew older, Alfred tried many times to win his uncle's affection, but failed. The only thing that might have succeeded would have been an honest affection for the old man, without hope of gain, and Alfred was far from feeling that, nor was he clever enough to simulate it convincingly. He saw that to scheme against his cousin was to court disaster, so he bided his time, outwardly friendly, inwardly hoping for Charles to commit some fault that would put him in his grandfather's black books.

The scandal with Lady Belinda had come on him like manna from heaven. On leaving school, Alfred had been articled by his uncle to a firm of London attorneys. The boy seemed clever enough, and thought that he would like to go in for the law. Who knew but that he might not rise to a Crown office, or perhaps stand for Parliament? Alfred, however, saw himself as too much of a gentleman to have to work for his living, and had risen but little. His uncle made him an allowance, and had promised him a sum of five thousand pounds in his will, and to his acquaintance he exaggerated this sum, and preened himself on his great expectations. He was not above using his noble cousin's name, either, when it suited him to do so, and Charles knew that this was so. Out of love for his grandfather he said nothing, but he did not receive his cousin.

Living, as he did, on the fringes of society, Alfred was not slow to hear news of any scandal. It was in any case almost impossible to keep any secret from servants, and most servants will gossip among their

acquaintance of the doings of their employers. Alfred
had for some time past kept up a discreet relationship
with a footman in Deverham's employ, offering a
reward for any information concerning his lordship's
affairs. The footman, who was paid in accordance
with the value of the news he brought, was not averse
to embroidering his tale, using his imagination freely
in the process. What Alfred heard was, therefore,
rather worse than the actual tale.

'And you say he sees this—Lady Belinda—very
regularly?'

'Oh, yes, sir, all the time, sir. Always off visiting
her, he is. I know it from the groom, sir.'

'And her husband? Does he know of it?'

'Well, as to that, I wouldn't like to say, sir. But I
do know she's a good many years younger than he is,
sir, and we all know what that means, don't we, sir?'
He leered.

'You forget yourself, fellow.' Uffington spoke
automatically, his mind busy on this new possibility.

'I'm sure I beg pardon, sir. I'm sure I wouldn't wish
to speak against her ladyship. Not that I blame the
master one bit, mind, for she's as pretty as a picture.'

'Seen her, have you?'

'Only from her carriage, sir. 'Course she don't come
to the house, with the master living alone and no lady
to be his hostess, stands to reason she can't, but she
has left notes, herself, at least three times that I know
of.'

'Has she indeed? Could you have had sight of these
notes?'

'Couldn't possibly, sir. More than my place is
worth, sir.'

Uffington sighed, and delved in his pocket for a handful of money. Pushing the coins slowly round the palm of his hand with the forefinger of the other, he reluctantly picked out five sovereigns. He held them loosely, so that the gold just glinted through, and looked at the footman.

'I would like a sight of those notes, if it could be managed,' he said quietly. The footman thought.

'Well, I don't know as they'd be very interesting, sir. I suppose I could try, for the master sometimes throws them carelessly to the fire and they lie under the grate. I can't promise nothing, though. And I should need to know that it would be worth my trouble, like. It'd be out of the house with no character, soon as winking, if I was to be caught. Now I can't afford that, sir.'

'Bring me what you can, and you shall not regret it,' promised Alfred.

He was in luck. A week later an ill-spelled note informed him that the footman had something of the greatest interest to show him. When they met, he proudly displayed three letters, two very crumpled and one still smooth, the creases sharp. Uffington held out his hand.

'I had a deal of trouble to get these for you, sir. Two was under the grate, like I said, and I can tell you I had a time getting them before the housemaid saw me. Not my job, doing out the fires, is it? As for this one, as is still fresh and nice, I took that from the master's pocket. Terrified, I was. I think you'll find it's worth your while, though.'

Alfred took out his pocket-book, and produced a bank note for ten pounds.

'The five sovereigns I promised you, you shall have for your trouble. That is all you have a right to expect. If, however, I find that the letter is as—useful—as you say, you shall have this, for your own, to keep your mouth shut about this.'

'Lor' bless you, sir, do you think I'm going to go blabbing about how I took private letters from my master's coat? You must take me for a flat.'

'Nevertheless, I must have your promise that it will be so, and I warn you that if ever our little transaction is known, I shall be aware that you have talked, since only you and I know of it. And then it will be the worse for you.' His face was fierce, and the footman quailed.

'I don't want no trouble, sir. I just wanted to do as you asked. Give me the five sovs, and I'll give you the letters. If you think they're worth more, that's up to you.'

He got his ten pounds. On examining the letters, Alfred found that the first two, carelessly discarded in the fireplace, were merely invitations, perhaps a little over-warm in their wording but, taken on their own, perfectly unexceptionable. The third, however, was a full-blown love letter. Charles had read it with disgust, and dismay, for he had not intended that the little flirtation he had started should ever be more than that. He had not allowed for the lady's relative inexperience, and the fact that until her marriage to her elderly and wealthy spouse she had lived very retired in the country, quite out of the way of sophisticated society. It was this letter which had shown him that he must at once end the affair, before all was undone. She offered herself to him unreservedly, as his wife if her husband would divorce her, or as his mistress in public or in secret, if he so wished. In her infatuation she placed herself completely in his hands, to break her fragile reputation if he would.

With the greater degree of cunning that had come to him with age, Uffington put the letters safely by for future use. Tempting though it was, he could not risk showing them to his uncle, for in trying to explain how he had obtained them he would render anything else he said to the old man suspect. While in some ways Simeon Moreton was not precisely a gentleman, he had a well-developed sense of honour, and would have shrunk from anything underhand.

Instead, Alfred visited his uncle, and during his visit confined his conversation to topics of general interest. Before leaving London, however, he had sent an anonymous note to the newspapers, along the lines that Lord D——, well known in society for his dashing ways, was at present honouring the house of Lady B——W——, in a manner which her husband might not entirely approve. Sure enough, the hint was taken and while he was there the little item appeared. Simeon Moreton always took a newspaper, for though his gout kept him very much confined to his own house, he liked to know what was afoot in the world. All that was necessary, when his uncle read the paper and furiously demanded of Alfred whether he knew what it meant, was to look very embarrassed, and appear reluctant to speak about it.

'Come now, nephew! I see that you know something of this matter! Out with it, man!'

'Well, Uncle, it is not really for me to be speaking of such things to you. Surely you had better ask Deverham himself? I am sure there is some perfectly rational explanation. It is probably some mistake, some error in the printing.'

'Don't give me error in the printing. There it is in black and white, as clear as can be. Lord D! That is meant for Lord Deverham, is it not?'

'I suppose it could be thought to be. But I am sure that Lady Belinda...'

'Lady Belinda, eh? So you do know what it's all about! Stop beating about the bush, then, and tell me, for I warn you I shall give you no peace until you do. It's no use trying to protect your cousin, though, damme, I like you better for it, and I am glad to see you have so much good feeling.'

Alfred smirked.

'I hope I would not say anything to make you think any less of my cousin.'

'I hope you would not be able to,' responded Moreton grimly.

With much simulated reluctance, Alfred allowed the story to be dragged out of him, knowing that it would have more effect that way than if he were to tell it all freely. Not that there was a great deal to tell, for he was not personally acquainted with Lady Belinda or her set. He did his best with the fact that Lady Belinda, though well born, had no money of her own, and had married Lord Waltham who was considerably older than she, and very rich.

At length he let slip that he had heard a rumour—just a rumour, mind, and probably no foundation to it—that the lady was about to be divorced by her husband. Simeon Moreton drew in his breath. To his way of thinking, divorce was a scandal so great that nothing could blot it out, and a woman who parted from her husband could scarcely be considered as part of the human race any more. However little she might be to blame—and it appeared that in this instance the fault was wholly hers—her duty was to remain at her husband's side. Even should he leave her, she should still consider herself as his wife, and live retired from the world in the hope that one day he might return to her. Even widows, in his opinion, had no business marrying again. To think that his only grandson, his heir, was contemplating marriage with such a one! If such a thing should come to pass, he would never receive his granddaughter-in-law, nor would he find it in his heart to forgive Charles. And it went without saying that his money would never be left so that such a household might benefit by it.

All this Alfred saw, and rejoiced in his heart while keeping his face set in lines of sympathy and sorrow.

'It may well be all a mistake!' he said in heartening tones. 'The Lady Belinda is very beautiful, I believe, and this is not the first time her name has been coupled with another's. I own that I had not heard any whisper of a separation, on other occasions, but rumour, as you know, sir, speaks often with a lying tongue!'

'No smoke without fire,' growled his uncle.

'But if it should be a very small fire?'

'A small fire may destroy a house, when once it is lit.'

Alfred was well satisfied with his work, and said no more, trusting to the old man's thoughts to do his task for him.

It worked well, and a letter was immediately written off to Charles, demanding an explanation. Alfred thought it expedient that he should be gone before his cousin arrived, and took his leave. He could do no more. His greatest ally now would be Charles' own pride. He had no way of knowing whether his cousin was really seriously involved with Lady Belinda, to the extent that he was willing to lose all for her sake. He very much feared that he was not. Nevertheless, the seeds of doubt had been sown in Simeon Moreton's mind. It was unlikely that Charles would take kindly to being interrogated by his grandfather, and there was always the possibility that he might lose his temper, as he had done when he was a boy with Alfred himself, and do or say that which the old man would not easily forgive. Whatever happened, it seemed likely that if ever any other chance presented itself Alfred would find it that much easier to use it, and to make his uncle believe him.

It was not long before his doubts were put at rest. He did not care to enquire of his uncle what was the outcome of Charles' visit, for he did not want to make his interest too obvious. He was relieved, therefore, to receive a letter from his uncle, referring to the subject himself. His nephew would be glad to hear, wrote Simeon Moreton, that Deverham had explained the matter fully to him. It was, as Alfred had suggested, greatly over-exaggerated, and Deverham had already, before his grandfather's letter had even arrived, extricated himself from the relationship.

It was a disappointment, but he had known from the first that it had been no more than an outside chance. Shrugging, Alfred drew from their hiding place Lady Belinda's letters, and re-read them for perhaps the twentieth time. A small smile crossed his lips. It would take careful handling, very careful handling indeed, but surely they could be made to work for him? He set himself to thinking of ways and means. It would not do to go about it too suddenly, and without being quite sure of his plans. There was plenty of time.

When he heard from his informant that his cousin had left London, and gone to Bath, he was not greatly concerned. To be sure, it seemed an odd place to go in March, when the Season would be commencing so soon, or at any other time of the year, come to that. Bath had long since fallen from its status as one of the most fashionable resorts in the country. Only the elderly went there, and such as really believed that the water could help their ailments, and dowdies on the fringes of society. Certainly not such as Deverham. Alfred assumed that some business, probably of his grandfather's, had taken his cousin there, and he would be gone for no longer than two or three days.

After more than a week had passed, he began to be surprised, and even alarmed. It was unheard-of that Deverham should forsake his friends and his accustomed haunts for so long. As yet no rumour had reached him of the presence of a beautiful young heiress in Bath, for those who had heard of it were not inclined to spread the news, since they had no wish to enlarge the field of contenders.

When ten days had gone by without word of Deverham, or any sign of his returning to London, Uffington could stand it no longer, but took leave of absence from his office and caught the next train to Bath. He had no very clear idea of what he should do when he arrived, but in the event it was unnecessary. Having left his bag in a cheap room at a small hotel near the station, he made his way up Manvers Street and Pierrepont Street, which he had been told would take him to the Abbey and Pump Room. He was just issuing from Pierrepont Street when a peal of silvery laughter, followed by a voice that he knew only too well, assailed his ear. Issuing from a little old building in the narrow street to his left was his cousin, and two young ladies, one of them decidedly beautiful and very fashionably dressed.

They were but a matter of yards from him. If it had been possible he would have turned, and darted back the way he had come, but his own sudden halt at the sound of their voices had attracted their attention. Deverham looked up and met his cousin's eyes. Not a muscle moved in his face, his expression did not alter, and yet Alfred knew that Deverham had instantly surmised why he was there.

There was nothing for it but to brazen it out.

'Cousin Deverham! I had not expected to meet with you here, like this!'

'Had you not? And yet I have been here for nearly two weeks, and Bath is not a large city.'

'So long a stay, Cousin? You are not out of sorts, I trust?'

'By no means. I don't know when I have ever felt better. And your visit—have you need to take the waters? An excess of spleen, perhaps?' he finished blandly. Uffington ground his teeth.

'I am here on business,' he replied shortly.

'Your own, or someone else's?' Charles was beginning to enjoy himself.

'Will you not introduce me to your charming companions?' Since Deverham was obviously not going to do so, there was a small satisfaction in forcing his hand.

'Certainly. Miss Winterbourne, Miss Florence, may I present my cousin, Mr Alfred Uffington. And now, we must be moving, for the wind is cold, and Lady

Winterbourne will be wondering what has happened to us. If you have nothing better to do, Uffington, I can recommend a visit to this little establishment. You may partake of Sally Lunn buns, which is a ceremony no visitor to Bath, for however short a time, should omit to enjoy. Good day.' Barely allowing time for the young ladies to make a small bow, Deverham swept his charges off, leaving his cousin gaping where he stood.

CHAPTER SIX

THEY returned one afternoon, two days after Alfred Uffington's sudden appearance in Bath, from a drive in the country. This was a great luxury to Patience, who seldom had the chance to go anywhere other than on foot, or to leave the confines of Bath. Her pleasure made her more lively than usual, and though the day was cloudy her quiet gaiety cast a glow over the proceedings. Even Deverham noticed that she spoke more than she generally did, and amused himself by provoking her into an argument as to the relative merits of Shakespeare and Dante.

What started as a piece of polite banter then became a serious discussion, passing somehow via *Vanity Fair*, published the previous year, to the Napoleonic era which of course they did not remember, but of which they had frequently been told by their parents and grandparents. Patience was interested to know Deverham's opinion on the recent events in Europe, for 1848 had been a year of many uprisings and revolutions on the Continent, and his position in society gave him more inside knowledge than she had been able to glean from the newspapers. She, in return, was able to enlighten him about the dreadful events at Chillianwallah only that January, when the Sikhs had been defeated. Her late brother's letters from India, carefully preserved by Lady Winterbourne, had given her an abiding interest in that country, and she was always careful to glean any scrap of information

from the newspaper, and from the conversation of
Bath acquaintances, one of whom was related to Lord
Dalhousie, the new Governor General of India.

They became so enthralled that for at least half an
hour they scarcely noticed the scenery through which
they passed, nor the sullen look on Florence's face.
She was accustomed to be the centre of attention, and
bitterly resented what she felt was Patience putting
herself forward, and showing off.

The gig, an unpretentious vehicle that Deverham
had hired, drew up in Gay Street.

'Are we here already? I declare, I had no idea,' said
Florence carelessly. 'Such lovely views as we have seen,
I was quite overcome with their beauty. I hope you
did not think me rude, that I was so silent on our
journey home.' This last was spoken with waspish
sarcasm, and both Deverham and Patience were
dismayed.

'My dear Miss Florence, I am afraid Miss
Winterbourne and I have behaved very shabbily towards you! We men are always the same, you know,
when we get on our hobby-horses, and find someone
kind enough to indulge us with the opportunity of
taking a canter on them!'

'I am sure I did not notice,' said Florence airily,
jumping down lightly from the gig and ignoring
Deverham's offered hand. Patience stepped more de-
murely down, unaided, since Deverham had turned
instinctively to follow Florence, who was already
walking up the steps.

'May I not come and drink tea with you, after
dinner? I have your grandmama's permission to do
so any evening. Perhaps I could read you some of the
poetry we were talking of. Would you like that?'

'Nothing would give me greater pleasure,' replied Florence coldly, without looking at him. 'Unfortunately, however, all this fresh air has given me the headache. I shall go to bed as soon as dinner is over.'

She went indoors, and he turned disconsolately away. Patience spoke softly to him.

'Do not mind her,' she pleaded. 'She is so very young, and her tastes do not run to reading. I should have remembered that. I expect it is the headache that has made her cross. She will be full of smiles again in the morning.'

He was too infatuated to admit that his idol had been cross, but too polite to agree to her wish that the conversation had not happened.

'I cannot regret having had the pleasure of so interesting a discussion,' he said warmly. 'I hope it did not weary you as much as Miss Florence.'

'By no means,' she murmured, and passed by him into the hall.

'You were not very polite, love,' she said mildly to Florence, who was pulling off her gloves with angry haste so that she might open a letter that was lying ready for her return.

'Well, you were not polite to me, prosing on in that boring way about such stuff. I wonder Deverham put up with it.'

'It was very bad of me, wasn't it? I will not do it again, I promise you.' Indeed, the pleasure of such intimate discussions was so keen that it was positively perilous to her fragile peace of mind. 'Do not be pulling at your glove like that, Florence, you will harm it. There, now, the button has come off. I will find it for you.'

'Do not trouble yourself,' said Florence, dropping the gloves on a little table and taking up her letter. 'I have plenty more pairs.' Patience thought a little sadly of the few pairs resting in their box in her room, and of how carefully she was wont to darn the tiniest hole, and colour the place with indian ink. She was bending to look under the table for the errant button which, in the troublesome fashion of its kind, had chosen to roll there and not into the open floor, when an exclamation from Florence made her look up. What she saw had her abandoning her search, and coming to Florence's side in time to support her as she swayed, white-faced, and nearly fell. Patience supported her with an arm round her waist, and guided her to a nearby chair.

'My dear child! Whatever can be the matter?'

Florence's lips trembled, and she could not answer, but pointed instead to the letter, which in her weakness she had dropped. Two tears made their way from her eyes and coursed down her cheeks.

'Your letter, of course. What is it? May I read it?'

Florence shook her head, and held out her hand for the piece of paper, which she folded with trembling hands and smoothed in her lap, her fingers passing over and over the surface of the paper as if to rub away whatever unpleasant words had been written on them.

'You must at least try to tell me, Flo, what has distressed you in this way. Mama is very good, and would never insist on seeing your private letters, but nevertheless she has a right to know with whom you correspond, particularly if there is something as serious as this appears to be. Would it not be easier to tell me about it, so that I may tell her?'

Florence drew a deep breath, and a little of the colour came back to her face. The tear marks were still on her cheeks, but she was more composed.

'Yes, I know all that. You shall read it in a minute, if you wish. Only I was so shocked, I hardly knew what I was doing. I will tell you about it, but not here!'

'Of course not, you are quite right. Do you go up to your room, and I will speak to Mama for a moment. She will have heard us come in, and will be surprised if she does not see us at all. Can you walk, now? You are not faint any longer?'

'No, I am well enough,' said Florence listlessly and, still holding her letter tight in her hand, she went slowly upstairs. Patience followed her to the first floor, where she found Lady Winterbourne, as she had expected, enthroned by the fire, and holding court to her new friend, that same lady to whom she had earlier recounted her sorrows in the Pump Room. She was a Miss Troston, who had come to live in Bath on the demise of her brother, with whom she had always lived. He had left her a modest sum, enough to keep her in the necessities, if not the elegances, of life, and she had fulfilled her dream of living in the city after many years of residing in an isolated village. Bath was to her a great metropolis, and she was deeply awed by Lady Winterbourne's rank, and her style of living. A simple soul, she seemed happy to hear the tale of Lady Winterbourne's trials and misfortunes over and over again, and each time brought forth an unfeigned sympathy and admiration that was incense to Lady Winterbourne's nostrils.

'Well, Mama, we are back again. I trust you have had a pleasant afternoon, for we certainly did!'

'Thank you, my dear. Miss Troston and I have been talking of old times, you know, and the time has passed so quickly I hardly noticed how long you were gone.'

'I am so glad! Good afternoon, Miss Troston. How are you?'

'Oh, very well, very well indeed, Miss Winterbourne! How could I not be? Your dear mother has been so interesting that I never spent so happy an afternoon! And then, of course, we have enjoyed such a delicious little repast! Everything so elegant! I am quite overcome!' Looking at the remains of the light repast, which seemed to have comprised buttered toast, crumpets, and sandwiches as well as two kinds of cake, Patience thought that she might well be completely overcome.

'Where is Florence? I do not see Florence?'

'I have sent her upstairs, Mama, for she has a little headache, and I thought it best that she should rest for a while.'

Lady Winterbourne was alarmed.

'A headache? I hope she is not sickening for anything. All this gadding about, mixing with one knows not whom, cannot be healthy. I have often said so. You must be sure she does not come near me, if she has taken anything, for you know how easily I catch things, and my constitution is not equal to it.'

'I think she is just a little tired, Mama,' soothed Patience. 'But you may be sure I shall not let her approach you until she is quite recovered.' Lady Winterbourne was satisfied, and Patience had the satisfaction of knowing that she might keep Florence out of her mother's sight until she had recovered her composure. Lady Winterbourne did not care to hear of other people's sorrows, and was inclined to regard it as an affront that anyone but she should admit to unhappiness.

Patience withdrew, and ran upstairs to her own room, where she swiftly put off her bonnet, and changed her outdoor dress of merino for an older afternoon dress of wool challis, and a plain lawn cap. She rang for tea to be brought to Miss Florence's chamber, and intercepted the housemaid so that she might carry the tray into the room herself.

Florence was seated by the fire, still in her outdoor dress and bonnet. Setting down the tray, Patience gently and quietly removed her bonnet as if she had been a child, and bent to unbutton and remove her boots, replacing them with the dainty kid slippers that Florence habitually wore indoors. Florence hardly seemed to notice, but submitted to what was done for her. She stared into the fire, her hands still smoothing the letter, while an occasional tear gathered and fell. Patience touched her hand, which was icy cold.

'You are very cold, dear Florence. Drink this tea, it will make you feel better. There is no hurry—I have told Grandmama that you have the headache, and we have nearly two hours until dinner.'

'I could not come down to dinner. I cannot eat.'

'Then you need not, but you must drink your tea, for it will do you good.' With unusual obedience Florence did so, and then a second cup. The obedience worried Patience more than anything else. It was so unlike Florence.

When the tea was drunk Patience moved the little table away, and drew up a stool next to Florence's chair. She laid both her hands on Florence's, stilling the distressed movement, and pressed them gently.

'Do you think you can tell me now, dear?'

'It is from Lavinia, my friend at school. You know we still write to one another.' She paused.

'And something is wrong?' prompted Patience. 'Your friend is ill, or in trouble?'

'In trouble, certainly. Her brother, Captain Curbridge, the one I . . . well, they have had word that his ship is lost.'

'That is very terrible! Miss Curbridge must be very unhappy. Was she very close to her brother?'

'I don't know. I don't think so. She is just my age, and he is twenty-five, so of course she did not see very much of him.' Florence spoke without much interest, and Patience, who had assumed that her distress was on behalf of her friend, began to realise that it was on Captain Curbridge's account that she was unhappy. It had never really crossed her mind that Florence's romantic escapade at school was any more than schoolgirl folly, but now it occurred to her that perhaps her niece's heart had been more touched than she had thought.

'Then of course you did not see a great deal of him, either.'

'Well, during the last few months I did. He was at home, you see, and Lavinia often invited me to visit with her. We went there nearly every weekend, for she had leave to do so. He is—was—very attentive to me.' She gave a little sob.

'Florence,' said Patience rather sternly. 'Did anything of a particular nature ever pass between you? You once said that he would have liked to ask your grandmama's permission to see you. Did he speak to you of love?'

'No, for he said I was too young for such things,' said Florence forlornly, 'but I think he would have liked to. He never said a word to me that you might not have listened to, and we were never alone together, at least not for more than a moment, by accident. Lavinia's mama was quite careful for that.'

Patience thought that she could not have been all that careful, since Florence was obviously able to make an assignation to meet Captain Curbridge for the illicit outing to the harbour which had alerted—and alarmed—her family. She also thought that it was not in human nature to pass up the chance of bringing such an heiress into the family.

'And you, Florence, what are your feelings on the subject? I know that it is said that a girl should have no thoughts of any man until she is given leave to do so, but I know well enough that such thoughts will come, and think no worse of you for that. Do you care for him?'

'I don't know!' Florence looked bewildered. 'I liked him, of course. He is—was—very handsome, and kind, and good, and I could not help knowing that he liked me very much. But I did not think... There was my coming-out to consider, and I was so looking forward to that, the new clothes, and London, and everything. He said I was too young, and I suppose I agreed with him. I know I was sad to hear that he had sailed, but I thought he would be sure to come back, and then I would see, but now... now I shall never see him again!'

'It is sure, then, that the ship is lost?'

'They think so. There was a storm, and the ship never reached its destination, though it should have arrived long since. And they have found pieces of wood, and one had the ship's name on it, that had come from one of the lifeboats. Oh, Patience! I can never look at the sea again! I thought it was so beautiful, but it is not!' She burst out crying, and Patience stood up to hold and comfort her. She thought it likely that the shock of the news had made Florence think more of her erstwhile lover than ever she had done before. She could only hope that she would not build up his memory into something it had never been.

Florence spent the next day in her room, and Patience gave a simplified version of the story to Lady Winterbourne, to account for Florence's grief.

'Naturally it is very distressing for the child, Mama. Her best friend at school, and a man whom she had known. We must be very gentle with her for a while.'

'I am sure I cannot see why she need make such a fuss,' replied her mother. 'Such things happen only too often, and a man who goes to sea is always at risk. At all costs, do not tell anyone of this. Lord Deverham would not like to know that she is weeping for another man.'

Deverham did, as a matter of course, call the following day. Patience met him with a tale of a trifling indisposition, and he responded by asking if he might have the favour of an interview with Lady Winterbourne. Patience, who looked at him with the eyes of love and missed no detail of his appearance, saw that he was dressed with particular care, and his boots surpassed even their usual well-kept gloss. A cold feeling stirred within her, and she strove to keep her voice even as she asked him to wait for a moment.

'Mama! Lord Deverham is below, and he particularly wishes to see you.' Lady Winterbourne sat up straighter, smoothed out the black silk of her skirt and adjusted her cap.

'Lord Deverham! And asking to see me! Patience, do you think . . . ?'

'Yes, I do. Oh, Mama, do you think this is right? She is still very young, and he knows her so little. Can they really make one another happy?'

'Why not? As to knowing her, how should any young man know the girl he proposes to? It is not possible that they should see very much of one another.'

'But so short an acquaintance! And Florence has been on her best behaviour since he arrived. He does not know what she is like. Will she ever make him happy?'

'You are by far too nice in your notions. It is not for us to tell him that Florence is wilful. She has her naughty ways, of course, but when they are married he will soon teach her to behave as he would wish. He will not be the first man to be caught by a pretty face.'

With a heavy heart, Patience returned to Deverham and bade him come up to the drawing-room.

Deverham followed her up the stairs, wondering as he did so whether Lady Winterbourne was likely to be in favour of his suit. That he was a good match he could not fail to know, but Florence was very young, and with her fortune and face might well expect to look even higher, and she had as yet had no opportunity to meet other suitors. He had written to his grandfather saying that he had met Miss Florence Winterbourne, and that she was as lovely as report had given her credit for. His grandfather had written back in the warmest possible terms.

...I have it on the best of authority that the young lady has at least a hundred thousand pounds, and, if she pleases you, I can see no reason why you should not put your luck to the test. Once she goes to London she will be besieged by men of all kinds, so you would do well to fix your interest with her now. If you should be successful, I may tell you that I shall at once make over to you a substantial portion of my business interests. I am an old man, and I have more than enough for my needs. No reason for you to wait until I turn up my toes!

There was more in the same vein. The offer was undoubtedly a generous one, and it was certain that nothing could please the old man more than to see his heir married so advantageously. It was enough to push Deverham, already fancying himself in love, into making his declaration in form.

Lady Winterbourne received him very graciously, and he saw at once that he need not fear any opposition in that quarter. He came to the point almost at once.

'It cannot have escaped your notice, Lady Winterbourne, that I find myself strongly attracted to your granddaughter. I think I may venture to say that she does not dislike me, though naturally no word of love has passed between us. May I have your permission to speak to her? General Thorpe will vouch for me, I know. Though I am not myself a wealthy man, I am my grandfather's heir. I have thought it proper to advise him of my intentions, and he writes most kindly, offering to give me a good part of my inheritance straight away. I would not like you to think that I am only interested in Miss Florence's fortune.'

'I am sure no one who knows you would think that, my dear Lord Deverham. It cannot be denied that the child will be very rich, and I myself am anxious to see her settled happily in life. I cannot, of course, answer for her, but I think she cannot be quite indifferent to you. As you know, she is a little unwell today, but if you will call, not tomorrow, but the next day you may have private speech with her.'

They parted with expressions of mutual esteem. Patience, unable to bear the sight of him leaving as the accepted lover of her niece, hid herself away until she heard the front door close behind him.

'You have known from the first that this would happen,' she told herself severely, pinching her lips and cheeks which were stricken white. 'It is ridiculous to feel like this. He will be in the family, and you will love him as a brother.' On this firm resolve she went down to the drawing-room, and endured her mother's raptures with a stoicism that an early Christian thrown into the arena with wild beasts might have envied.

Florence, when told of the good fortune that had befallen her, was listless but acquiescent. She had overcome the first shock of the news, and was making a real effort to overcome her grief. Patience saw it, and felt both surprise and respect. She thought that this hard lesson might yet be the making of Florence.

'Lord Deverham will be coming back in two days, and you must have an answer ready for him. You know Grandmama would never compel you, and you are very young to be engaged. If you wish it, you may ask him to wait a while, say a year, and then ask you again. It will be perfectly proper to do so.'

'I do not mind that. I should prefer to have it all settled. I should like to be Lady Florence,' she admitted naïvely.

'You would be Lady Deverham, you know,' gently corrected Patience. 'Your title comes from your husband, not your father.'

'What matter, so long as I am "my lady"? I may have a house in town, and give parties, and dress up every night.'

It seemed rather an empty way of considering a marriage, but Patience was resolved to be gentle with her, and did not remonstrate. She reflected that it was impossible that Florence should not learn to love Deverham very well. She herself could imagine no greater bliss than... She pulled herself up sharply.

Offerings of flowers were brought twice a day from Deverham to the supposed invalid, and it had to be admitted that bouquets of hothouse roses and lilies helped to distract her, and offered a foretaste of the delights of marriage to a man who was accustomed to live in the first style of fashion. When the second day dawned Florence dressed herself with particular care, and waited in the drawing-room, surrounded by his bouquets. There was a knock at the door, and soon Deverham was with her.

Florence received his protestations of love with some complacency, and a lack of confusion that might have daunted him, had he not put it down to her innocence and inexperience. He saw that she was far from head over ears in love with him, and was inclined to like her the more for it. In true form, he went down on his knee to offer his hand to her, and with shy grace she put her own in it. He pressed it to his lips.

'You have made me the happiest of men, my dear,' he said, rising to his feet again and seating himself next to her. 'I hope that I shall be able to make you as happy.' He drew from his pocket a magnificent sapphire and diamond ring and her eyes sparkled as he placed it on her finger. Though she owned a great deal of jewellery that had belonged to her mama, she had never been allowed to wear more than a modest necklet of pearls.

'A sapphire, for your eyes,' he said. 'It should by rights have been an amethyst, but I wanted nothing but the most precious for you.' She thanked him with more warmth than she had hitherto displayed, and he thought fondly what a child she was.

'I will not press you to set too early a date for our marriage,' he said nobly.

'Oh, no, for I want to spend the Season in London. I have quite set my heart on it!'

'Then I will not spoil it for you. Perhaps, if it is not too soon, we could be married in September. We should then have good weather for our honeymoon tour. I should have liked to have taken you to Italy, and to the lakes, but of course that is not possible as things are at the moment. We might go to Scotland, though, which I believe is very beautiful. A cousin of my father's has a castle there. Should you like that?'

'Oh, yes. I am sure I should.'

She did not sound very enthusiastic, but he put that down to maidenly shyness. Very soon he rose to take his leave, promising to visit again the next day.

'I expect you would like to be rid of me now, so that you may tell your grandmother and your aunt.'

'Yes. Thank you, Lord Deverham.'

'It will be proper for you to call me Charles, now,' he pointed out.

'Oh, I couldn't!' she said involuntarily. He laughed.

'I hope you may soon learn to! I should like to see those pretty lips frame my name.' He embraced her tenderly, kissing her brow and cheek, since she did not offer her lips, and he would not frighten her by being too passionate. Then he was gone, and Florence was left moving her hand in a shaft of sunlight, so that she might admire the glints of light from her new ring.

Lady Winterbourne was jubilant. Florence would be safely off her hands, and it was, moreover, a match such as no one could fault. A husband in the nobility, with a wealthy grandfather to boot! If she could have had her way the marriage would have gone ahead without any delay, in spite of the fact that Florence still lacked a month of her seventeenth birthday. She herself, she reminded Patience when she remarked on the matter, had been married at eighteen, and what could have been happier? That Florence was not precisely head over heels in love did not weigh with her a jot. Love was something that happened after marriage, if one were lucky.

'You don't think that is a little old-fashioned, Mama? You remember how delighted we all were when the Queen married Prince Albert, soon after we came to Bath, to think that she was able to make a love-match.'

'We are blessed in having a Queen with so strong a sense of duty. I am quite sure that as Queen of England, even at that young age, she would not have permitted herself to fall in love with anyone who was unsuitable.' Lady Winterbourne was not to be persuaded. In her eyes a decided preference, a similarity in age, fortune and status, and above all the approval of the families were surely all that was, at this stage, required.

'It is not as if Deverham were an old man,' she pointed out when Patience said that a difference of thirteen years was not exactly similarity. 'He is a young man still, and in my opinion marriage with a man slightly older than herself is just what Florence needs. Why, she is steadier and quieter already.'

It was true. Florence was a great deal quieter than before. She bore the inevitable congratulations that were showered upon her by her grandmother's friends with admirable composure, showing none of that jubilation that might almost have been expected from one who was about to make so good a marriage. The Bath set, some of whom had hoped to have their own relative the one to win so golden a prize, nevertheless forgave her her choice and pronounced her a very ladylike young girl. Patience was not so sure. Florence never, now, spoke of Captain Curbridge, or of her friend Lavinia, but her aunt saw a look in her eye that gave her reason to suppose that now, when it was too late, this sorrow had taught her to know the secrets of her own heart. She could only hope that, in learning to love one other man better than herself, Florence would move on to love her husband in the same way.

Deverham wrote at once to Simeon Moreton, who replied in ecstatic terms, and with golden promises. He also wrote a very civil letter to Lady Winterbourne, and a loving note to Florence, his new granddaughter, as he called her. He begged that they might come and visit him as soon as might be, for he longed to make the acquaintance of Florence, and while he could not hope that his poor house would be worthy of Lady Winterbourne, nevertheless everything would be done for her comfort if she would deign to honour his humble roof. No mention was made of Patience, who rightly but reluctantly concluded that Mr Moreton had never heard of her, and did not know of her existence.

Lady Winterbourne was pleased with the letter, which she felt showed a proper respect for her rank.

'I do not, in general, care to make long journeys, or to stay in any house other than my own. On this occasion, however, it is my duty to do so, and I can assure you, my dear Deverham, that I shall grudge no effort on my granddaughter's behalf. It is very proper that she should make the acquaintance of Mr Moreton as soon as possible.'

'I know that my grandfather will be very happy. I am sure he will soon learn to love Florence almost as much as I do.'

'And then we shall go to London, shall we not, Grandmama?' Florence was anxious that her visit to London should not be long delayed. April was upon them, and the Season starting.

'I suppose it must be so. Though why you must do it, now that you are engaged to Deverham, is a mystery to me. Would you not prefer to remain here? I am sure Deverham will not mind staying on, and you would see a great deal more of one another. Or you might stay on with Mr Moreton, if you wished. I cannot see the need to go to London now. You might be presented next year, as Lady Deverham.'

Florence looked mutinous.

'You promised that we might go up for the Season, Grandmama. Surely you will not change your mind now?'

'Since you make such a point of it, I suppose it must be so. But it is very odd.'

'I think that Florence should have her Season, ma'am,' put in Deverham. 'It is a great thing for a young girl, you know, and she is sure to be the belle of the year. You would not wish to deny her that! Besides, she may find someone far more eligible than I, and end up a duchess! She must have her chance!' He spoke in jest, but Florence merely gave a little smile, and it was left to Lady Winterbourne to protest that she was sure Florence could never find anyone else to love when she was lucky enough to be engaged to Deverham.

It was agreed in the end that they would leave for Manchester as soon as might be—which would not be very soon, Patience knew, for it would take a great deal of work to get her mother ready for such a journey. They would have a short visit of two weeks with Mr Moreton, during which time Deverham undertook to arrange for his man of business to find them a house in London, engage servants, and have all ready for their arrival. They might then go straight in, with none of the problems and discomforts that usually attended on such a move. Lady Winterbourne could not be delighted, but she saw that it was not going to be possible to omit a visit to London, so she resigned herself, thinking that at least Deverham would be able to deal with the details that she would otherwise have found so taxing.

Patience, in private, pleaded with her mother to be allowed to remain with Mrs Anstruther, in Bath or at her home if she should return before Lady Winterbourne came back. In vain she pointed out that she had not been invited, and that Mr Moreton might not care to include her.

'You know very well that if you were not invited, it was merely an oversight on Mr Moreton's behalf. He would be most embarrassed to know that you had stayed behind.'

'But you have heard from Deverham that he is a gentleman of solitary habits! It will be bad enough to have two strange females staying in his house, without a third arriving of whom he has never even heard!'

'In my day, girls did not refer to their mothers as "strange females".'

Since Lady Winterbourne almost never made a joke, Patience treated this one with the requisite appreciation.

'You are so droll, Mama! But you know what I mean. I should so much prefer not to visit Mr Moreton.'

Lady Winterbourne's flash of good humour did not last long. She had a great dislike of being thwarted, and was not accustomed to it.

'And I prefer that you should. How would it be if I were ill? It is likely, after the journey, that I shall be quite prostrated for at least two days. Who is to care for me, if not you? There is the journey, besides. You cannot imagine that Florence would stir herself to look after me.' It was in vain that Patience pointed out the excellence of Florence's maid. Lady Winterbourne was accustomed to being cared for by Patience, and no one else would do. Patience, who had known that there was not much hope, gave way and turned her mind to packing.

This necessitated a great deal of care. Patience was relieved to know that Florence's maid could be trusted to look after her mistress's things, for there was more than enough to be done for Lady Winterbourne. Almost every gown she possessed must be brought out, unwrapped from its brown paper, and considered. Since those which were of silk had had their voluminous skirts unpicked from the waistband, to enable the fabric to be rolled and prevent folds from cracking, Patience was forced to employ a sewing woman to assist with the task. The black sewing was so tiring to the eyes. Her own wardrobe was not so difficult, since she had few gowns, and they were for the most part in practical colours and fabrics. Much to her astonishment, Lady Winterbourne decreed that Patience should have some new, for Manchester and for London. Patience accordingly found herself the proud possessor of a new merino day-dress, of a deep rose pink, a lighter summer walking-dress of silvery green cambric, the colour of young apple leaves, and two silk evening gowns of blue and light pink.

'You are not to be buying those dreary colours you generally wear, Aunt Patience,' decreed Florence. 'I declare I should be quite ashamed of you, particularly in London. If Grandmama will not pay for them, I shall do so myself.' Patience was touched, and gratified. Although the basic motive was perhaps a selfish one, nevertheless she had never known her niece display so much generosity. It was not that she was mean with her money, for her trustees made her such a generous allowance that she would always be prepared to give if asked. Merely, she had rarely before noticed anyone's wants but her own.

As a crowning glory, Lady Winterbourne disinterred, from the sandalwood chest where they had been shrouded in silver paper and packed with rose bags against the moth, four magnificent shawls, actually from Kashmir itself and not the Norwich or Paisley ones made in their imitation. They had been sent home to his mother by poor Augustus, when he first went out to India with his Florence, and Lady Winterbourne had treasured them. Miraculously, after so long, they were found to be quite free of damage by moths, and the fine, soft wool and silk still glowed with vibrant colours. Even Florence, who had several fine Norwich shawls, drew in her breath in admiration and longing.

Two of the shawls were in sombre tones, and Lady Winterbourne decided that it would not be inappropriate for her to appear in them. The other two were brighter colours, and Lady Winterbourne, as a great favour, presented one to each of the girls. Patience had never received so valuable a gift from her mama, particularly as it was not her birthday or Christmas, and she was quite moved, so Lady Winterbourne was perfectly satisfied with the effect of her generosity.

For his own part, Deverham would have been perfectly happy, in view of Florence's youth, for the engagement not to be publicly announced, but merely made known among their own circle, but Lady Winterbourne, who perhaps wanted to be quite sure that there would be no opportunity of a later denial, was insistent. Notices were therefore sent to all the newspapers, and so it was that Alfred Uffington learned of his cousin's good fortune. It need not be said that he was far from delighted.

CHAPTER SEVEN

PATIENCE viewed the visit to Manchester with dread. When she remembered how many times in the past she had longed for the chance to see the world, any part of it, that lay beyond Bath and its confines, she could have wept for her own simplicity. Now, it was true, she would see something of that great manufacturing town, one of the sources of her country's new greatness and prosperity, and afterwards she would see London, which before had been beyond the dizzy heights of imagining. With what pleasure, now, would she seize the chance to remain in the cosy familiarity of Bath!

Half worn out with the frenzy of the preparations, and with the difficult task of keeping her mother calm and as cheerful as she would ever allow herself to be, she found that the journey passed by as a blur. She had always viewed travelling by railway as the height of modern luxury, and under Deverham's sheltering wing it was certainly that. It was with the deepest relief that she was able to leave to him the unknown details of tickets, timetables and reservations. He bespoke an entire first-class carriage for Lady Winterbourne, Patience, Florence and himself, with second-class seats for the two maids and his own manservant, whose strength and patience were severely tried by the quantities of luggage without which neither Lady Winterbourne nor her granddaughter considered it possible to travel.

Patience was so taken up by her mother's needs during the journey that she scarcely had time to think of their destination. Fortunately Florence was in the sunniest of moods, having received only that morning the most magnificent set of pearl ornaments from Mr Moreton, with a kind note saying that he could not wait for her arrival to present them to her. She chattered happily to her betrothed throughout the journey, showing none of the trepidation natural to a young girl going to meet so important a future relative, and Patience was only too glad that Deverham was diverted by her childish talk, and that the two of them were happily occupied.

By the time they were approaching Manchester they were all tired. In Lady Winterbourne this took the form of gently voiced but ceaseless complaints, while Florence grew demanding and pettish. Deverham humoured her as gently as he could, but Patience could have slapped her when she remarked, for perhaps the twentieth time, that she was tired, and bored, and were they nearly there? She saw Deverham's lips tightening, and hurried to speak.

'If you are so tired, dear, will you not come and sit here, by me, and try if you cannot close your eyes for a little while? You know Lord Deverham has told us that there is less than an hour before we reach Manchester, and then there is the journey to the house. You must be looking your best to meet Mr Moreton!'

'You know I cannot sleep sitting up,' snapped Florence, 'and, besides, if I put my head back my hair will be disarranged, and I shall arrive looking a fright! Anyway, I have the headache.'

'Nobody,' remarked Lady Winterbourne to the world at large, 'nobody knows what I suffer from headaches. I hope I am not one to complain, but the pounding behind my eyes...I hope you will never suffer so, Florence.'

'Oh, Grandmama, you always think you have things worse than other people,' said Florence crossly. This was undeniable, but tactless, for it led Lady Winterbourne to hold forth for several minutes about her delicate health, enumerating the instances when the doctors had remarked that they had never known anyone to suffer as she had done. Florence was building up steam to make some devastatingly frank and undutiful remark, and Patience delved again in the bag she had packed for the journey with things she thought she might need.

'Mama, I have here some of the peppermint drops that you like. You know the doctor said they were the very thing for soothing the nerves. Florence, if I roll my shawl very carefully, you may put it behind your neck, and I think you will be able to rest your head without untidying your hair. I will bathe your forehead, and if you close your eyes it might refresh you.' Firmly she administered a large peppermint drop to her mother, who found herself unable to speak round its dimensions, and was able to settle Florence comfortably. Peace was restored, and unknown to herself she gave a little sigh.

'And what of you, Miss Winterbourne? Have you nothing in your bag to administer to yourself?'

She had almost forgotten Deverham, sitting quietly in his corner of the carriage, and jumped when he spoke quietly. She looked up to find his eyes, friendly and amused, fixed on her, and gave a shy smile.

'I am quite well, thank you, Lord Deverham. May I perhaps offer you a peppermint drop as well?'

He laughed quietly. Lady Winterbourne was dozing, her head falling back, and Florence seemed to be resting also.

'Do you think I require one, Miss Winterbourne? Perhaps you are afraid that if I talk I will wake our companions.'

'As to that, they cannot sleep much longer, for we must be nearly arriving. I should not care for your tongue to be hindered then, sir, for I must tell you that I rely on you to see us safely off this train, and also to keep Florence amused.'

'For the first, I cannot believe that you could not organise the whole, so competent as you are. As to Florence, will she require so much entertainment?'

She saw that she had erred, and hastened to make amends.

'By no means, but of course she will be interested to hear what you have to tell her of the city as we pass through it. Shall we pass any of your grand-father's factories as we go? I know his house is on the outskirts, but we must travel through the city to reach it, must we not?'

'We will pass one, but I do not think Florence is likely to wish to hear about it. She is so young, and delicate, I cannot think of her in connection with business of that kind. I own I have always found the mills very interesting, and as a boy it was a treat to be allowed to visit them.'

'You have done so? How I envy you!' She spoke without thinking, and regretted it instantly, for it would have been better for her own peace of mind if she spoke to him as little as possible. She could not deny to herself that her first impression of his handsome person was in no way tarnished by knowing him better. He was an intelligent and interesting companion, and she had learned to value his judgement and enjoy hearing his opinions.

'If you would like, I could take you to see them one day,' he offered diffidently. 'I did not think that ladies cared for such things.'

'Not all, perhaps, but I own that I find them fascinating. I have heard and read a good deal about the new manufactories, and the conditions to be found in them. I should like to see them for myself.'

'Then you shall. I think you cannot but be impressed, when you do, and while I know that conditions in such places are sometimes very shocking, you will not find such things in my grandfather's mills. He, you know, is not ashamed to say that he has risen, as it were, from the ranks, and he regards the care of his workpeople as part of the debt he owes to them and to himself. He was strongly in support, for instance, of limiting the number of hours worked by women and children. He himself had been doing so for some time before the Act last year.'

'You must be very proud of him.'

'Yes, I am, for there is no humbug about him at all. You will like him, I think, for now I come to think of it you are much the same.'

'No humbug—only humbugs!' she quipped, taking out her bag of peppermints again. He laughed.

'Now I suspect I have been talking too much! I will take one, and guarantee to swallow it or chew it up before the time comes to alight!'

Patience closed her eyes and pretended to sleep, for with every such exchange she found herself more and more drawn to him. She reflected a little sadly that he did not find *her* too delicate to be connected with, or to visit, a factory. She hoped very much that the chance to visit one would be granted her, but vowed that she would only do it if she were accompanied by someone else. Apart from anything else, Florence was inclined to resent any such attention being paid to another than herself, and she must not upset Florence.

As the train began to slow, Lady Winterbourne awoke with a jerk, and Patience was fully occupied in reassuring her that nothing was to be forgotten, and in helping Florence to tidy her already tidy hair, and set her bonnet on becomingly.

It was dusk as they emerged, yawning and stiff, from the train, and once again there was the usual bustle over luggage—was Deverham quite sure his man had counted the pieces? Florence could not see the box that held her best bonnets—was Patience sure nothing had been left behind in the carriage? Lady Winterbourne could not account for her muff—until all were safely stowed in the carriage that had been sent from Moreton Grange to fetch them. Patience, squashed into a corner so that her mother and niece might have more room for their skirts, could see little as they drove, and retained only a confused impression of roofs and chimneys against a darkening sky. Then at last the wheels were crunching on gravel, and welcoming lights were ahead.

Their welcome was as warm as they had been led to expect. Mr Moreton himself, though crippled by his gout, hobbled into the hall to greet Lady Winterbourne with a deference that delighted her, shook his grandson's hand with warmth and bestowed upon Florence a hearty kiss, which Patience was relieved to see she took in good part. His comments on her beauty were almost too fulsome, but

Florence revived like a wilting flower after rain, and sparkled happily.

There was a momentary awkwardness when Mr Moreton failed to greet Patience. This was not surprising, since nobody had thought to apprise him of her existence, and until the moment when Deverham brought her forward he had taken her for Lady Winterbourne's maid. When her existence as a member of the family had been disclosed to him, however, he made up for his lapse by a frank apology that pleased Patience, though her mother was inclined to look askance.

'You'll have to forgive me, my dear, for I never knew of your existence until this moment! Never knew her ladyship had another daughter, for to tell you the truth, I'm not much acquainted with the great ones of the land!'

'Well, if you were, you would still not have known of me, for I am afraid I am only a little one of the land! I am very sorry, sir, to be here, as it were, uninvited. I hope it is not inconvenient.'

'Far from it, my dear. I hardly know what to do with this great house, all by myself, and it will be good to have a few more people in it, for once. Those people of mine have next to nothing to do. Do them good to have to earn their keep, for once!' This was said with high good humour, and Patience saw that he was proud of his house and his servants. The room to which Patience was conducted was furnished with a richness that she had never before experienced, and she spent a fascinated quarter of an hour exploring it when she was alone, before going to see her mother.

'Only fancy, Mama! Turkey carpet throughout, and the walls hung with silk! The curtains are velvet, like

yours, and so heavy I wonder that they can pull them
at all! And such a fire—the room was as warm as if
it were July!'

'It is certainly very comfortable,' admitted Lady
Winterbourne, who was lying in a soft wrapper, with
her stays loosened, while her maid saw to the un-
packing of her things. 'Of course, it is all very vulgar,
but one cannot wonder at it. A man of the people,
of course, but such a character!' Patience was glad
that her mother had chosen to be pleased with her
host, for she was not in general inclined to be civil to
anyone who, in her opinion, smelled of the shop. Mr
Moreton's relationship with Deverham, however, more
than offset his unfortunate antecedents, and she was
obviously going to think of him as an eccentric.
Patience could only hope that he would not notice,
or that, if he did, he would not mind.

She need not have worried. Simeon Moreton was
so delighted to have under his roof the widow of a
baronet that he would have accepted almost any
amount of condescension on her part. While he had
resented the unspoken criticisms made by his own son-
in-law, because the late Lord Deverham had been, in
his opinion, a fool about money, for Lady
Winterbourne he had nothing but respect. She was
everything, in his opinion, that a titled lady should
be, and he would have been disappointed if she had
been less haughty.

With Florence he was almost gloating in his delight. His fulsome compliments would have embarrassed anyone with more modesty, but since Florence
herself thought that her own beauty was probably the
most important thing in the world, she accepted them
happily.

Dinner, which had been held back until their arrival, was a very grand affair. A short rest and a quick change into evening dress had done little to refresh the ladies, and Patience for her part would have been glad of a light supper and an early night. Instead, their host's generous spirit, and his estimation of what was owing to his guests and to the spirit of the occasion, led him to set before them no less than seven courses, with their accompanying wines. The food was rich and delicious, but Patience could scarcely swallow it, while the light from what seemed like thousands of candles as well as several lamps glittered on the silver with which the table was loaded in a way that made her head spin. Lady Winterbourne, who had slept a good deal on the train, was fortunately enjoying herself in her favourite way, recounting the tale of her troubles, in a suitably expurgated version, to an enthralled Mr Moreton, whose unfeigned interest and sympathy quite won her, and led her to describe him to Patience, when they finally withdrew for the night, as a very good sort of man, and remarkably gentlemanlike.

Florence had also slept, and with the resilience of youth had come downstairs in her pale blue silk gown looking as fresh as a daisy, as Simeon delightedly informed her. She had pleased him mightily by putting on the pearls he had sent her, and though Patience thought them perhaps a little ostentatious for a girl not quite seventeen, she could not deny that they glowed against Florence's white skin, while the pear-shaped drops of the ear-rings made her long neck look even longer.

'There, now, if they aren't just the thing for you!' exclaimed Mr Moreton when he saw her. 'Nothing but the best, I said, and you may be sure these are the best. A pretty penny they cost, and I don't begrudge a bit of it, for they'll keep their value, you'll see.' Such an open way of speaking made Lady Winterbourne stare, but Florence hardly regarded it.

'They are very pretty, and just what I like, for Grandmama won't permit me to wear my mother's jewels yet. Thank you, sir!'

He chuckled, and rubbed his hands in delight. 'Diamonds, I wanted, but the lad from the shop said no, it must be pearls, and dash it all, he was right! I'm not too proud to take a word of advice, for I don't always know what's what, in that line, and I'm not ashamed to own it. Now should you find me doing or saying something that don't seem to you quite the thing, my lady, just you up and tell me. I shan't take it amiss!' Patience stifled a giggle at the sight of her mama's face when thus adjured, and spent a happy ten minutes imagining the possibilities of such an offer. With regret she acknowledged to herself that Lady Winterbourne was unlikely to avail herself, knowingly at least, of the invitation.

Fortunately Patience was allowed to sit quietly through what seemed like an interminable dinner, for Mr Moreton talked to Lady Winterbourne, and Florence monopolised Deverham's attention completely. He did, it was true, attempt several times to include Patience in their talk, but Florence pouted, and Patience let him see that she was happy to be quiet. When the ladies withdrew, Simeon poured himself a glass of port, and gestured to his grandson to take a chair next to him.

'Pour yourself a glass, lad, and we'll drink another toast,' he said. He had already proposed, and drunk, several toasts throughout the meal, and Deverham feared that he would suffer for it in the morning.

'I am glad to see you in such good health, Grand-father,' he said tactfully, filling his glass and absently setting the decanter down out of Mr Moreton's reach.

'Never felt better, my boy. From the moment I heard you'd got yourself paired up with the heiress, I took a turn for the better. They say a light heart makes for a healthy body, and by God! my heart has been light these past days. You've done well, my lad, and been lucky too. She's a real little beauty, and young too. Young and beautiful girls with fortunes attached to them don't turn up too often, I can tell you!'

'I am a very lucky man,' agreed Deverham. 'I am glad she meets with your approval, sir.'

'Approval! That's mild. And she's well connected, too! That's what I can't get over. That Lady Winterbourne may be a widow with hardly twopence to rub together, but she's related to half the great houses in England, I hear. Pity about her daughter, though.'

'I think Lady Winterbourne is exceedingly lucky in her daughter,' said Deverham. 'Without her she would be uncomfortable indeed. You should have heard her ladyship on the train! Between the two of us, sir, she was well-nigh unbearable, for I've never spent so long cooped up with any woman before, but Miss Winterbourne knew just how to handle her. She is an excellent daughter.'

'Yes, yes, I'll take your word for all that, but she's a poor-looking thing, isn't she, and getting a bit long in the tooth. She'll not find a husband too easily, I'll bet.'

'I do not think that Miss Winterbourne is in the market for such a commodity,' responded Deverham, with a spark of anger that surprised him. His grandfather was expressing thoughts which he himself had had when he first met Patience, but he had forgotten now that he had ever had them. He had no memory of the fact that when he had first met Patience he had felt some pity for her, seeing that by comparison with Florence she was so very plain and ordinary looking. He had never heard the expression 'homely', but if he had done he would unhesitatingly have applied it to Patience, since in his eyes she was one of those girls who were destined to stay at home and care for their elderly parents, while declining into a useful but dull old age.

He was not aware how it was, but by degrees this opinion of her had undergone a subtle transformation. For some time now he had become accustomed to watch her, and enjoy the glow in her lovely eyes when she was happy, and their sparkle when she was amused. He did not realise how much of his enjoyment of their joint outings had come from her quick and enquiring mind, but he knew that one of the things he was looking forward to was seeing her in London, and hearing her opinion of what she saw and heard there. He wanted to take her to the theatre, to the opera, to the museums and art galleries, for he was sure that she would revel in such treats.

Now it came to him for the first time that others, besides himself, might find her entertaining and attractive. It was true that all young women should be looking to be married, and while she was unfortunately situated in her lack of fortune, she might still find someone who would be willing to overlook that and offer her marriage. Somehow the thought disturbed him, and he was almost vexed with himself. He had seen enough of Lady Winterbourne to know that she was not an easy person to live with, and surely he should be glad if Patience were to receive a respectable offer. As her nephew by marriage, it might be possible for him to settle something on her, since his grandfather was being so generous. Then, at least, he would have some power to approve, or possibly disapprove, of any suitor who might present himself.

The subject of these thoughts, all unaware of their trend, would have been horrified had she known of them. Patience was in the drawing-room with her mother and Florence. The former was nodding over her cup of coffee, and the latter was sighing, in some boredom, and endeavouring to amuse herself by catching the light in the fine diamonds set into the clasp on her pearl bracelet.

'It is very dull here. I hope we shall not stay too long. I shall tell Deverham that I would like to go to London sooner, perhaps next week.'

'That would scarcely be very civil to his grandfather, when he has been so kind to you, and means to be so good to Lord Deverham.'

'Well, he could come to London, if he liked.'

'I hardly think he is well enough, and come to that, your grandmama must have time to recover from this journey before she undertakes another one. Besides, the house will not be ready.'

This was a more cogent argument in Florence's eyes.

'No, I suppose not. But what are we to do here? I do not think that Mr Moreton has any acquaintance that we should care to know. I wonder what the shops in Manchester are like?'

'Should you be interested to visit a factory? Lord Deverham was kind enough to say that we might, if we wished.'

'Goodness, whatever for? From what I could see from the carriage they were ugly enough from the outside, without going into one.'

Patience reflected that she should not be surprised by such a reaction, and offered her niece a book of engravings that lay on a small table nearby. The choice proved to be an unlucky one, for Patience had not noticed that the subjects were ships, and included among them was a picture of the very vessel that had been lost with Captain Curbridge. Florence, tired with travelling, burst at once into tears and fled from the room. Patience was obliged to leave her to the ministrations of her maid, for the outburst had woken Lady Winterbourne, and the gentlemen could be heard approaching. Patience soothed her mother, made excuses for Florence being too tired to stay up, and poured tea when the tray was brought in. Mr Moreton looked disappointed, so Patience exerted herself to amuse him, finally having the notion of asking him whether he played at cribbage.

'My dear Miss Winterbourne, you could not have made a more inspired remark, or one which you will not live to regret more sincerely! I should warn you that my grandfather plays with fiendish cunning! I have never managed to beat him yet!'

'Ah, but then he has never played with me! I think I may say I have been well taught, for I am used to play with General Thorpe, in Bath, and military tactics, you know, must prevail over civilian skill!'

'Played with old Thorpe, have you?' Mr Moreton was gratified by the mention of his friend. 'Military tactics may be all very well, my girl, but give me good business sense any day! Now, where have they put that confounded board?'

Patience did her best, and managed to win one game out of three, which her generous host was pleased about.

'Can't abide playing with a fool!' he exclaimed. 'Well done, my lass—I beg pardon, Miss Winterbourne, I should say.'

'Please do not alter your mode of address on my behalf, sir,' she begged. 'I have never been called a lass before, and I take it as a great compliment. Besides, you called me a great many other things besides, during that last game, and most of them were much worse than that!'

He was conscience-stricken.

'There, now, wasn't I telling you to let me know of it, if I didn't behave like a gentleman? What will her ladyship think of me?'

'Well, she won't think anything much, for she is nine-tenths asleep, and if you will excuse me, I think I must be bidding you goodnight.'

'If I said anything I shouldn't——'

'My dear sir, you called me nothing that was not deserved, and I have not enjoyed a game so much for a long time! Pray do not give it another thought. I hope we shall be friends, and friends never mind such things, you know!' She roused her mother gently, and led her from the room. Mr Moreton looked thoughtfully after her.

'That's a good girl. A very good girl. Plain, of course, but none the worse for that. We must see what we can do for her, when you go to London, my boy. Would she take it amiss, do you think, if I were to settle some money on her? I can spare it, after all, and if it would serve to help her find a husband——'

'I think she would take it very much amiss,' said Deverham crossly, quite forgetting that he himself had been formulating the very same plan.

'Well, if you say so. But I think it's a pity.'

Fortunately for Patience, Lady Winterbourne was too sleepy to wish for any conversation, and soon dismissed her daughter in favour of her maid. Patience peeped in at Florence, and was relieved to see that she was sleeping soundly, her tears over. Patience wondered very much whether her niece's heart had really been touched, or whether her sorrow was the natural sentimentality of a young girl for an older man who had taken notice of her. It was true that Florence did not seem exactly heartbroken, and such outbursts as that of the evening were rare. Nevertheless, Patience was learning that Captain Curbridge was far from forgotten, and she felt that the gaiety Florence showed when talking of her London Season was sometimes a little forced, as though she was using it to drive away unpleasant thoughts.

Alone at last in the luxury of her own room, Patience slowly undressed. She did not have her own maid, and though her mother's was willing to help she preferred to manage for herself as far as possible, for she cherished these moments of solitude. The fire had been newly made up, and she enjoyed the unusual warmth of the room, as, tired though she was, she examined her travelling dress for marks, and brushed it carefully. She felt restless, unable to settle, and the accustomed tasks soothed her. When at last she climbed into bed she felt the tension ebbing from neck and shoulders, and sank with relief into sleep.

CHAPTER EIGHT

THE following morning, Lady Winterbourne's worst
fears were realised, and it was with gloomy satisfaction that she reported to Patience that she felt decidedly unwell. One look at her told Patience that for
once she was not exaggerating. Her eyes were too
bright, and her cheeks too flushed. When Patience
took her hand it felt burning hot.

'Mama! You are so hot, I am sure you have a fever.
You must return to bed at once.'

'I do not want to.' Lady Winterbourne, now that
she was really ill, was inclined to be frightened. She
did not want to admit how unwell she really was.
Having slept badly, with disturbing, uncomfortable
dreams, she had been relieved to find that it was
morning. For all her complaints, she seldom had any
illness worse than a slight cold in the head, and like
many healthy people was inclined to resent her body
for the symptoms it was experiencing. 'I am not hot
at all. On the contrary, I feel quite cold, and I will
stay here by the fire. Only, my legs are aching, and
my head, and I do not want to move.'

Since she was already reclining on a comfortable
sofa, Patience thought it best to let her have her way
and, making sure she was well covered and shielded
from draughts, told her maid to stay with her mistress, and give her as much to drink as she would take.

She would normally have stayed with Lady
Winterbourne, but here as a guest in the house it

seemed better that she should attend breakfast, at least on the first proper day of their visit. Downstairs she found Deverham just starting to eat, and they were joined almost straight away by Florence. Deverham served them both from the array of dishes on the sideboard, and Patience out of habit busied herself with pouring tea and coffee.

'I expect Lady Winterbourne prefers to breakfast in her room?' asked Deverham as she passed him a cup of coffee. He scarcely noticed that it was made just as he liked it, but was conscious of a feeling of comfort. Patience looked serious.

'I am afraid my mother is not well this morning.' Neither of her auditors was very surprised: they had spent most of the previous day hearing how travelling upset Lady Winterbourne.

'She will like to remain in her room for today, I expect. Please ask the housekeeper for anything that you think she might like. It was a very tiring journey yesterday, and I know she is not accustomed to travel.'

'I am afraid it is rather worse than that,' said Patience. 'I own that I thought at first she was just ... tired, but she is feverish, and complains of aching in her head and limbs.'

Florence looked alarmed.

'A fever? She really is ill, then?'

'I think she is, but I am sure that a few days' rest will put her right. She is much stronger than she thinks, you know.'

'But she might be infectious!' Florence was looking really worried, and Deverham looked at her fondly.

'You must on no account attempt to nurse your grandmother, Florence, however much you might wish

to. She would not wish you to take her infection.'
Florence looked her surprise.

'Nurse her? I should think not! I cannot possibly
be ill now, and besides, that is for Patience to do.'
Patience blushed for her, and looked down at her lap,
unwilling to see the look of surprise and sorrow on
Deverham's face. She had known that it would not
be possible to hide Florence's selfish nature from him,
and was almost glad that he had seen it, for it was
not fair that he should marry her blindly.

'It would worry your grandmother to have you ill
too,' said Deverham gently, looking for an excuse for
her. 'Otherwise, I suppose you would wish to be with
her?' Florence saw that she had erred, and gave him
a sweet smile.

'Of course I would! Only, I have never looked after
anyone who is ill, and Patience is so good at it, you
know! She nursed me, when I had measles as a child,
and was so kind!'

He was pleased.

'I thought I could not be mistaken in you. Of
course, you are far too young to have any experience
in nursing.'

Patience thought sadly of the times she had nursed
her mother through real or imaginary ailments, and
of how she had cared for her when her brother died.
She had been younger then than Florence was now,
but nobody had said that she was too young or inexperienced for the work. She gave herself a little
shake.

'I hope very much that Mr Moreton will not take
the infection. It would be too bad to bring such a gift,
when he has welcomed us so kindly!'

'Oh, it would take more than that to lay him low.
The gout is all that ails him, and most of that he brings
on himself, for he will not do as the doctor orders
him! Apart from that, I have never known him to
have a day's sickness in his life! He will be most distressed to hear of this. Should I call the doctor, do
you think? He would not wish to be remiss in any
such attention.'

'Thank you, you are very good. I will see how she
is after breakfast. At present I have left her with her
maid, and she is resting on a sofa. It may well be that
she is only over-tired. As you say, she is not used to
travelling.'

On returning to her mother's room after breakfast,
however, Patience found that her optimism had been
ill-founded. Lady Winterbourne had fallen into a
troubled doze, but woke when her daughter entered,
and tried to sit up. She fell back on to the cushions,
with a little moan.

'Mama! You should not try to get up! I am afraid
you are not at all well.' She went to her mother, and
laid a hand on her forehead, which felt hotter than
ever. Lady Winterbourne pushed her hand away, and
pulled herself up again more slowly.

'I wish you will not fuss so, Patience! I assure you
I am not at all unwell, merely a little tired, and the
jolting of the train has made my joints ache. I shall
be quite well directly, if only you will leave me to rest.'

'Of course, Mama, but would you not rest more
comfortably in your bed than on this sofa? See, it is
all ready for you, and it has been nicely warmed, so
you will not feel cold leaving the fire. Come, may we
not help you back?'

Lady Winterbourne submitted reluctantly, protesting all the while that she did not wish to go to bed, and that she was not ill. When Patience unwisely suggested calling the doctor, she cried weakly and flatly refused.

'See a strange doctor, who does not know me or my constitution at all? I wonder at your suggesting it, Patience. If our own Dr Jenkins were here, perhaps, that might be different, but a stranger! A day's rest is all I need. I wish you will go away, for you make my head ache with all your chatter.'

Patience did as she was bid, but she was a good deal alarmed. She could see for herself that her mother was ill, and had never known her to refuse to see a doctor, stranger or otherwise. In the past there was nothing she had liked better than to interview a new physician, and tell him every detail of her past and present symptoms. That she would not see anyone struck Patience as more worrying than anything else, and she determined that if her mother were no better by the following day she would take it upon herself to summon him, and bear the consequences.

She made light of her worries when she went downstairs again, however, for it seemed a poor return to their host's hospitality to make too much fuss just yet. He was very solicitous and, when Patience unwisely referred to her mother's reluctance to see a strange doctor, immediately offered to send to Bath for Dr Jenkins.

'No need for her ladyship to worry! I can send a man for him, easy as that, and have him here by tomorrow morning! Just say the word, Miss Winterbourne, and it shall be done.'

'It is so good of you, sir, but I could not allow it! Dr Jenkins is a busy man, and has many patients to attend. He could not leave them all and come all the way here, just for Mama.'

'He'd come soon enough, if he were paid,' he responded drily. 'What's the point in having all this money, if you can't get what you want?' he added simply. Patience could not but be amused.

'You must not say such things, or you will have me expressing a desire for all sorts of exotic things!'

Mr Moreton was pleased. He loved to surprise.

'Name them!' he begged.

'Oh, now I feel like the princess in the fairy-tale! Shall I ask for the phoenix, or a unicorn, or merely a tidy little dragon to light my fire for me?' He was disappointed.

'Now you're joking. But if there is something . . . ?' He looked so hopeful that she was touched.

'I shall do my best to think of something,' she assured him. She reflected that it was a good thing that Florence was walking in the garden with Deverham, for such an invitation would have been disastrous in her hearing. She was too greedy, and had not the wit to hide her greed, and would have been dropping artless requests for all sorts of expensive trifles, which Patience would have had to persuade her she might not yet accept.

At that moment a servant entered with the morning's post, which had to be brought from Manchester and never arrived before the middle of the morning. Patience withdrew to a chair by the window, and busied herself with some sewing, so that Mr Moreton might feel at liberty to read his letters. With a word of apology he leafed through them, putting most of them to one side without so much interest, but examining one with an air of surprise.

'You will excuse me if I read them, my dear? There is one here in a hand I do not know.'

'Pray do not regard me, sir. Would you wish to be private? I can easily go elsewhere.'

'No need, no need. I am sure it is nothing of importance.' She concentrated on her needle, but a few moments later he exclaimed so loudly that she ran it into her finger as she started. She dropped her work hastily, so that she might not get blood on it, and looked up at him. What she saw in his face made her forget her finger, and jump to her feet to go to him.

He was ashen, his eyes blank and staring, and his fingers slowly tightened on the paper he still held until it started to tear.

'Mr Moreton! Sir! Are you ill? Oh, may I call for anyone?' This brought his attention back to her, and reached out his hand for her wrist, gripping it painfully.

'No! No one! No one must know of this!'

'Shall I leave you?' She was unwilling to do so, for there was a blue look round his mouth that she did not like. He considered her for a moment, his eyes searching her face with a kind of despair. He still held her wrist, and the strength of the man who had spent his life working with his hands was in that grasp, though she scarcely felt the pain. He shook his head, and let her go.

'No. Stay. Pour me a drink.' His hands dropped, and his head, as he again looked at the letter he still held. Patience ran to the side-table, and slopped some spirit into a glass. She held it to his lips as he sipped, and was glad to see the blueness receding. At last he

took the glass into his own hand, and finished it.
When he held it to her for more she did not demur,
for she felt that at this moment his gout was of sec-
ondary importance. When he had drunk a second,
though smaller glass, he looked up again, as if asking
what he should do now.

'I am afraid you have had a shock, sir.'

'A shock! You might well say so. Aye, I've had a
shock, right enough.' His voice, which was usually
modulated carefully, had relaxed into the accent of
his childhood, and he gave a grim smile. 'You're a
good lass, and I'll tell you straight out—I don't know
what I should do.'

'If you do not, I am sure I am not fit to help you.
May I not call for Lord Deverham? Surely he would
be the one to help you now.'

'No!' The word was almost shouted. He heard the
loss of control, and corrected it. 'No, you must not
call him. Not him, of all people.' He fell silent, looking
at his letter, and for the first time Patience saw him
as an old man.

'If it concerns Lord Deverham, as I suppose it must,
then I think he should know of it,' she said with gentle
persistence.

He glowered at her.

'And I tell you I will not have it!'

'That is for you to say, naturally. But I do not think
I should be discussing this with you. I will withdraw.'

'No. Don't go.' She did not look surprised or annoyed at his tone of command, but gathered up her
sewing and sat herself in her former place, slightly
turned from him to show that while she might obey
his order to stay, she would have no further dis-

cussion with him about his letter. He studied her for a moment, and gave a little laugh.

'Stubborn little thing, aren't you?'

'I hope I am not, sir. Of course I must do as you tell me, for you are my host, and older than I. But I will not do that which I feel to be wrong.' She continued to make her neat stitches, with an air of composure than impressed him. He drew a breath.

'Miss Winterbourne, I see that there is more to you than I thought.'

'That is probably true of most people, sir.'

'You seem so meek, but there is a core of steel underneath. I like that!'

'I am most gratified.'

'Come, do not be angry with me. I should not have shouted at you, I know, but I am an old dog, and too old to learn new tricks. I must speak of this to someone, and I think I may trust you. You will not refuse to help an old man, will you? You see I ask you with all humility.'

She could not refuse him.

'You will speak of this to no one?'

'If that is what you wish. But I should prefer not to know of it at all.'

'So should I, my dear. Leave that confounded fiddling, and come and sit by me.'

Obediently Patience did as she was bid. He looked down into her face for a few moments. His own was unreadable, and she strove to hold her eyes steady as he glared at her. At length he grunted, and held out the letter.

'Here. You had better read it.'

'Are you quite sure? If it does not concern me——'

'That is exactly why I want you to read it. You are not involved in all this. You might see it clearly, as I think you have a habit of doing, do you not?'

'I hope so. Very well, I shall read it.'

After the first few lines the words blurred. She closed her eyes tightly, so that she saw bright, coloured patches behind her eyelids. Then she opened them again, and forced herself to re-read.

In bold, feminine hand the letter was unequivocal. Phrases jumped up at her. 'My lover', 'with child by him', 'certain it is his', 'swore he would be true to me', 'my husband will divorce me'. And the signature, Lady Belinda Waltham. Baldly spelled out, no possibility of misunderstanding or error, and yet . . . and yet . . .

'I do not believe it.' Her own voice came out so firmly that she startled herself. Nevertheless, she said it again. 'I do not believe it. It is not true.'

'But the letter!'

'I know. But, sir, you know him better by far than I do. Can you believe in this?'

He looked uncomfortable, miserable.

'Once, I would have said, of course not. But now . . . it is true, you know, that they were—friends.'

'Friends? No more than that?'

'So he said. But there was gossip. A deal of gossip. People talking about her, and him. I heard about it— never mind how. I couldn't believe it then, but it was in the newspapers, in black and white. I sent for him, and charged him with it, and he could not deny it.' She made a tiny sound, and he looked at her. Her face was white, her lips compressed to still their trembling. 'You are shocked. I should not be talking of these things with you; it is not fitting.'

'It is a little late to be thinking of that now,' she said harshly. 'He admitted it—that they were...lovers?' She brought the word out with difficulty.

'No, that's just it. He said they were friends, admitted that he had flirted with her, but that it was no more than that. He was angry that I had thought badly of him. And I believed him. Then.' He fell silent, staring into the fire.

'Then you must continue to believe him now.' Whatever she thought in her innermost heart, she must fight for him now, fight to save his inheritance for him. Whatever he had done, she could not cease to love him. Her heart was so entirely given that she thought she could forgive him almost anything. At all costs he must not lose all for the sake of such a past mistake. Loving him as she did, she could not in any case believe him capable of such behaviour.

'But the letter? Why should this woman write this, if it is not true?'

'Spite, and jealousy? If she has heard that he is to wed another, she might act so to ruin him in your eyes, and in Florence's.'

'But to compromise herself like that! If this letter became known, true or not, she would be ruined for ever in the eyes of the world.'

'I suppose that she trusts you will not wish the story to become known any more than she does.'

He looked at her shrewdly.

'You seem very certain that he is innocent. Fired up at once, didn't you? Why would that be, I wonder?'

Patience forced herself to meet his gaze levelly. He held her eyes in his, and she could feel the colour rising in her cheeks, but would not look away. He gave a little frown, and patted her hand.

'I beg pardon, my lass. I should not have said that. You would stand up for anyone you believed in, I suppose.' Her cheeks were still hot, but she knew that he would never refer to anything he might have learned from his reading of her face. There was a kind of sorrowful pity in his glance that hurt her more than anything, but she lifted her chin and would not give in to it.

'I hope I would. And as Lord Deverham is to marry Florence, I think of him as a member of my family. I would not wish anything to mar that marriage.'

'Nor would I, girl. She's a very good match for him. It was me as put it up to him. Heard about her from old Thorpe, I did.' She had suspected as much, but still felt a kind of wry amusement at the way she had engineered her own downfall.

'You will say nothing to her, then?'

'Neither to her, nor to him. I don't know what to believe. You have talked me round, I suppose, but still . . . I'm not sure.' He looked at the letter in his lap.

'Do not read it again. Let me put it where it belongs, in the fire,' she begged, but he shook his head.

'Not so fast, lass, not so fast. I'll not do that yet.'

'Then put it away, at least. I heard voices. Florence and Deverham will be coming in very soon.' He pulled himself to his feet, wincing at the pain.

'I cannot see him now. I will go to my room. You may say what you choose.' He limped out with all the speed he could manage, and Patience was alone. She would have given worlds to retreat, also, to her room, and have a good cry, but instead she forced herself back to her window chair, and took up her discarded needlework. There was a little spot of blood on the white cambric. Patience felt that she would never be able to look at this handkerchief again without remembering the events of the morning. She would have liked to have thrown it into the fire, needle and all, but she gritted her teeth and carried on with hemming the edge.

Deverham and Florence accepted without question that Mr Moreton had returned to his room. Deverham knew that his grandfather had taken much more wine than was good for him the night before, and was surprised that he had ventured downstairs at all. He was not alarmed to hear that the older man wanted to see no one—not even his grandson. When his gout was bad Mr Moreton's temper was much inclined to the irascible, and he preferred to see as few people as possible.

After luncheon Patience excused herself, and made her way to her mother's room. Under the circumstances it seemed scarcely necessary that the engaged couple should need to be chaperoned. In spite of the morning's letter she saw nothing to indicate that Deverham was likely to let his ardour run away with him, and since she knew that Florence was no more than lukewarm in her feelings she felt justified in agreeing to their going out riding together in the afternoon, as Florence had expressed a wish to do. Patience knew that she had a new habit, very becoming, that she wished to show, and thought that her niece would be too worried about spoiling its fine cloth and immaculate cut to take any foolish chances on horseback.

She was right. The house, though not far from Manchester, was within easy reach of some very fine countryside. Once they were beyond the limits of the estate, Deverham led the way down a prettily wooded ride which led to a stretch of more open country. It was a fine afternoon, and Deverham had missed his riding while he had been dallying in Bath, and felt his spirits lift.

'Shall we gallop?' Already he could feel his horse urging forward.

'Oh, no, if you please. I do not care to gallop. It is not very ladylike, is it?'

With some disappointment he reined in his horse.

'I suppose you are not used to country rides. Did you get much riding when you were at school?'

'Oh, yes, Grandmama said I should learn to ride, as it is a useful accomplishment. Some of my friends used to invite me to go with them, too, and sometimes we made up expeditions to the country. But I do not like to go fast: one can so easily become unbecomingly heated, and the wind plays havoc with my hair.'

Deverham agreed sombrely that it would be a pity to untidy her immaculate appearance, and they continued on their way. After a short while they came to a rise in the ground, which afforded good views of the surrounding countryside. Deverham pointed out such places as might be of interest to her.

'Oh, yes, it is very pretty. Quite charming, indeed,' agreed Florence, looking at him coyly from beneath her lashes. He realised that she was expecting a compliment.

'Beauty is in the eye of the beholder, they say,' he said gracefully, 'but in this instance, I should rather say that Beauty *is* the beholder.'

He was rewarded with her most brilliant smile.

'Why, Lord Deverham, you say the prettiest things! I am glad you like my habit. It's new, you know, I haven't worn it before.' She smoothed the deep green velvet with more affection than she had bestowed on the horse, which had earlier received a perfunctory pat.

'Yes, very becoming,' he said wearily. Florence did not notice his tone.

'I had intended to save it until I went to London,' she prattled on, 'but I thought you would like to see it. I am particularly pleased with the hat, for I think it is very fashionable, though I did buy it in Bath. Still, if I see one I prefer when I am in town I can always buy it.'

He turned his horse.

'If you look this way, Florence, you will have a good view of Manchester.'

'Oh, yes, how interesting. Of course, for *really* fashionable hats and bonnets, one has to go to Paris.'

'I expect you would like to go there, some day. We might go there on our wedding trip.'

'How I should love that! I want to be a credit to you, you know, and then I should be really fashionable. Perhaps I might become a great hostess, and hold salons.'

Deverham was shocked to find himself thinking that with her conversational powers there was not much chance of that, and resolutely banished the disloyal thought as they turned for home. As they went back at the desultory amble that was her preferred speed—trotting, she said, was too bumpy and might spoil the precise angle of her hat—he strove to find some common ground in what they had read, for he was

passionately fond of books. The effort was vain.
Florence never attempted anything more taxing than
a French romance, or a book of fashion plates. Seeing
the mutinous boredom on her face, he brought back
her smiles by talking of London life.

'If you are intent on setting yourself up as a hostess,
I must see that you meet Harriet Ashburton.'

'Lady Ashburton? Are you well acquainted with
her?'

'Tolerably well, though I could not say that I am
really one of her set. I was once lucky enough to meet
Thackeray there, though.'

Florence was not interested in writers.

'What is she like? She is very tall and plain, is she
not? She must be quite old by now.' To Florence,
anyone over the age of thirty was practically in their
dotage, and she plainly could not understand how
anyone who was not beautiful could be so successful.

'I would not call her beautiful, but she is very witty,
and clever. I have to admit I live in terror of incurring
her displeasure, for she can be very sarcastic! She has
always been very pleasant to me, however, and I have
several times visited their place in Hampshire, the
Grange.'

'The Grange? That does not sound very important.
I thought Lord Ashburton was very rich?'

'He is. Do not be deceived by the name; it is very
grand indeed. Great high bedrooms, with vaulted
ceilings, and the main rooms with painted frescos on
the ceilings and all hung with the most magnificent
paintings. Constant activity, too, with guests always
arriving and departing.'

Florence sighed with delight.

'And what about London? Does she entertain there?'

'Oh, yes, at Bath House. You may meet anyone you have ever heard of there.'

'And the Queen, and Prince Albert?'

'They visit only the most exclusive houses, of course, and only care to meet those who are thoroughly respectable. That is as it should be, but I believe it is the Prince, rather than the Queen, who is so strait-laced. He cannot relax, you see, even in male company, and I am afraid he is not much liked. People fear he has too much influence over the Queen, and I am afraid he and Palmerston are heading for a battle royal, if you will pardon the expression.'

Florence was not interested in politics.

'Grandmama says he used to be known as Cupid.'

'Palmerston? Yes, I believe so, but that is all in the past. I believe he is truly happy with his Lady Emily. He always was devoted to her, even before she was widowed.'

'But they are so old! I cannot but be embarrassed at the thought of a marriage between a man and a woman in their fifties, and she a grandmother!'

By now they had reached the gates of the house, and within a few minutes were in the stable yard. Assisting Florence from her horse, Deverham knew that she was coyly aware of his hands holding her, but found himself unmoved. To his horror, his main sensation was one of relief, that the ride was over, and the strain of making conversation at a level that she liked was finished.

Patience found her mother a little better. A long sleep and several cups of tea when she awoke had refreshed her, she said. She showed no inclination to get out of bed, however, and Patience was thankful, for she could see that the improvement was only small. The fever was perhaps a little lower, but Lady Winterbourne confessed that she still ached, and that it hurt her to move. Patience stayed and made desultory conversation, relieving the maid who had been with her mistress all the morning.

After a while Lady Winterbourne's utterances grew fewer and slower, and Patience saw that she was feeling drowsy again. She sat very still, and presently a little snore told her that the invalid was again asleep. She did not move, for she was glad of the chance to sit and think, though her thoughts were not happy ones. She could not bear to believe that Lady Belinda had written the truth, and yet why should she write so, if not? Even in Bath, Patience had heard of the beauty who had taken the world by storm, and two years later had gratified her impoverished family by making such a brilliant marriage. Surely she had a great deal to lose by writing such a letter, and nothing to gain even if it were true. Two tears forced themselves out of her eyes, and she wiped them impatiently away. At that moment there came a low knock at the door, and a housemaid put her head round it, peeping in to see whether Lady Winterbourne was awake. Patience put her finger to her lips, and moved silently to the door.

'Excuse me, miss, but there's a lady downstairs, and she's asking to see you.'

'To see me? But who is she?'

'I don't know miss. She wouldn't give her name, just said she had to see Miss Winterbourne, and it was very important.'

'But I know no one in this part of the country!'
The maid did not reply, but looked at her helplessly.

'There's no one else to see her, miss,' she hissed.
'Master's in his room, and his lordship and Miss
Florence have gone out. Mr Nateby's put her in the
morning-room. Please come, miss!'

Patience turned to look at her mother. Lady
Winterbourne was sleeping peacefully, and there
seemed no other choice.

'Very well, but you must remain here, and fetch me
if my mother should awaken. I am sure there is some
mistake, and I shall be back almost at once. It cannot
be me she wanted.'

She hurried down to the morning-room. A slender
figure turned as she entered. The stranger was dressed
in an ill-fitting gown of a rather worn appearance,
and a battered bonnet, over which had been placed a
thick veil of very good lace, which assorted oddly with
the rest of the clothes but served to hide the lady's
face completely. She stepped forward, and Patience
noticed almost without being aware of it that both
her boots and her gloves were of the finest kid, and
looked almost new. She frowned in suspicion.

'Miss Winterbourne?' The voice was low and
breathless, but well bred. Patience was now sure that
her unknown visitor was masquerading in borrowed
clothes.

'I am Miss Winterbourne.'

'Oh.' The stranger seemed disconcerted. Patience
waited in silence. Slowly the other lifted back her veil,
revealing a white and tear-stained face of remarkable
beauty.

'You are really Miss Winterbourne?'

'I can assure you that I am. But you have the advantage of me. Will you not tell me who you are? And why you are here?'

She gave a little sob.

'You must forgive me—I had to come. Oh, I think I shall go distracted. You do not know who I am, do you? I am—I am—Lady Belinda Waltham!'

CHAPTER NINE

WHATEVER she had expected, it was not this. Patience pushed the door shut behind her, not realising that the catch was stiff and that the door swung open again a few inches. She came forward, looking at Lady Belinda's face, beautiful in spite of her recent tears. Seeing her like this, Patience knew that she could not find it in herself to hate her. She came forward and took the costly veil from hands that were unconsciously twisting and pulling at it. Her voice was soft and calm, the voice that she was accustomed to use to Lady Winterbourne when she was in what her maid privately called 'one of her states'.

'Will you not sit down?' she asked prosaically. 'You do not look well, and I think you must have had a difficult and tiring journey. May I ring for some refreshment?'

Lady Belinda looked at her in horror.

'Refreshment? How can you think of refreshment at a time like this?'

'I think it would do you good.'

Lady Belinda sat down and stared at her, then began to laugh rather hysterically.

'Oh, heavens, I have done all this for nothing. You do not know who I am, and the letter cannot have been sent. I am undone, and to no purpose!'

'On the contrary, I know exactly who you are, Lady Belinda, and your letter arrived this morning. Forgive me, but in your present condition, do you not have a duty to take more care of yourself? Rest a little, and let me ring for some tea.'

Her voice was still kind, but Lady Belinda shrank from her as her laughter turned into a storm of tears, and she buried her face in her hands and rocked backwards and forwards. Patience came to sit beside her, not attempting to touch her until the violence of her sobs had abated to hiccups. Then she gently undid the strings of the hideous bonnet, and laid it aside, offering her guest a plain but serviceably large handkerchief, and went to pour her a small glass of wine. Lady Belinda wiped her eyes, drank the wine, and then sat up straighter.

'You are very kind. You say my letter has been received, and you obviously know its contents. Have you read it?'

'Yes, I have read it.'

'And who else?'

'No one but Mr Moreton. I was with him when it arrived, and in his shock he asked me to read it. I shall not speak of it to anyone, and I do not think he will either, at least for the moment. He has gone to his room, to think what must be done. Would you like to see him?'

'No! No, I could not face him. I should not know what to say to him.'

'The truth, I hope. Is not that why you are her?'

'Yes, I suppose it is. I had to write it, but after it was done, I got to thinking. He never did me any harm, and I could not bear it ... so I told my husband I had to visit my old governess, who was very sick, and came.'

'Not by yourself, I hope?'

'No. I brought my maid. These are her clothes.
Mine were all too fine, and I did not want to attract
attention.'

Patience went to the thing that was puzzling her
most of all.

'Why did you ask for me?'

'I did not know whom else. I did not dare see Mr
Moreton, and I thought you must know about it, or
if you did not, I would be able to warn you before
anyone said anything. But you are not at all as I
thought you would be. You will not—not cast him
aside, will you? You will still marry him?'

Light dawned. Once again, Patience realised that
her existence had been unknown. As the elder,
Patience was of course Miss Winterbourne, and her
niece Miss Florence Winterbourne, but since Lady
Belinda had not known that Florence had an aunt,
she had naturally asked for the only Miss
Winterbourne she was aware of. Patience thought it
fortunate that she had done so; she would not have
liked to place any reliance on Florence behaving sen-
sibly or discreetly in such circumstances. She framed
her reply with care.

'I think the marriage will still take place.'

'Thank God for it. Then I have not done too much
harm.' Now that her first anxiety was allayed, Lady
Belinda was studying her with some interest. Patience
thought with hidden amusement that if she had heard
Deverham was to be married to a young and beautiful
heiress, she must be experiencing quite a surprise.
Lady Belinda was worldly wise, however. She knew
well that the possession of a handsome fortune bestowed beauty and youth on the possessor, at least in
the mouths of those laying suit to her.

'If you are feeling better, will you not tell me how you came to write to Mr Moreton? If you do not wish to see him, I will tell him about it for you.'

Lady Belinda hung her head.

'I suppose I must. That is why I came, after all. But it is very hard. I am afraid I have behaved very foolishly.'

'Who of us has not, at one time or another? You and Deverham were friends, were you not? He has admitted as much to his grandfather, for there has already been an attempt to stir up trouble between them.'

'Has there? I did not know that. I wonder if that man Kingston...but I must go back to the beginning.' Her fingers began to twist together, and Patience took her hands into her own and held them.

'Do not be distressed. You have been so brave coming here today. I will not believe any harm of you.'

'I do not deserve such kindness. It is true that everyone was talking of us. You must know that my husband is somewhat older than I, and I was...bored. I had everything I had always thought I wanted, money, jewels, clothes, but it seemed so empty, somehow. My husband was kind to me, but he is a busy man, and he left me with too much time on my own. Deverham is younger, and handsome, and we danced and flirted together. No more than that! You must believe me! That was bad enough, that I should flirt with another man, but it was all words, like a game.'

'I understand. I believe you.'

'A game.' Lady Belinda gave a bitter laugh. 'A game that no one can win, though I thought I had done. I did not even know the rules! I thought that Deverham loved me. It is known that he has never lost his heart to any woman, but I took his pretty speeches for more than they meant. Looking back, I am so ashamed, but I boasted of it, to my friends. I thought I had done that which so many had failed to do, and I was proud. I thought that I loved him, but it was all the idea of love, of a grand passion, that I wanted.'

'You are not the first young woman to fall into such a trap,' said Patience comfortingly. 'You must not blame yourself too much. So you boasted to your friends, a little, and they talked?'

'Yes. Charles came to see me. He was very angry. He said things . . . I cannot tell you. It was terrible. I told him that I loved him, and he laughed at me.'

'That was unkind.'

'No, he was right. It was madness. He said he would not see me again. My husband was away, there was nobody there. I wrote to him—mad, stupid fool that I was—I wrote that I would go with him, let my husband divorce me and marry him, or go with him as his mistress, if he chose.' She wept again, but quietly.

'And then?'

'He wrote back. He apologised for his anger, but he said again that we must not meet any more, except as acquaintances might in company. He said that he did not love me, not like that, and that he thought I did not really love him either. He was kind. He told me that my husband had deserved better than this. I was angry, for a while. I would have done anything, then, to hurt him. I had offered him myself, my name, my reputation, everything, and he had spurned them! But he was right. Then, a little while later, I found that I was expecting a child, my husband's child, and

suddenly everything was changed. Now, I look back
at how I was, and I wonder if I am the same person.
Can you understand that?'

Patience wrinkled her brow.

'I think I can. You are not your own person any
more, now, are you? You belong to the child, as it
belongs to you. You have to think for both of you,
for the moment, instead of just for yourself.'

'You do understand. I thought you would. Forgive
me, but ... Deverham is very lucky, I think.'

'I hope he thinks so too.'

'And you love him, don't you? More than I ever
did, I know.' Patience could not reply, but her companion read her answer in her eyes, and in her trembling lips. 'I am sorry, it is not for me to speak of it,
but I see that I am right. You do love him.'

Patience lowered her eyes before that searching
gaze.

'He does not know. He does not love me.' Her voice
was low.

'But you are to be married?'

Patience had almost forgotten her masquerade, and
caught herself up short. 'Mr Moreton wished it,' she
said evasively.

'You forget, I know Deverham well. He would not
be pushed to propose marriage to any female, however
his grandfather might threaten or cajole. He is one
who goes his own way! He must like you a good deal,
at least.'

'Oh, yes, I think he likes me,' responded Patience
dully. 'But, Lady Belinda, you have not finished your
tale. I still do not know why you wrote to Mr
Moreton.'

'Oh, dear, I had forgotten I had not told you. I spoke of the letter I wrote to Deverham, did I not? Well, it fell into someone else's hands. A man called Kingston—at least, so he said.'

'How did he get it? Surely Deverham would not have given it to anyone?'

'He said he had, but I did not believe him. He was— oh, I don't know, horrible. I suppose he must have stolen it. He is the sort of man who might easily bribe a servant to do that sort of work. He showed me the letter, to prove that he had it, and he was gloating. He saw that I was *enceinte*, and said that everyone would think the baby was Deverham's, even my husband. I was so horrified, I believed him. I suppose if I had held out, maybe I should have been believed, but there would have been a scandal, at the very least, and I do not think I could have borne it. He made me write to Mr Moreton, and told me what to say. He said that if I did not, he would show my letter to my husband. You must see, I could not risk that! I know it is hard to believe, from my conduct, but I am fond of him. He is so pleased and proud to be a father, and it would be the end of everything. Even if he did not utterly cast me off, which I think he would not do, for he is really very kind, he would no longer trust me. He would send me to live in the country, and maybe take my baby away from me when it is born, and I could not bear it! You see, I had to do as he said!'

'Yes, I can see how it was. This Kingston, you did not know him at all? I wonder if that is really his name? Why should he wish you to do this?'

'How should I know? I don't suppose for a moment that his name is really Kingston, and his face did seem a little familiar. I suppose I must have seen him, somewhere, but I do not know who he is, only that he hates Deverham. He did not care what happens to me, so long as he harms him. I did as he said, because I was so frightened, and he took me by surprise, but after he had gone I kept thinking about it. I just could not do it! I could not stop the letter, for he took it away with him to post, so I just made up my story for my husband, and came up here right away. And now, I don't know what to do!'

'You have already done a great deal. It is brave of you to try to put things right.'

'But that man, Kingston, he still has my letter! And he will use it, I know he will. What is to be done?'

'We can do nothing, ourselves. We must tell Deverham.'

'Tell Deverham? I could not! He will be so angry! I do not want to see him. You are engaged to him, would it not be better if you told him?'

'My dear Lady Belinda, you must speak to Deverham yourself! He will not be angry with you, I am sure of it, but you must tell him about this man, this Kingston. You must tell Deverham!'

Unnoticed by either of them, the door opened.

'Tell me what?' asked Deverham with deceptive mildness, closing the door firmly behind him and making sure that this time, at least, the lock caught. The two women stared at him in horror. Of them both, Patience was the more flustered. He had heard something, but how much? How long had he been there?

Long enough, obviously.

'My dear Lady Belinda! What a pleasant surprise to see you here!' She cowered away from him, mistrusting that bland tone. 'And you have something to tell me? I am glad, my dear Patience, that you do not wish to keep secrets from me,' he continued, taking Patience's unresisting hand into his own and raising it briefly to his lips. 'It augurs very well for our future—relationship.' The pause was infinitesimal. Patience felt the colour flaming in her cheeks, she could not raise her eyes to look at him. He kept a firm hold on her hand, and gripped it encouragingly, giving it a little shake and her a warm smile. Lady Belinda took refuge in a further burst of tears. He remembered with irritation that this was a common trick of hers.

'Come now, Belinda! It is too late to weep,' he said, forcing himself to speak gently. He had in fact been standing outside the door for some while, and had heard things which had given him much food for thought, but he did not wish either lady to know this. Perhaps there was also, in the back of his mind, a wish to punish her ladyship, just a little, for what she had done.

Seeing that he was not to be moved by tears, Lady Belinda took courage and told him everything that she had told Patience. At the end of it she was weeping again, in true contrition, and he stifled his irritation to reassure her.

'I am so sorry! I would give anything for this not to have happened,' she sobbed.

'I know, and you have gone a long way to make amends by coming here. Heaven send we can get you back home with your husband none the wiser! We must be as brief as possible. Tell me of this man who came to you.' He already had no difficulty in guessing his identity, and her description confirmed it.

'My not-so-dear cousin Alfred,' he murmured to himself at the conclusion. 'I might have known that he would try some such trick. I suppose he has heard the news of my marriage, and is desperate to discredit me, at least in my grandfather's eyes, if not in yours, my dear.' Patience had sat silent throughout the recital, and had taken the earliest opportunity of removing her hand from his clasp. If he had noticed it, he did not react. Now she looked at him with a little flash of anger in her eyes. It seemed to her that he was getting unnecessary enjoyment out of the situation in which they found themselves. She was not to know that he looked on her with different eyes, and that the endearment came naturally to his lips. He gave her the smallest smile of encouragement, and she sat up straighter, trying not to let him see how embarrassed she was.

'What is to be done?'

'The most important thing, I think, is to see that Lady Belinda gets back home as soon as may be, and without anyone knowing where she has been. If that cannot be achieved, nothing else is to any purpose. I only hope that the fatigue of the journey has done no harm.' To Lady Belinda herself he said, 'Since I take it that you do not wish to see my grandfather, a short letter explaining that your first was untrue and that you were coerced into writing it should suffice to set his mind at rest.'

'There is no problem about my return. My old governess does in truth reside not too far from here, and my maid and I are staying with her. I will willingly write to Mr Moreton, but what of Mr Kingston— your cousin, I mean? If he should learn what I have done . . . he still has my wretched letter! How could you let it fall into his hands?'

'How indeed? It was lost from my pocket, when I went to destroy it. It would seem that not all my servants are as trustworthy as I would like to think them. You may rest assured that the culprit will be brought to book. You may also be assured that I shall deal with Cousin Alfred. You have nothing to fear from that quarter.'

Looking at his face, Lady Belinda gave a little shiver. She thought that she would not like to be in Mr Kingston's shoes when Deverham found him.

The letter was soon written, and the hired gig which had brought Lady Belinda summoned from the stable yard. She replaced her bonnet, light-hearted now that all her troubles seemed to be at an end.

'Is it not terrible? It is one that my maid was about to throw away, for the straw has been rained on so many times it has quite lost its shape. I do not think I have ever worn such a thing in my life! But my own are far too smart, for Lord Waltham likes me to be well dressed,' she added naïvely. Patience smiled.

'You look beautiful even in that bonnet,' she said. 'I hope you will soon be safe at home with him, and happy again.'

'Well, I mean to be, for I hope I am wiser than I was. We are to go away now, to his house in Yorkshire for a while, but we are sure to meet when I return. Will you come and visit me, and see my baby?'

'If I can,' answered Patience carefully. 'I know that I should like to.'

'Come, the gig is here,' interrupted Deverham. 'I do not wish to be inhospitable, but I think you should leave. We must not risk anyone else seeing you.' Lady Belinda kissed Patience.

'You will be happy too, I am sure of it,' she whispered. Patience blushed vividly, and Lady Belinda threw her veil over her head and tripped happily out to her conveyance. Deverham spoke softly to the butler, enjoining him to silence with the other servants as to their visitor. Patience turned to go, but Deverham saw her and stopped her.

'You do not think you can slip away like that, when I have had no time to thank you? You have been a true friend.'

'I hope I shall always be that,' she said soberly. 'You must forgive me for my deception of Lady Belinda,' she continued with difficulty. 'She asked for Miss Winterbourne, you see, having no knowledge of my existence. I didn't realise, at first, that the mistake had been made, and when I did . . . I thought it better to deal with it myself, and not involve Florence. I am afraid I appeared very interfering. It was quite by chance that I saw her letter, and would not have read it if Mr Moreton had not insisted.'

'I know you would not, though it is well for me that you did. And you did not believe the letter?'

Her cheeks grew faintly pink again, but she met his eyes without flinching.

'I did not think that you would abandon a woman so lightly. That you would flirt with her, yes, but not that you would leave her *so*, to bear the consequences of her folly.'

'I am not sure that Florence would have been so understanding.'

'She is very young,' pleaded Patience. 'It is better that she should not know of it. You will not tell her, will you?'

'Do you not think that a husband and wife should have no secrets from one another?'

'They should not, and when you are married no doubt the right moment will come for you to tell her about it. But for the moment it would be better that she should not know.'

He had to agree with her. That day had been the first time he had spent much time alone in Florence's company. She had talked easily enough—on subjects that interested her—but she had shown no desire to learn about the things that interested or concerned him. He could not imagine how she would have re-acted had she been present when Lady Belinda's first letter arrived. He did not flatter himself that she was violently in love with him, but her pride and sense of possession were very strong, and he did not think she would have been complaisant.

'I must go after my cousin, before he has time to expect me. He will know that the letter has arrived, but not that I have been able to connect him with it, as yet. But he may have some servant in the Walthams' house who will tell him that Lady Belinda has been away. It might put him on his guard. I think I should go at once. Will you give her second letter to my grandfather? There is no time for lengthy explana-tions now, but you can make all right with him.'

'Of course I will. In fact, I will take it to him at once. Do not worry—he was not willing to distrust you, and will be happy to know that he did not need to.'

'I cannot talk to you now. When I return will have to do. Do not let them all wear you out, between them! I shall be back as soon as I may.'

She caught at his sleeve.

'Be careful! He must hate you a great deal, he will be dangerous! You must take care!' The muscles under her hand were reassuringly hard. He smiled and took her hand, raising it once again to his lips. This time she kept herself under firm control, neither blushing nor allowing her hand to tremble in his. When he released her she took the letter and went with what dignity she could manage up the stairs, knowing that he was watching her. Once out of sight, round the corner, she pressed her hand to her cheek, cherishing the memory of his touch. She wondered how long he had been standing outside the door. Long enough to know that they were supposed to be betrothed, at least, but surely not long enough to have heard anything else? She could not know.

Deverham, watching her go, could have enlightened her, but would not have done so. When he and Florence had returned from their ride, Florence had at once run up to her room to have her maid remove some splashes of mud from the skirts of her new habit. He, following more slowly and in a mood of slight gloom, had been attracted by the sound of his own name, spoken in female accents that were strangely familiar and yet unexpected. Recognising the voice of his erstwhile friend, Lady Belinda, he had shamelessly stayed to hear what was afoot. It had not taken him long to find out, and he had also heard enough to know that Patience, whom he had hitherto regarded as an amusing companion who happened to be a female, was in love with him.

In the suddenness of this revelation, the thought of Florence never crossed his mind. Deverham was human enough to be flattered, the more so as he had never rated his own charms particularly high—it was part of his appeal, though he did not know it. He was accustomed to being courted for his position, and for the wealth that would one day be his, but he had never been able to think that such flattery was for the man himself, without the glitter of rank and money. The fact that he had made no effort to attract or to interest Patience made it somehow more touching, as did her obvious certainty that her regard would never be returned. He saw that she loved him enough to want him to have whatever his heart desired—and that if that desire was for her niece, she would do her utmost to see that he achieved it. He did not think that anyone had ever cared for him in quite this way.

As he made preparations for a swift departure, he thought about her. He remembered the times when her quiet, dry humour had made him laugh, and her quick intelligence had given him pleasure in their discussions. He thought how she had striven to meet his gaze candidly and openly, and admired the self-control which would not let her betray any response to his kiss, though he had not missed the glow of warmth in her eyes. He had for some while ceased to think of her as plain and insignificant, and now he could think of nothing but that shining look, which glowed like sunlight in his mind. She could not, of course, compare with Florence for beauty, but after their ride, and his experiences with Lady Belinda, he was beginning to think that female beauty, however pleasing, was far from being the most important attribute a young lady could possess.

What Patience had, he realised, and what her niece signally did not possess, was character, and a particularly pleasing one, at that. The glow of warmth he had just seen in her eyes seemed suddenly infinitely preferable to the sparkling, shallow prettiness of Florence.

CHAPTER TEN

DEVERHAM wasted no time. Running up to his room,
he swiftly changed from his riding clothes, threw a
change of linen and a few other necessities into a bag,
and then hesitated. Opening a locked drawer in his
table, he drew out a small pistol, which he regarded
for a moment. It was unloaded, but he left the am-
munition where it lay, and eventually stuffed the pistol
into the depths of his coat pocket before taking up
his bag, cramming his hat on his head, and running
downstairs again. He had left orders that a horse was
to be saddled for him, which he would leave at an inn
where he was known near the station. He wanted to
go as quickly and as unobtrusively as possible.

He had time, during the journey, to formulate some
sort of plan. Reaching London, his first move was to
the nearest men's outfitters, where he purchased a
dark-coloured muffler. This he wound round neck and
jaw in the manner of a man who is suffering from a
heavy cold or a toothache, and thus hoped to obscure
his identity, at least while his hat covered his dis-
tinctive head of hair. He kept away from his club, his
house, and other known haunts, lest he should chance
to run into anyone he knew, and instead went to a
cheap chophouse in an out-of-the-way corner of the
City, neither too near nor too far from his cousin's
lodgings. There he found a quiet corner, and dined
well enough. Once it was dark he left again and, with

his hat well pulled down and his muffler pulled up, he patrolled the streets around Uffington's home.

His patience was at length rewarded. Loitering on a street corner, feigning to admire the fly-blown display of pipes in a shop window, he first heard and then saw his cousin approaching. Deverham hunched his face further into his muffler, and watched the reflection come nearer and pass him without pause. Alfred, he saw, was looking mighty pleased with himself. His attire proclaimed that he was dining out, and he floated by in a cloud of scented pomade that made Deverham's nose wrinkle involuntarily. He watched the other man until he was out of sight, and then made his way to the lodgings.

He had never had occasion to visit there before. It was a large, dingy house, the door and window frames sadly in need of a coat of paint, with grubby net curtains sagging inside the windows. Deverham knocked.

After a considerable wait, the door was opened by a young maid, hardly more than a child, who gaped adenoidally at him and tried in vain to straighten the cap that covered her unkempt hair. Deverham smiled at her, and she looked alarmed.

'Good evening. I should like to see Mr Uffington.'

She thought for a moment. 'You can't. He ain't in.'

'What a pity. I particularly wished to see him.'

The maid looked at him consideringly. 'You ain't a bailiff?' she asked craftily.

He smiled again. 'Do I look like one?'

'No, but you never knows. Up to all tricks, they are.'

'Mr Uffington often has bailiffs calling on him, does he?'

'No more'n the rest. Clever, he is.' She paused, considering his cleverness and finding some reflected glory in it. Deverham put his hand in his pocket and pulled out a sovereign, holding it carelessly so that the dim light from the hallway caught on the gold. Her eyes widened.

'I should like to wait for Mr Uffington. I can assure you I am not a bailiff. In fact, he is a relative of mine.'

Her eyes were fixed on the coin, hardly hearing what he said. He held it out and she snatched at it, then stepped back to let him in.

'I shouldn't really, but the mistress is out, and if you keep mum she'll never know. You won't tell?'

'Not if you don't.' He thought with relief that it was to be easier than he had first thought. She led the way up to the pair of rooms on the first floor.

'Shall I light a candle?' She was obviously reluctant to do so, and he had no desire to give his cousin the warning of light shining beneath the door when he returned.

'No, the fire is lit, I will wait by that. I don't mind sitting in the dark. I want to surprise him, you see. He is not expecting me.' He held out another coin and she looked at him knowingly.

'You won't make no noise? Mistress don't like no trouble in the house. She says she has to keep a good reputation. No fighting or nothing.'

He considered.

'You think I have come to fight him?' She looked at him with old eyes in a young face.

'Reckon you haven't come as a friend, even if you are a relation. I don't care, s'long as there's no trouble with the mistress. Like to see him beat, I would. Never gives me nothing but bad words, and once he tripped me when I was carrying the coals upstairs. Went everywhere, they did, and I nearly lost me place for it. Took me a week to get the place clean again. Just because I answered him back, like.'

Deverham was not surprised. It was just like Alfred to exact such a revenge on someone smaller and weaker than himself. He and the servant-girl exchanged grins of complicity as he found himself a comfortable chair where he would be hidden by the door as it opened.

After she had gone he conducted a thorough search of the rooms. They were full of little comforts—even luxuries. Alfred did not stint himself, though the drawer full of unpaid bills showed that he could scarcely afford it. Deverham was not very surprised that he did not find Lady Belinda's letter. He had not expected his cousin to leave it about; it would almost certainly be kept on his person. He made up the fire quietly, then sat down and stretched out his long legs, preparing to wait in comfort.

Tired from his journey, he slept a little, waking in the near darkness to hear footsteps on the stairs, a heavy tread. The fire had sunk to a dim glow. Silently Deverham pulled in his legs, and eased himself more upright in his chair. The door opened and Deverham felt, rather than saw, his cousin enter. A waft of cigar smoke now mixed with the previous odour of pomade: Uffington had dined well, and the cigar glowed between his fingers as he crossed the room to light first a candle and then a lamp on a table near the fire. Having done that he turned, and caught sight of Deverham sitting upright but comfortable by the now closed door.

'What in the name of . . . Deverham!'

'The same, dear cousin.'

Uffington bared his teeth in a grin.

'Such an honour! To what do I owe it? I understand you are to be married—and to an heiress, too!
My congratulations, coz.' His mind was working furiously. Obviously Deverham knew of the letter to his
grandfather. He could not, surely, know of any connection with himself? He might guess at it, but there
could be no proof. He could brazen it out.

Deverham stood up, and walked lazily over to his
cousin. Alfred looked up at him as he approached,
and found himself swallowing nervously. He remembered all at once the incident in their childhood, when
Charles had attacked him. Now Deverham was no
longer a child but a man, taller than he and with broad
shoulders that owed nothing to his tailor. Alfred
swallowed again.

'How did you get in, anyway?' he demanded rather
shrilly. 'They had no business allowing it—you might
have been anybody! I shall have to complain!'

'It might have been anybody—and I fancy you
would have preferred it to be anybody. Anybody at
all. Even a bailiff.' Deverham's voice was contemptuous. He did not raise a hand, but Uffington shrank
back.

'I really must ask you to leave. It is very late. We
can have nothing to discuss at this hour.'

'I couldn't agree more,' Deverham unexpectedly
agreed. 'Nothing at all to discuss. So if you will just
give me the letter, I will be on my way.'

Alfred felt the blood draining from his face. He
edged back, wondering desperately whether he could
seize the poker to defend himself.

'Letter! What letter?'

'You know very well. Lady Belinda's letter to me.
Will you give it to me, or must I shake it out of you
like the little rat that you are?'

'You have no right to insult me like this! No right
at all!' Bargaining for time to think, Alfred took
refuge in bluster. Deverham ignored him, but continued to hold out his hand.

'The letter!' he insisted doggedly.

'I tell you I haven't got any letter! I don't know
what you're talking about!'

Deverham took another step forward, looming huge
and menacing in the lamplight, and Alfred recoiled
again. 'Don't you touch me! Lay one finger on me,
and I'll call for the police,' he snarled. Deverham
curled a contemptuous lip.

'Still a coward, aren't you, Cousin,' he remarked.
'Call the police? I should like to see you do it. For
the last time, will you give me that letter?'

'I will give you nothing!' Seeing that he was not
going to be hurt, Alfred let the insult go by and allowed his manner to return to its usual sly truculence.
He thought that he had the upper hand, for he was
quite sure that Deverham would not risk allowing his
affairs to become public knowledge. He prepared
himself to bargain, determined to sell Lady Belinda's
letter as dearly as might be, and was horrified when
his cousin turned away from him.

'Very well.' Deverham picked up his hat, muffler
and gloves, and prepared to depart.

'Where are you going?' Alfred's voice was shrill
with shock and surprise.

'Going? Why, I am leaving, of course. You do not
think that I came here for the pleasure of your
company, do you? On the contrary, I find it objec-

tionable in the extreme. If you will not give me the letter, there is no purpose in my staying any longer. I shall return to Manchester.'

'But...but...Lady Belinda...your marriage...your grandfather...'

'You need not concern yourself about any of that,' said Deverham carelessly, pulling on his gloves and preparing to put on his hat. 'It may be that my marriage will not take place, for quite different reasons, but whether or not it does, my grandfather knows precisely what has happened.'

Alfred turned pale.

'He can't! He can't possibly! He can't know about her letter——' He stopped speaking, inwardly cursing his unruly tongue for betraying him. Deverham raised a sardonic eyebrow.

'But you know nothing about that, do you, Uffington? Surely that is what you told me. You must see whether my grandfather will believe you. In the light of what Lady Belinda has told him, I think it unlikely, don't you?'

Shaking, Alfred groped for a chair and fell, rather than sat, into it.

'She has told him...everything?'

'Everything,' replied Deverham, clapping his hat on his head and reaching for the door.

'Stop! Wait!' The words were almost a scream. Deverham let his hand drop from the handle, but did not turn.

'I believe I have already mentioned that I do not care for your company. I have nothing to stay for.'

'But the letter! I have Lady Belinda's letter!'

'I know that very well, in spite of your denials.'

'Do you not want it? I thought you came here to get it.'

'I did, but since you seem so attached to it, you may keep it. I cannot conceive what use it may be to you.'

'But . . . your good name . . . and hers . . .'

Deverham turned slowly, and looked at his cousin.

'If you publish that letter, or use it in any way against me, you will very soon find yourself in a court of law, facing a charge of blackmail, which you well know is regarded in a very poor light, and carries a stiff sentence. Do not think that my good name can suffer from anything you may say about it. Both my grandfather and my bride have faith in me, and know very well that I am innocent in this matter. As for Lady Belinda, what do you stand to gain? I shall speak to Lord Waltham myself. He is not a fool. He and his wife will be journeying abroad very soon, and I think you will find that he will not hesitate to prosecute you if you attempt to blackmail him.'

Alfred sank his head into his hands. His dream of money was dispersing like mist in the sunshine of reality. Deverham, who had a very good idea of his feelings, thought that the softening-up process was working well.

'What am I to do? I must have money! Waltham will pay me for that letter, will he not?'

'He might do so,' responded Deverham carelessly, 'but I doubt whether he will give you a great deal. And then, he has a good many friends, you know, and not a little influence. A word in the right ear, a little money spread around, and who knows how long you will live to enjoy your windfall? A dark night, a knife in the back . . . it is all too easily done.'

Uffington raised a livid countenance.

'But . . . but that would be murder! He would not!
He could not!'

'I would not care to bet on it, but it is your life,
after all,' said Deverham smoothly, raising a hand to
cover his twitching lips as he thought of Lord
Waltham, that pillar of the community and stalwart
member of the Church, behaving in such a way.
Alfred, who did not know Lord Waltham at all,
looked shocked.

'But murder, Deverham! You would not let him
murder me, your own cousin?'

'Kindly refrain from reminding me of our relationship. It affords me no gratification at all.' Deverham's
voice was cold and hard. 'The thought of such a
murder shocks you, does it not—because the victim
is your own precious skin. Yet you set out to kill the
happiness of many people. To ruin Lady Belinda, to
destroy the future of her unborn child and condemn
them both to a lifetime of opprobrium which you must
know they do not deserve—is that not murder, of a
kind? And your uncle, my grandfather, a man who
has never shown you anything but kindness and generosity—did you stop to consider the effect of your
letter, and the fact that a shock like that could well
kill a man of his age and infirmity? Is that not murder,
or does that name only apply to your own demise?
My own happiness, and that of my future wife, though
I rate them lower, still hold some value, but to gain
your own sordid ends you would not give them a
second thought. You are utterly contemptible.'

Alfred cringed back in his chair, raising his hands
as if to shield his ears from the low-voiced tirade.

'It's all very well for you,' he mumbled bitterly. 'You have never known what it is to have no money. It all comes so easily for you—money, title, even a rich wife. It's not fair.'

'I don't suppose it is, but who ever told you that life is fair to anyone? I did not ask to be born rich and titled, but since I am I thank God for it, and hope to do my best to live up to my name and fortune, and to accept the responsibilities of my position. If you had been less envious and grasping, and prepared to work for what you want, you would not have found my grandfather, or myself, ungenerous. As it is, I wash my hands of you.'

'But I tell you I must have money! I have had some heavy expenses of late——'

'Spending money on the strength of your expectations, were you? How very like you that is. Well, you are a fool and a knave, but for the sake of our relationship I am prepared to be generous. I will give you five thousand pounds, in exchange for Lady Belinda's letter, and your written confession.'

A spark of hope gleamed in Alfred's eyes. He considered. Five thousand pounds was a fraction of what he had hoped to gain, but it was better than nothing. It would pay his debts, or those of them that were inescapable, for he had no intention of wasting good money on anything he could get out of. He nodded slowly.

'Very well. But it must be at once.'

'You shall have a draft on my bank the moment the letter, and your confession, are in my hand,' said Deverham, laying down his hat and pulling his gloves off once again. 'Sit down and write it now, for I want to see what you put.' Unwillingly, Alfred did as he was bid. His cousin stood over him, reading every word as it was put down, and making quite sure that nothing was omitted from the shabby account. When it was finished Alfred scrawled his name at the bottom, waved the paper in the air to dry it, and with an attempt at insouciance offered it to his adversary.

'There you are, then! How about my money?'

Deverham re-read the confession slowly, not deigning to answer. He held out his hand again.

'The letter,' he said shortly. Alfred drew it from the inside pocket of his coat, and after checking to see that it was indeed Lady Belinda's letter Deverham strode to the fire and put the paper in it, holding it down with a poker until it was completely consumed. Then from his own pocket he drew a banker's draft, already prepared. Uffington took it greedily, checking it as carefully as his cousin had done the confession.

'It is quite correct,' said Deverham coldly. 'You need not fear that I have cheated you.'

'Very sure of yourself, weren't you?' muttered Alfred morosely. 'Had it all ready, I see. What if I had refused to play ball?' He recoiled again at the angry glitter in Deverham's eyes.

'I should have strangled you, Cousin, and saved myself the five thousand pounds,' he said quietly, and Alfred could not doubt that he meant it. His hands crept nervously to finger his neckcloth. 'As I shall do,' continued Deverham in a deceptively gentle voice, 'if ever you should cross my path again. Be warned! This time, I have dealt gently with you. Another time, it will be far different. You poor fool, Lord Waltham would not stoop to harming one hair of your head, but I would have no scruples—none at all! I should not employ another man to do my dirty work, either, for it would be a pleasure, believe me, to do the deed myself.'

Alfred shivered, but tried to hide his fear. He had no doubt that his cousin meant every word that he said. 'Since that is how you feel, I have no wish to have any further dealings with you. England is a poor place, after all, and my talents have never been properly recognised. I shall go abroad, I think.'

· 'That's the idea—travel...for your health,' said Deverham unpleasantly. Taking up his hat and gloves he was gone before Alfred could say another word, leaving him staring at the wisps of ash that drifted up the chimney from the fire, and then at the precious draft in his hands. It occurred to him that there was nothing to stay for. He had little of value here—if he were to go now, tonight, he would save himself the cost of paying the arrears of rent that he owed. As he started to sort through his belongings, picking out those of the most value in his new life, there came a well-known knock at the door, and his landlady entered.

'Your gentleman guest left word that you would be wanting to leave, so I'll take what's due to me now, as it's convenient,' she announced, planting herself firmly in the doorway and eyeing his preparations with a knowing glance. Alfred ground his teeth with rage, feeling in his pocket for the last of his ready money. Arms akimbo, she watched him, then counted the money that he handed to her with an attempt at bravado that he could not but be aware fell sadly flat.

'And a month in lieu of notice, if you're wishful to leave at once,' she reminded him. Tight-lipped, he counted it out, and she left, looking grimly satisfied. Ruefully he surveyed the small sum left to him. He could do nothing, now, until he had possession of his windfall. Still, since he was leaving openly he could afford to sleep there, and pack his things properly for his journey. He would need to make an early start, though, if he was to escape his other creditors. With a sigh he started his packing once again.

Leaving the shabby lodging house, Deverham halted under the light that gleamed from the doorway of a nearby public house, and looked at his watch. It was not late—barely half past ten—and although he was tired he had a fancy to see all this business finished once and for all. Taking a chance, he hailed a cab and directed it to the Walthams' house. Arriving, he was pleased to see that lights gleamed from many of the windows, indicating that the household had not retired to bed. Knocking at the door, he asked for Lord Waltham, to the butler's surprise, and a few minutes later was greeting him in the book-lined library.

Walking forward, Deverham offered his hand, and after a barely perceptible hesitation his host shook it. His face was grave, and his greeting unsmiling, but he asked Deverham to be seated civilly enough, and offered him a drink.

'Hear what I have to say first, and if you wish to give me a glass of brandy after it, I will not refuse,' said Deverham ruefully.

'I am not sure that I wish to hear it,' Waltham returned, taking his seat again.

'I think, if you will listen to me, you will not regret it,' said Deverham. He then related, in a much simplified form, the history of Lady Belinda's infatuation, laying great stress on the harmless nature of

the friendship, and suppressing the content of her in-
criminating letter, saying only that in her innocence
she had phrased the note too warmly, and that by
misfortune it had fallen into the hands of his un-
scrupulous relative.

When at last he fell silent Lord Waltham stirred.
He had sat very still during the recital, his eyes fixed
on Deverham's face, and now he continued to regard
him without speaking. Deverham met his look without
embarrassment, and after a few moments the other's
face relaxed its grim look. He stood up and, still
without speaking, went and poured two glasses of
brandy. Deverham gazed tactfully into the fire, and
affected not to notice that the other kept his back
turned for longer than would normally have been
necessary to fill two glasses, or that a handkerchief
was discreetly used to remove a certain brightness from
his eyes. They raised their glasses in a silent toast, and
sipped companionably.

'I shall always be grateful for what you have told
me,' said Lord Waltham at length. 'I knew or had
guessed a large part of it, and I am thankful to know
the truth of the matter. The fact is, I fell for a pretty
face, as many have done before me, and did not stop
to think that I might not have enough to hold her.
No fool like an old fool, they say, and I was beginning
to think I was that old fool.'

'By no means,' Deverham assured him. 'I believe
your wife to be most sincerely attached to you. She
never cared for me, you know, not really. The thought
that she might lose her place in your heart, and in
your home, frightened her badly, and taught her to
know her own feelings. I am sure nothing like this

will ever happen again, particularly now that you will have a family to keep her busy.'

'I will not tell her that I know, at least not yet.'

'No, that might be for the best. The time will come when you can speak of it, both of you, and even laugh at it, but for the moment she has had too much upset. Take her to the country, and cherish her, for she did indeed act with much courage, and loyalty, to help me.'

'And the young lady—your betrothed—is she content? She has not let all this upset her?'

Deverham looked rueful.

'She does not know of it. But I am not sure . . .' He fell silent, staring into the fire. He could not say that he was no longer sure of his own wishes, and yet he knew that he could no longer go forward with the engagement he had so hastily and thoughtlessly entered into. He rose to his feet.

'It is late, and I have had a somewhat strenuous day! You will excuse me if I leave you now, for I must return to Manchester as early as possible tomorrow.'

They shook hands, and with more good wishes he left the house. Deverham went, not to his home, but to his club, where he could obtain a bed for the night with the minimum of fuss. In spite of his tiredness, however, it was long before he slept. He thought of Florence, believing herself about to make a brilliant marriage. While he did not think her heart was touched, he knew that she would not give him up without a struggle. As a gentleman, was he bound to hold himself to his word? Then he thought of Patience, and wondered whether she, too, was thinking of him. He let his mind dwell on her. The way she could sit so still, her hands so peaceful and quiet in her lap; the curve of her cheek; the graceful turn of her head when she looked up at him; the way her eyes glowed with happiness, or sparkled with laughter. For him, the beauty of her mind and spirit were expressed in all these things. Smiling, he turned his head into the pillow, and slept.

CHAPTER ELEVEN

HAVING left instructions that he was to be woken betimes, Deverham surfaced blearily from the depths of sleep to what seemed like a thunderous knocking at his door. Bewildered for a moment, he stared around him, wondering where he was and what he was doing there, then memory returned and he sat up as the elderly boots came in with his hot water. The mists of sleep receded as he made a hasty toilet, downed his breakfast with a good appetite but at some speed, and hastened to catch his train. Lucky enough to have a carriage to himself for the first part of the journey, he resumed his sleep, and arrived much refreshed in Manchester. Repairing to the inn where he had stabled his horse, he drank a swift mug of ale while it was made ready for him, and then he was on his way home.

He strode into the house in good spirits, but was brought up short by the butler's long face.

'What's amiss, Nateby?' he asked, as the servant relieved him of his outdoor things, and the small bag he had taken to London with him. 'Is it my grandfather, or her ladyship?'

'I'm sorry to say it's both, my lord. Master took bad with his heart after you left, and hasn't left his bed since, and her ladyship has taken a turn for the worse. The doctor has been here, to both of 'em.'

'Well, out with it, man. What did he say?'

'He says as if Master stops in bed, and keeps from worrying, he'll do all right, but if he goes on this way, he won't answer for the consequences. And worried he has been, my lord! There's no doing anything with him, and it's only Miss Winterbourne as he'll let care for him. Not even *me*!' Deverham saw that the old man was greatly hurt and made haste to soothe him.

'There are times when a woman's touch, you know, can do wonders, and Miss Winterbourne is very used to dealing with invalids. But what of Lady Winterbourne?'

Nateby shook his head.

'That's just it! Proper poorly she is, and doctor didn't say much, but he didn't look too happy, I can tell you. She's in a high fever, and does nothing but call for Miss Winterbourne all the time, till it's a wonder the poor lass isn't half distracted with it!'

Deverham frowned.

'Do you mean to tell me that Miss Winterbourne has had the nursing of both of them, for the past two days?'

'Aye. Her ladyship's maid sits with her ladyship, when she's asleep, and Mrs Nateby and I do what we can for the master, but it's her they both want. Fair worn out, she is.'

'I should think she might be! And what of Miss Florence?'

Nateby said nothing, but the corners of his mouth turned down and he nodded towards the sitting-room. Deverham strode to the door and went in.

His betrothed, most elegantly gowned and with her dusky curls immaculately dressed, sat gracefully before the small fire. An embroidery frame, a half-finished novel, and a book of engravings had all been cast aside, and bore mute witness to her boredom, but at present she was engaged in nothing more exact-

ing than admiring the way the firelight struck sparks
from her ring. She looked up when he came in, and
her face lit up with pleasure, in a way that it had
seldom done before when she saw him.

'Deverham! How pleased I am to see you! You
cannot imagine how I have missed you, for with
Grandmama and Mr Moreton ill, and Aunt Patience
busy looking after them, I have been so bored! You
cannot imagine how tedious it has been, for there is
no one to talk to, and the shops are too far away to
visit, and when I asked Aunt Patience if she could
not spare an hour or two to come into town with me
she was quite disagreeable.'

He looked grave.

'I am sorry to hear that you have been bored. You
must have been worried about your grandmama, were
you not?' There was almost a note of pleading in his
voice; it was hard to believe that so lovely a creature
could be so heartless.

She did not hear it, however, and responded
blithely, 'No, for she is always saying she is ill, and
nothing ever comes of it. I am sure it is only a cold,
or some such thing, and you know I could not risk
going near her and catching it. Not now, when we are
about to go to London.' She came towards him,
holding out her hand and inclining her cheek for his
kiss. His own hand was cold as he took hers, and his
lips barely brushed her skin. She was hardly aware of
his coolness. 'Where have you been, anyway? No one
would tell me anything. It is not very gallant, to go
off like that without a word of farewell.'

'I had some urgent business in London,' he said
shortly.

'Well, I forgive you, for this once, since you hurried back so quickly. But do not do such a thing again, I beg you! There can be no need to visit London now, when we will soon be going there together.'

'We cannot go while your grandmother is ill.'

'Oh, I am sure she will soon be better,' she said airily. 'Will you not sit down? Tell me about London—did you see anyone important?'

'You will excuse me for now,' he said brusquely. 'I must see how my grandfather is.'

'Oh, yes, I had forgotten he is ill too. I would have gone to see him, only I thought he might have Grandmama's cold, and I knew you would not want me to risk the infection.'

'If you had taken the trouble to enquire,' he said, not troubling to hide his anger, 'you would have learned that his trouble is with his heart, and is not at all infectious.'

She pouted.

'Now you are angry with me, and it is not fair! I am no use in a sickroom, I would only be in the way. Do not look at me in that horrid, cross fashion!' She stamped her foot and the childish gesture, which might have angered him, softened him with its reminder that she was, after all, hardly more than a spoilt child. He took her hand and patted it consolingly.

'There, now, I am not really cross with you. But I must go and see my grandfather. I shall see you later.'

He made his way swiftly upstairs, and entered his grandfather's bedroom after the most perfunctory of knocks. Patience was sitting with the old man, and one glance was enough to show him that both of them had suffered. Mr Moreton's face had a greyish tinge that he had never seen in it before, and the hand he stretched out to his grandson had a tremor and weakness in its grasp that filled him with foreboding. Patience was very pale, with deep purple shadows beneath her eyes, and to his anxious glance she seemed to have lost weight, and developed hollows in temple and cheek that had not been there when he left. After one swift glance at him she murmured an excuse and left the room. He would have followed, but his grandfather's weak grasp on his hand tightened, and he turned back to the bed.

'Tell me,' commanded the old man. 'Tell me what happened.'

Deverham sat down on the edge of the bed, and held the old hand in a warm clasp.

'There is nothing to worry about, sir. All is well.'

Mr Moreton gave a small, satisfied smile, and closed his eyes for a moment. When he opened them, his colour looked to be better already, and there was a lively spark in his look.

'Been setting the world alight a bit, haven't you? Didn't I tell you to have nothing to do with married women?'

'Yes, and how right you were, sir.'

'That's generous, lad, but the blame doesn't lie with you, or with her, poor young thing. It lies fair and square with that scoundrel, Alfred. To think that my own flesh and blood could behave so...' His struggle for words strong enough to express his feelings brought on a fit of coughing, which alarmed Deverham. When the paroxysm had subsided, however, and his grandfather had grudgingly taken a few sips of the cordial left on a small tray by the bed, he seemed no worse. Deverham gently pushed him back against the pillows again.

'You must not allow him to upset you, Grandfather. As I have said, it is all over now, and no harm done. I fancy we will see and hear no more of my cousin, for some time at least, for I think I have contrived to frighten him enough to keep him out of the country for a few years. And you may be sure that I shall do nothing, in future, to give him any handle by which he may find a way of hurting us.'

'My own sister's boy!' mourned Mr Moreton.

'Hers, yes, but also the son of the man she married. You know you would have kept her from that mistake had it been possible, and when she would tie herself to him, you helped them more than they had any right to expect. You should hold yourself blameless in this, for you have deserved far better than you received for your generosity.'

'He was a wrong 'un from the start, I am afraid.'

'Yes, he was. Now he has the means to make a fresh start, in a new place. Maybe he will make something of himself yet. But do not let us be talking of him any more. I have seen Waltham, and made all straight with him, so you must make haste to get well again.'

'For your wedding?'

'Perhaps.' The older man gave him a sly look, and Deverham wondered how much he had noticed. Not much escaped those eyes, he knew only too well. 'The fact is, Grandfather, I am afraid I am not as sure as I was that Miss Florence and I should be happy together. I am sorry if you are disappointed, for I know how much the match pleased you.'

'No need for that,' responded his grandfather gruffly. 'I'd not see you pushed into any marriage against your will. But I thought you cared for the young lady? She's pretty enough in all truth.'

'She is very beautiful, and I must admit I was dazzled by her, at first. But I have come to think that I need more than just beauty in a wife. The truth is, we have nothing in common. I am afraid we should be fighting before six months were out.'

Mr Moreton nodded slowly.

'I've not had much chance to get to know her yet. She seems a sweet enough girl, though very young, of course. But it's your life, and you must do as you think best, lad. I won't deny it was what I wanted for you, for she'll have a tidy fortune to bring with her. But there, I'm not precisely a pauper, and you've no need to marry for money, after all.'

'I am glad that you take it so well. You know that I want to please you, but in this one matter I could not go against my own feelings. I wish to say nothing against the lady, but I feel sure that her own heart has not been touched. There is a hardness, a lack of sympathy, in her, that I cannot like. I am afraid she has been of no comfort or assistance in this house, while you and her grandmother are ill.'

'I've not seen the girl, and that's a fact, but to tell the truth I didn't want to see anyone. I was so shook up by that letter, you know, that I was afraid that I might say something to give away more than I should about the matter, and I was that scared that Miss Florence would find out about it. There was only Miss Patience that knew, and she looked after me a treat.'

'What a very good girl she is, sir!'

Mr Moreton shot him one penetrating glance. Unwell though he was, it had not escaped his notice that Patience, while stubbornly defending Deverham's behaviour, was reluctant to talk about him, and invariably changed the subject if he attempted to do so.

It came as no surprise to him that she, brought up as she had been among the old dowdies in Bath, should find herself attracted to his handsome heir, and he honoured the courage and the delicacy of mind that would not allow her to betray her feelings. How far Deverham himself was aware of it he did not know. He had, he thought, done enough meddling in his family's affairs, but the last few days had served to make him very fond of Patience, and he could not resist praising her a little.

'Oh, aye, she's the real thing, all right. They say as good as gold, don't they, and she's gold all through. Not much to look at, perhaps, but a real lady.'

'She cannot, I own, be compared with Florence for beauty, but to my mind she has a beauty of her own. Those eyes, you must own, with such softness and brilliance, and her voice is so particularly pleasing. I am sure you must have remarked it.'

Mr Moreton closed his eyes, so that his grandson should not see the gleam of pleasure in them as he listened to these eulogies. He was surprised and pleased to find that the boy, as he still thought of Deverham, had the wit to look beyond a quiet exterior.

'I have tired you, sir, with so much talking,' Deverham blamed himself. 'You should not have let me run on so.'

'Not at all. Your visit has done me all the good in the world, more than any of this muck the doctor keeps giving me. But I won't deny I am a little sleepy now. I'll rest for a while. But mind you come and see me again later on! I want to hear just what you said to that scoundrel, and what he had to say for himself. Frightened him, did you? Well, he always was a coward. I could almost wish I could have been there to see it!'

With a satisfied smile Mr Moreton settled himself down among his pillows. Deverham waited for a moment until the breathing slowed and steadied. Tired he might be, but the old man did look better now that the problems were resolved. Quietly he left the room, and went to see how the other invalid was progressing.

Reaching Lady Winterbourne's door, he met the housekeeper, issuing from the room in a waft of camphor, lavender and balsam. Her face was grave, and when Deverham asked if he might enter she shook her head.

'I don't like the look of her at all, my lord. Her fever's very high, and most of the time now she's wandering in her mind. It seems to upset her to have anyone in the room but Miss Patience, though her maid and I do what we can to help.'

'This is terrible! What does the doctor say?'

'Not a great deal, though I can see he's worried. The trouble is, it seems to bother her when he comes, and that only makes her worse.'

'We must send for her own doctor, from Bath. Find out his name from Miss Patience, and I will see to it at once.'

Her face brightened.

'Very well, my lord. Master did say something about that right at the beginning, when her ladyship was first unwell, but with him taking to his bed, and all, it quite slipped my mind. Let's hope he'll be able to help.'

'And meanwhile you must see that Miss Patience does not make herself ill as well. See that she has a glass of wine with her meals, and be sure to see that she drinks it, and takes some nourishment. I thought her to be looking most unwell when I saw her just now in my grandfather's room.'

'It's true she's hardly slept these last two nights, for her ladyship calls for her constantly, and then she's been so good with Master! Now you're back, I hope Master'll pick up a bit, and she'll be able to rest, if it's only to lie down on the sofa in her ladyship's room. I will say, though she's only a little bit of a thing, she's strong,' added the housekeeper, with all the respect of one worker for another. The housekeeper bustled off about her business, and Deverham waited for a while outside the door. There was no sound from within, and at length he took himself off, realising that Patience had enough to worry her at present.

The rest of the day was uncomfortable. The only useful thing he could think of doing was to amuse Florence, and keep her entertained, which was not at all to his liking. Nevertheless, knowing that Patience would be happier to know that her niece was occupied, he set himself to spend time with her. It was too late in the day to go far, but he persuaded her to walk in the garden with him, and set himself to listen to her chatter. He marvelled, as he did so, that he could ever have fancied himself in love with her, for almost every word she spoke revealed her self-absorption, and the woefully empty mind that passed lightly over the surface of life, skimming like a butterfly from one drop of sweetness to the next, and ignoring all that did not provide instant gratification. By the evening he had a pounding headache, and Patience had still not emerged from her mother's room. He had to be satisfied with sending messages of sympathy and support to her, and sought his own bed, after spending an hour with his grandfather, with some relief.

The morning brought little to brighten it. Only the continuing improvement to Mr Moreton's health caused a gleam of pleasure, but the weather was cold and wet, and Florence, thwarted in her desire to go shopping by Deverham's flat refusal to leave the house while Lady Winterbourne was so ill, was indulging in a fit of sulks.

For Patience, sitting at her mother's bedside, it seemed like a dark tunnel through which she had to grope her way, with no prospect of issuing into the light of day. Her whole body ached with fatigue, but when she did lie down on the little bed that had been set up in the room she found herself unable to rest. Either her mother's fevered mutterings roused her from a fitful sleep, or the silence when she did not speak made her fear that the worst had happened, and had her rising every few minutes to check that the laboured breathing still continued. She had never known her mother to be so ill, even during that dreadful time when her brother had died, and she was filled with fear for the future. To be sure, her life with her mother was dull, and not always happy, but it was all that she knew. For all Lady Winterbourne's constant complaints about her health, it had never occurred to Patience that she would not live for many more years yet. Feeling as she did, it was out of the question for her to live with Florence and Deverham. She supposed, drearily, that in the end she must make a home with her sister Julia, and strive to make a useful life for herself in Sir John's parsimonious household.

Deverham's messages, and the news that he had sent in haste for Dr Jenkins from Bath, brought her some comfort, and she tried to be glad when she heard that her niece was spending much of her time with her betrothed. At least she did not need to worry about Florence behaving badly, as she was apt to do if she thought she was not receiving her full meed of attention.

The day wore drearily on. In a daze of exhaustion Patience sponged her mother's hot, dry face and hands, tended the simmering kettle that supplied the pungent steam that she hoped would ease her harsh breathing, and strove to administer the cooling drinks that the doctor had prescribed. In her rare moments of lucidity, Lady Winterbourne's eyes fixed on her with a look of fear and entreaty that went to her heart, but these moments came less and less often.

The hours seemed to drag, and yet the dusk came upon her before she was expecting it. The housekeeper arrived with a tray for her, and gave her the welcome news that Dr Jenkins would be arriving first thing the next morning. Patience tried to smile, but she could see that the servant shared her own fear that such help as he might be able to give would be too little, or too late, to be of any use.

Mrs. Nateby laid the tray on a little table.

'I know you don't feel like eating, miss, but you must keep your own strength up. There's some good soup, now, that Cook's sent up special, and a nice piece of chicken, nothing too heavy. Do see if you can't get them down you, and a glass of wine, that his lordship poured with his own hands, and says I'm to see you drink. Do try, now, miss!'

With a shaky smile Patience took up the glass, and
sipped at it. With her not having eaten for some while,
or slept, it made her head spin a little, but it warmed
her so that she was able to drink most of the soup,
though the chicken was like sawdust in her mouth.
The housekeeper stood over her as she ate and drank,
and nodded her head, pleased to see that she had taken
something.

'Now you lie down on the sofa, miss, and let me
put this rug over you. I'll stay here, and watch her
ladyship. I can sit here, by the screen, so she won't
see me and be distressed by the sight of a stranger.'

'I am afraid she would scarcely be aware of it,' said
Patience sadly, submitting to the housekeeper's edict
and laying her throbbing head, heavy with the fumes
of the wine, on to the pillow. She tried to sleep,
knowing that she must, and did fall into a doze for
a while, and at midnight, a little refreshed, she rose
and sent Mrs Nateby to bed, saying that she would
watch for the rest of the night. The housekeeper was
reluctant to leave, but since the patient was lying
quietly she consented to go, on the understanding that
she was to be sent for should there be need.

In the small hours, Lady Winterbourne grew restless
again, muttering and tossing her head. Patience strove
to quiet her, replacing the covers that she pushed away,
and in the end holding the unquiet hands in her own
to keep them still. With the first light of dawn she
saw a change in the face that she had watched for so
long. The little frown between her brows smoothed
out, the muttering ceased, and Patience was able to
release her hands and lay them quietly on the smooth
sheets. As she hung over the bed in the first rays of
sunshine that crept between the heavy curtains, her

mother opened her eyes and, for the first time for many hours, looked at her peacefully and with comprehension.

Then Lady Winterbourne's eyes closed again. She gave a deep sigh, and turned her cheek a little into the pillow. Patience leaned over her, studying the peaceful face, and taking the quiet hand that lay, wasted and white, against the silk of the covers. Overcome with weakness and emotion, Patience sank to her knees by the bed, and let her tears fall on the white linen sheets.

She did not hear the door open quietly as Mrs Nateby stole in, nor her exclamation of distress as she saw the quiet bed and the kneeling figure beside it. The housekeeper hurried to fetch Deverham, who in his own anxiety was already up and dressed. The bustle disturbed Florence, who threw on a heavy silk robe and hurried after them. At the door of her grand-mother's room she peeped fearfully round them, and gave a wail of anguish.

'Oh! She is dead! It is not fair! She cannot die now, when I am about to be presented! Oh, Patience, you should have looked after her better! I shall never forgive you, never!' She burst into angry tears, which Patience scarcely heard. She lifted her head from the bed, and they saw the tears on her pale cheeks. Deverham gave an exclamation of anger, and dealt a hearty slap to his betrothed's cheek, shocking her into silence. She stared at him in horror, one hand to her reddening cheek, her breath still coming in gasps.

'That is enough,' he said sternly. 'If that is all you can find to say, you had better take yourself off. You are not needed here.' She began to cry again, but more quietly, turning for sympathy to the housekeeper. She, however, had been as shocked as he by the unseemly outburst. Nevertheless, she knew her duty, and with tightened lips she laid her hand on the girl's arm.

'Come along, miss. You've had a nasty shock. I think you'd better come back to your room, and have a lie-down.'

'But—he hit me!'

'Well, miss, there's some as would say he had reason to,' was the grim response. Seeing that she would get no sympathy, Florence acquiesced and allowed herself to be put back to bed, with unwonted obedience. Deverham did not hear them leave.

'My poor darling,' he said, starting forward. But the face that Patience lifted to him, though wet with tears, was smiling tremulously.

'She is sleeping,' she said softly. 'The fever has broken, and she is just sleeping.'

Scarcely daring to believe her, he approached quietly. As he grew nearer, he saw that the body he had thought to be motionless was breathing, quietly and easily, and when he reached out to take her hand from Patience he found it cool to his touch. Patience still knelt by the bed, the tears flowing unnoticed down her cheeks. Scarcely knowing what he did, but with the instinct to comfort and cherish strong within him, he gathered her into his arms, lifting her slight form bodily from the floor, and holding her cradled against him. She resisted a little, but her small strength was used up, and she subsided against his strong shoulder as he carried her to the sofa.

There he sat down, keeping her tightly in his arms and setting her on his knee as if she had been a child. Like a child she wept her tears of joy and relief, and he stroked her hair, murmuring endearments, until she was quiet. He was still, afraid that she would withdraw from his arms, but to his surprise she still lay against him, her head in the hollow of his shoulder.

'Little love, little darling,' he whispered, much moved. She did not stir, and with a wry smile he realised that she was fast asleep.

Slowly and gently he laid her down, drawing the rug over her and smoothing it round her shoulders. She gave a little sigh that was half a sob, and murmured his name. Bending down he softly kissed her cheek and her lips, then, with one last glance at the sleeping Lady Winterbourne, crept from the room.

CHAPTER TWELVE

WORN out with watching, Patience slept unmoving until the arrival of Dr Jenkins from Bath. She awoke to find his kind, familiar face looking down at her, and smiled sleepily up at him.

'Well, I am glad to see that my services are no longer required! Her ladyship should do well enough now, with the good nursing I know you will give her.'

'Oh, Dr Jenkins, I am so sorry you have had this journey for nothing. But how glad I am to see you! Has Mama woken yet?'

'No, I merely looked at her as she slept. Sleep is what she needs just now, but when she wakes I will examine her properly. Just now, though, Miss Winterbourne, it is you I want to deal with. What do you mean by wearing yourself out like this? I take leave to tell you that you do not look at all well.'

She laughed at his scolding.

'There is no need, I can well imagine that I look quite dreadful. I am only tired, however, and I assure you that you are not about to have another patient on your hands.'

He was glad to see her so cheerful, but would not leave it at that.

'Nevertheless, I must insist that you go to bed. To your proper bed, mind, and in your nightgown, and you are not to stir until tomorrow, at the very earliest. Otherwise, I shall not be answerable for the consequences, and I should have Lord Deverham breathing fire at me, for not taking better care of you.' She blushed, and he laughed. 'When I arrived, his first care was that I should see you! When I said I must look to her ladyship first, he looked quite startled, and I do believe that he had forgotten her completely.'

Patience was unable to answer him, and busied herself with the fastening of her indoor slippers so that she had an excuse to hide her face. She had very little memory of the events of the morning, but a dim recollection of his holding her in his arms, and calling her his darling, sent a tingle of excitement through her body. This she sternly repressed, telling herself that it was no more than an attempt to comfort her. Nevertheless, her eyes were bright as she looked up again at the doctor.

'Be off to your bed, young woman,' he ordered, twinkling back at her. 'I shall stay here with her ladyship, and see to her when she wakes. And what's more, I shall forbid her to call for you, too.'

Still half asleep, Patience left the room and made her way to her own bedchamber. Here she found the housekeeper, busily warming the bed.

'Oh, miss,' said that good woman, the ready tears springing to her eyes, 'I'm that pleased, I don't know what to say. I quite thought her ladyship had passed on, when I saw her lying there so quiet, and you on your knees. And now here's Dr Jenkins, and our own doctor here too for the master, though he's well on the mend now, and all is turning out so well! I don't know when I've been so thankful, and that's a fact!'

Seeing that Patience was still half asleep, she helped her to undress as if she had been a child. A cup of warm milk stood to hand by the bed, and she stood over Patience while she drank it, and snuggled obediently down among the pillows. Closing the curtains against the sunlight, Mrs Nateby withdrew, and Patience was asleep again before the door had closed behind her.

Dr Jenkins took his leave during the afternoon, satisfied that both his patients were doing well. Obedient to his instructions, Patience remained in bed, eating a light meal in the evening and falling asleep again almost at once, when she was told that Lady Winterbourne was making good progress, and that her maid was sitting with her.

The following morning she awoke at first light. Lying in bed, luxuriating in the warmth and softness, and feeling the strength returned to her rested body, she came fully alive for the first time since her mother's illness. Today she would come downstairs again. She would see Deverham. The thought carried ecstasy and dread. Had she really heard him call her those loving names, and had he really held her in his arms? Perhaps in her exhaustion she had dreamed the whole. If that were so, she must prepare herself to see him again without embarrassment. She could do it. She must do it. Restless, she climbed from her bed and drifted to the window, pulling back the heavy curtains and pushing open the casement. Her hair, for once unrestrained by the neat plaits she generally put it into for the night, lifted in the waft of cool, fresh air that came in from the garden below.

The sunlight that streamed from a cloudless sky gilded the heavy dew that lay on the fresh green of the new grass, on the tender young leaves just unfurling on the chestnut trees, and lit up the daffodils that clustered under the trees until they glowed like little lamps. The twitter of birdsong enhanced the stillness, and the piercingly sweet scent of spring filled her with joy. Suddenly she felt that she must be outside, she could not stay indoors any longer. Swiftly she washed and dressed herself, pulling one of her new gowns from the cupboard with the feeling that its soft, pale colour was the only thing worthy of such a shining morning. The soft green cambric felt deliciously light after the heavy fabrics of winter, the wide skirts floating above her petticoats. It was ornamented all down the front with rosettes of the same material, graduated in size from the small ones on the bodice to the larger ones on the skirt, for all the world like clusters of newly opened leaves. She brushed her hair, bundling it into a silk net rather than taking the time to pin it up. She retained enough sense to put a stout pair of shoes on her feet, then, snatching her Kashmir shawl from its careful wrappings, she flung it round her shoulders, and slipped quietly down the stairs and out into the garden.

Once outside, she could have been the only person in a newly created world. Putting from her all thoughts of past and future, content to enjoy this gift of a beautiful spring morning, she wandered happily off. The garden was a large one, and she was soon out of sight of the house. Forsaking the trim lawns and tidy borders, bright with bulbs but bare of other plants, she went through the shrubbery, passed by the gate of the walled kitchen garden, and on to the orchard beyond. Here the grass grew lush, bright with dandelions like little suns, and little wild daffodils that had more grace than their sturdier garden cousins. The apple blossom was no more than a promise in the tight buds on the twigs, but two fine cherry trees were tasselled with snowy flowers, and a breath of perfume from the bank beneath them told her that there were violets as well as the celandines and primroses that she could see. With a happy sigh she bent to gather them.

Deverham was also awake early. Florence had kept to her room all the previous day, whether out of anger or from shame at her own behaviour he did not know. He passed his time with his grandfather, who was feeling so much better that he was demanding to leave his bed. It needed all Deverham's considerable ingenuity and strength of character to keep him content in his bed, and when he finally went to sleep Deverham was only too happy to take himself to his room at an early hour. Now he was up, though it was not yet seven, and waiting impatiently for the chance to see Patience.

By a quarter past seven he could wait no longer, and sent Mrs Nateby to see whether Patience was awake yet. She returned almost at a run.

'She's gone, my lord!' she puffed. 'Her bed's cold, she must have been up for some time. I expect she's downstairs, though I'd have thought I would have seen her.'

Deverham ran downstairs and conducted a swift search, but Patience was nowhere to be found. Shaken from his usual calm, he found himself wondering whether she had run away from him. Perhaps he had frightened her, the day before? He turned blazing eyes on the astonished housekeeper.

'She must be found—immediately! Summon all the servants, and send them out at once!' Mrs Nateby stared at him.

'Whatever for, my lord? She won't have gone far, with her ladyship still so weak, and all. It's a lovely morning. She'll have gone out into the garden. Do her good after being cooped up all these days. You sit down and have your breakfast, and she'll be back soon enough, you'll see!'

Ignoring the main part of her speech, Deverham seized on the one word that was of interest to him.

'The garden! Of course, that's where she'll be!' He ran from the room, leaving the housekeeper a prey to interesting surmise.

In the hall he met Florence, who had arrayed herself carefully and was set on charming him out of his anger. She had the wit to see that she had behaved in a way that was beyond the bounds of what was acceptable, but it never occurred to her that a sweetly phrased apology, with perhaps a few contrite tears, would not set all right. Deverham, however, scarcely noticed her, and would have passed her by without a word had she not caught at his sleeve.

'Oh, Deverham, I am so glad to see you! You are not still cross with me, are you?'

He looked at her with eyes that scarcely saw her.

'Cross with you? No, I am not.'

'Then will you not keep me company for breakfast? I must learn to pour the coffee just as you like it.'

He thought that he had never known her to bother with his coffee before, but that Patience always gave him his cup just as he preferred it.

'I am afraid I have not time, just now. If you will excuse me, I must go. Your aunt is in the garden, and I must find her.' Unceremoniously he removed his arm from her clasp, and when she did not move set her firmly to one side and went out, leaving her open-mouthed behind him.

Once in the garden, he soon found the marks of Patience's footprints in the dew of the grass. Calmer, now, he followed her, not wishing to startle her when he did come upon her. He saw how she had wandered from place to place, moving from one clump of flowers to another. At last he saw her, standing half turned away from him and very still under the larger of the cherry trees. Her face was lifted to the song of a blackbird, the bird glossy dark among the snowy blossom, and she was quite unaware of his presence. He stood still and watched, as with unselfconscious grace she reached up her hand to the branch above her. He thought she would pick some blossom to go with the handful of primroses and violets in her hand, but she merely caressed them, lifting the hanging heads to enjoy their beauty.

He did not speak or move, but as if she had become aware of his gaze upon her she turned and looked at him. A glow of colour rose in her cheek, but her eyes did not fall. She looked steadily at him with the look that he loved, gentle and brave, and his heart turned over. Stepping forward he spoke her name, and opened his arms as she came into them with the lovely inevitability of a bird coming home to its nest. He gathered her to him, flowers and all, and exulted as, with no false modesty, she lifted her face to his kisses, and returned them with fervour.

After a few minutes he became aware that something was tickling his chin. Lifting his head, he saw that it was a violet, one of the posy that she still held. Unceremoniously he removed them from her grasp, and dropped them on the grass before putting his arms round her again. She gave a small exclamation of distress.

'They were for Mama!'

'Damn Mama,' he said. Patience accepted this shocking remark with equanimity.

'I can always pick some more,' she said calmly, 'and I am glad to have my hands free,' she added, reaching up to caress his cheek. Greatly enchanted by this forward behaviour, he kissed her fingers, then tilted her face so that he could kiss her lips again.

'Well!' A shocked gasp behind him made them both jump. 'Deverham! Aunt Patience!'

They both turned. When he had not returned Florence, intrigued and piqued by Deverham's behaviour, had decided to follow him. Now she stood, her face white with anger and shock. Unconsciously she was gripping the ring that Deverham had given her, and his lips twitched at the sight. Patience, shocked out of her enchanted world, became aware that she was behaving with the greatest impropriety, that her skirt was muddy and wet where she had knelt to gather her flowers, and that the silk net had slipped off and her hair was hanging in disarray down her back. She was not, of course, aware that her face was radiant. Her cheeks pink with embarrassment, her lips rosy from Deverham's kisses, she glowed with a beauty that Deverham, looking from aunt to niece, thought that the younger girl would never achieve.

Florence, who had never thought that any man would even notice another woman when she was by, was shaken to the depths of her being. That Deverham did not love her was nothing, but that he should choose her old, dowdy Aunt Patience instead was more than she could bear. Lost for words, she turned and began to stumble back to the house. Patience, swiftly bundling her hair back into its restraint, fol-

lowed her, and Deverham, who was the least perturbed of the three, walked after them.

By the time they reached the gardens by the house
Florence had had time to collect her thoughts.
Stopping short of the french windows that led into
the breakfast-parlour, she turned to face them.
Deverham had taken Patience's hand, and they were
shamelessly walking together, thought Florence, as
though they were already engaged, or even married!
Well, she would have something to say about that,
she thought.

'I suppose you have not forgotten, my lord,' she
began, her voice high and hard, 'that we are
betrothed?'

'Not exactly forgotten,' said Deverham in a considering tone that was calculated to annoy her.

'Then, my lord, I must ask you why you are behaving in this shameless fashion with Another!'

'A little less melodrama, if you please,' he said with
an air of amusement. 'There is no need to address me
as "my lord" with every other breath. And this is not
Another, but your own Aunt Patience, to whom you
owe both respect and gratitude.'

'Respect! Gratitude!' Florence's voice rose again.
'I should respect her when she behaves like a hussy?
And gratitude, when she has insinuated herself between us? I do not know how she has managed to
turn your head so, my l... Deverham, but I should
remind you that she has no fortune, not one penny,
and if you think I might give her some of my money
you may think again!'

With an exclamation of disgust Deverham stepped
forward, but Patience restrained him.

'It is true that we have behaved badly to you, Florence. I am afraid I was—carried away.'

'You had better watch that you are not carried away any further,' spat Florence viciously. 'He may treat you as he has treated me, cast you aside!'

'Like a worn-out glove?' asked Patience in some amusement.

'It is all very well for you to make a joke of it. You have not been wronged as I have.'

'Wronged?' put in Deverham. 'I think you have had a narrow escape. Do you really think we should have been happy together, if this wretched engagement had run its course? Do you seriously tell me that you love me?'

'Love you?' Florence was surprised. 'I like you well enough. And I should like to be married, and have a title, and a place in society.'

As before, the childishness of her response softened him.

'All this you may have, in time, without tying yourself to me. I would be the last to deny that you are a very beautiful girl, and with your fortune you may have your pick of the eligibles. Who knows, you might even become a duchess!'

This exciting possibility served to divert Florence's mind for a moment.

'Are there any unmarried dukes at present?' she asked naïvely.

'Several,' he assured her. 'And I am well acquainted with at least two, and will promise to introduce you, if you will agree that we should call an end to our betrothal.'

Her mouth took on the stubborn line that Patience knew only too well. She was very conscious of the open french windows, and all the other open windows that looked on to this part of the garden. Neither Florence nor Deverham made any attempt to moderate their voices, and she was tolerably sure that there was not a servant in the house who was not listening, openly or otherwise, to every word that passed between them. She attempted to urge them into the house, but Florence was deaf to her.

'End our betrothal?' she cried in ringing tones. 'And have you announce another, straight away, and to my aunt? Never!'

'For heaven's sake, Florence,' said Patience crossly. 'May we not at least go indoors? I have no wish to have my affairs made public knowledge, and I would have thought you would not either.'

'But then I have done nothing to be ashamed of,' said Florence smugly. 'Besides, I have said it now, and that is all there is to it.'

'It most certainly is not,' said Deverham. 'I shall not stir from this place until we have this cleared up. You have admitted that you do not love me; you know you may easily marry to better advantage, and with someone you can care for.'

'No, not that,' she said in a hard voice. 'I have done with love. I cannot imagine feeling that for anyone, now. I shall marry where it suits me.'

'Then why cling to this engagement?'

'Because it has been announced,' she replied, astonished that he should need to ask. 'What would people say, if we break it off at once?'

'What does it matter? I am happy to take the blame, for I am well aware that I was at fault ever to ask you, when we hardly knew one another. No blame will attach to you.'

'But when they see that you prefer Aunt Patience to me, I shall be a laughing stock! To have my own aunt preferred to me! And she is so old, and dowdy, and little, without even a penny to bless herself with! I won't have it, I tell you! I just won't have it!'

Patience, fortunately, rated her own attractions so low—and was in any case as surprised as Florence to find that Deverham loved her—that she was quite unmoved by this speech, but Deverham was furious.

'You won't have it! What you will have, my girl, and what you should have had many years ago, is a damned good hiding!' He stepped forward as if to administer his rough justice there and then, and with a squeak of dismay Florence fled. Between tears and laughter, Patience clasped Deverham's arm when he would have followed.

'Charles! You cannot! She is overwrought!'

'Come now, Patience, really! You did not think I would touch her, did you? But it will do her no harm to think that I might.' They followed Florence into the breakfast-room, where they found she had taken her stand, with prudent defiance, behind the snowy reaches of the table. With the greatest courtesy, Deverham held a chair for Patience, then stood ready beside the one Florence, on the rare occasions when she was downstairs for breakfast, used. She eyed him dubiously, and he held out his hand with a wry smile.

'There is no need to be afraid, my dear. Your aunt will protect you.'

'I do not need her protection! I am very well able to take care of myself.'

'Then why are you still standing over there? Come and sit down, like a good girl.'

'I am not a good girl! I mean...I do not choose to sit down with you!'

'Then I fear I must eat my breakfast standing up, unless you leave the room. Not that I am complaining,' he pointed out carefully, 'I merely mention it in passing.'

'Breakfast! I do not know how you can think of eating!'

'I know, dreadful of me, isn't it? I am afraid that I am really remarkably hungry, and I fear that I must be completely lacking in sensibility.' He filled a plate generously from the selection of dishes that were keeping hot on the serving table, and under Florence's horrified but fascinated eye proceeded to eat, with great aplomb, his plate balanced neatly on the mantelshelf. With a great effort, Patience controlled her amusement.

'Lord Deverham,' she said severely, 'kindly refrain from teasing her. Florence, you would do very much better to sit down, and have a cup of tea.' She took a slice of toast, and began prosaically to help herself to butter and honey.

'I do not *want* a cup of tea.' Florence, trying to sound dignified, simply sounded sulky even in her own ears. 'Oh, very well, I will sit down, then.' She did so, and at once Deverham brought his plate to the table, and joined them.

'That is better. Perhaps now we may talk about this in a sensible fashion.'

'There is nothing to talk about. You have asked me to marry you, and I am wearing your ring. You cannot back down now.'

'Of course I cannot. No gentleman could. You, however, may do so without reproach. No one who knows me would be surprised that on better acquaintance you should have decided that we should not suit. For we should not, my dear.'

'And have you marry Aunt Patience out of hand? Never.'

Patience found that the piece of toast in her hand was like ashes in her mouth, and laid it down.

'What are you saying, precisely? Do you mean that you will not release Deverham unless we give our word never to marry?'

Florence had not really considered the matter deeply.

'Well, I don't know about never. But certainly not until I am married.'

'People would only say that I married your aunt in despair, after you had cast me off.'

'No, they would not,' Florence said shrewdly. 'There are plenty of other women in the world you could marry in that case. No, they would guess that you preferred her to me, and they would laugh at me.' She was close to tears. 'I don't know how you could, Deverham! I was being good, and polite, and you must admit I am much prettier than Aunt Patience!'

It was impossible to reason with her in such a mood. Patience put a cup of tea down within her niece's reach, and after sniffing into a lace-edged handkerchief Florence absently picked it up and began to sip at it.

'You do not love me, do you, Florence?'

'No, I suppose not, but I like you well enough.'

'Should we continue with this marriage, it would be the beginning of a lifetime of unhappiness for all three of us. Surely you cannot want that. You are so very young. You have hardly met any men yet. One day, quite soon, perhaps, you will find someone you can both like and love, and if you are married to me, what then?'

'I don't want to marry you now. But I do not want to end our engagement, now that it has been announced. At least, not until I have found someone else.'

'How is that to be done, when you are known to be engaged to me?'

Florence looked at him helplessly, tears welling in her eyes.

'I want to go to London! I want balls, and masquerades, and dinners, and the theatre! I want to make my curtsy to the Queen, with a train three yards long, and plumes in my hair!' She sounded so like a child longing for a treat that Patience was almost sorry for her.

'I don't see why you shouldn't have all that,' she said slowly. Florence's tears vanished like snow in the sunshine, and she looked up hopefully. 'After all, the arrangements are made for the house in London, and it must be nearly ready. We cannot think of going until Mama is recovered, of course, but after that, surely we should carry on? After all, if you want to meet a more suitable husband, where could be better? All the eligible young men will be up for the Season, and with your looks you should be one of the beauties of the year.'

'Far be it from me to cast a blight on your happy dream, but, since Florence is known to be engaged to me, it is hardly likely that any gentleman who can call himself such will make advances to her.'

'No, I know. I am afraid we shall have to act a little,' said Patience. 'At least, you will have to.'

Charles groaned.

'Do not tell me, I am cast for the villain of the piece. I can feel it in my bones.'

'Well, yes. You must be very stern, very possessive and strict. You will make everyone pity Florence for being tied to someone so much . . . so much older, and she must appear to be frightened of you.' Patience paused as Charles buried his face in his hands. 'You will not mind too much, will you?'

Deverham raised a face suffused with suppressed laughter.

'Mind? Why should I mind? You do not think, perhaps, that people might find this change of character rather sudden?'

'Oh, no, for you have recently reformed, have you not? And men of—mature—years, who fall in love with young girls, are apt to behave so, I believe.'

'Enough! I feel like a grandfather! I am not so very old, you know.'

'No, of course you are not.' Patience was soothing, as to a captious child. 'But you are much older than Florence, after all. Then, you see, if Florence should find someone else, no one will be surprised that she should prefer him to you.'

'My reputation, then, is to be sacrificed to Florence?'

'No, no! Only think how people will pity you when she casts you off.'

'Like a worn-out glove,' interpolated Charles, his sense of humour getting the better of him.

'Precisely so . . . an *old* worn-out glove,' agreed his beloved calmly. 'Then, of course, when you marry me, they will pity you even more, because you have

obviously been so disappointed in love that you are
prepared to accept anyone!'

For the first time he was not smiling.

'I will not have you say such things,' he said sternly.
'And not for Florence or anybody will I allow people
to think that you are second-best for me, Queen of
my heart.'

To his surprise this elicited a short burst of ap-
plause from Florence.

'Very pretty—much nicer than anything you ever
said to me,' she approved. 'You must certainly marry
one another...eventually,' she finished firmly. 'I think
your idea is very good, Aunt Patience. Only you must
not be looking at one another like that, or making
flowery speeches, or you will be giving the whole thing
away.'

'One other thing,' Patience continued, with becomingly pink cheeks. 'I think it would be better if
we did not tell Mama any of this.'

'Oh, no, she would never be able to act her part,'
agreed Florence. 'And besides, she won't be very
happy at the thought of losing you, even to
Deverham,' she added. Patience sighed.

'I am afraid you are right, but at the moment that
is the least of my worries.'

'Oh, do not worry! I think it will all be great fun!
I have always loved acting, and I am very good at it,
you know. It will all go just perfectly!'

Patience could only hope that she was right.

CHAPTER THIRTEEN

LADY WINTERBOURNE, convalescing, was as demanding and difficult as Patience had known she would be. With a bona fide illness behind her, she was querulous, affectionate and irritated by turn, insisting on Patience's almost continuous presence by her side, and expressing plaintive wishes for unseasonable delicacies that would have led a lesser cook than Mr Moreton's to give a month's notice on the spot.

Wrapped in a cocoon of happiness, Patience dealt with her mother serenely, and with a glow in her eyes that any observant beholder would have recognised instantly. As it was, Lady Winterbourne attributed the happiness that she did dimly notice to relief at her safe recovery, and made the most of it.

Florence and Deverham were less happy. Deverham was annoyed that his love seemed to spend all her time in her mother's sick-room, being bullied, and that he hardly ever saw her alone. Florence, for her part, was bored and restless. In the interests of their continuing pretence, and to relieve Patience of another demanding relative, Deverham took it upon himself to keep her amused. It was not an easy task. Now that she was no longer interested in capturing, and keeping, his interest, she was no longer the amiable, agreeable girl he had first met.

'Riding? Oh, Deverham, you know I do not care for riding. It is so uncomfortable, and so boring, and I dislike the aroma of horse about my person.'

'Come, now, Florence, it is good exercise for you, and who knows but that it might be useful? When you marry your duke, you are bound to have to spend some time in the country with him.'

'But I shall not have to ride. I shall have a carriage, in fact several carriages, and grooms and coachmen, when I want to go out.'

'You will get very fat.'

Florence looked down at her trim waist, scarcely needing the restraint of a corset to pull it to the desired shape, and smiled smugly.

'I have always been slim, and I have never taken very much exercise. Besides, once I am married, what does it matter? Nobody expects a wife to keep an eighteen-inch waist for ever.'

'Nevertheless, we are bound to be here for a week or two yet, and what are you going to do with yourself? I know very well you are bored.'

'Bored! I should think I am. If only we could go to London now! You cannot imagine how I am looking forward to it!'

One or two expeditions were made to Manchester, but these were not a success, since Florence's main wish was for shopping, and she found nothing there that satisfied her exacting tastes. Mr Moreton had few friends, and after Florence had been taken to pay two or three calls she declared they were old-fashioned and boring, and would not go again. In the end Deverham was driven to entertain her with a fund of London gossip, of which his past activities had given him a useful store. Much of it, of course, was unfit for girlish ears, but he succeeded in distracting her for an entire afternoon with the stories.

'The Earl of Jersey's daughter? And she actually eloped? I never heard about it.'

'It must be nearly four years ago now. You were just a young schoolgirl then.'

'And she was just my age?'

'Lady Adela? I think she was seventeen, the youngest daughter, of course.'

'And he? Quite unsuitable, I suppose?'

'I never met him. He was a captain in the 11th Hussars, Ibbetson, his name was, and the family never knew of the acquaintance. I believe he used to speak to her in the Park, when she was out walking with her maid, and I have heard that he used to watch her window with a spy-glass, and make signals from his veranda, for he lived nearby.'

'How romantic! Where did they go?'

'They eloped from Brighton, and he carried her off to Gretna Green, and then across the Channel. Of course the Earl was furious, and Lady Jersey in hysterics, but there was not much to be done. In the end they had to make the best of it, or lose their daughter completely.'

'But if they had not, she would have been ruined, for no one would have received her. How dreadful! I cannot imagine taking such a risk.'

'It took some living down. Lady Jersey appeared at the Drawing Room, later on, positively bedecked with diamonds, tiara and stomacher, and a cloth of gold train. But, of course, the matrons always appear in their grandest toilettes on such occasions.'

'But surely the Drawing Rooms are for the débutantes. They should be the most dressed up.'

'Well, it is their day, of course, but a terrible ordeal, I should think. By the time they have sat in a coach in the Mall, being ogled by the populace, freezing or roasting according to the weather, then waited in some ante-room, worrying about walking backwards in a train three yards long, when they make their curtsy they are ready to drop. The married ladies, on the other hand, may simply air their most expensive gowns, and outshine the Queen's jewels with their own.'

'Do they do so?'

'Sometimes. Of course she is rather small, and next to someone like the Marchioness of Douro she looks a little dumpy.'

'Well, when I am presented, I shall make quite sure that people are looking at me, not anyone else. And I shall not worry about my train. We used to practise at school, sometimes, and I am very good at it.'

With conversation kept at so trivial a level, it was not surprising that Charles was frequently driven to take sanctuary in his grandfather's room. Mr Moreton was making a rapid recovery, and it was becoming increasingly difficult to persuade him to stay in bed quietly. Charles did not attempt to hide the present state of affairs from him.

'So! Fallen for the other one, have you? I wondered.'

'You do not mind, Grandfather?'

'And if I say I do?'

'Then I am sorry, but it will not make the slightest difference to me or to Patience. Without her I could not be happy, however rich, and though I should dislike to lose your affection, she is more to me than anyone.'

'Bravo! I never thought to hear you say such things about any woman. That other little piece was all very well, but I do not care about you marrying a fortune. All I want is to see you settled, and done with this racketing around. I want to see my great-grandson, before I'm done.'

'And so you shall! But I have to tell you, there is a problem.'

'Her ladyship? She'll come round.'

'No, my erstwhile betrothed. She does not wish to marry me, but she will not end our engagement. She cannot bear the thought of her aunt marrying me.'

'It's a pity we made things public, then, but that can't be helped. What will you do?'

Charles explained Patience's plan, and Mr Moreton laughed himself into a state that had his grandson alarmed for his health.

'What wouldn't I give to see it!' he exclaimed when he had recovered his breath.

'Then why not? I know they would welcome your presence in London.'

'No, lad, no. I'd never be able to keep a straight face, for one thing, seeing you playing the heavy husband, and you'll all have enough on your plates without my letting the cat out of the bag.'

Charles had to admit that he was right. Patience, when next she visited Mr Moreton, had to endure a great deal of teasing, but she could forgive everything when he gave her a hearty hug and a kiss, saying with blunt good humour, 'Anyone who can bring a look like that to Charles's eyes is right with me. I believe I saw it coming before he did! Welcome to the family, lass.'

With a tremulous smile Patience wiped her
brimming eyes, as ever more easily moved by kindness
than by scolding.

'I am afraid it is rather a muddle, sir.'

'Not of your making, my dear. I trust to your sensible head to see that all goes well. Will you manage
it, do you think?'

'I think that with her looks and fortune, Florence
will be besieged by men of all ages. My only fear is
that she will not find one whom she can love. I cannot
allow her to marry just anyone, because he happens
to have a title, so that I may be happy. I am afraid
she is quite silly enough to marry for the sake of a
great name, and a place in society.'

'Not exactly silly, more hard-headed, I'd say.'

'But she is so young! I must protect her, for no one
else will, except Charles, and he cannot do much.'

Mr Moreton was beginning to look dubious.

'I don't want you and Charles to have to wait too
long. It's time he settled down, and I'm not getting
any younger. As I told him, I want to dandle my great-
grandson on my knee.'

'And so you shall,' she said warmly, her cheeks
rather pink. 'You must not let yourself be bothered
by all this. Set your mind to getting better for our
wedding!'

By the time Lady Winterbourne was fit to travel,
the house in London was pronounced ready to receive
them. The journey, managed as before by Charles,
proceeded uneventfully, and very soon he left them,
tired but elated, to return to his lodgings. Florence
was in seventh heaven.

'Is it not wonderful, Grandmama? Such a very good
address, and everything just as it should be. Tomorrow

I must go shopping, and order some new gowns. Those I have are all very well, but they will not do for London.'

Lady Winterbourne, who had been recruiting her strength on a sofa, became visibly more animated.

'Do not, I beg you, Florence, buy anything without consulting me first! For your first Season, and at your age, you must study simplicity. Nothing too ornate, I beg you, or too brightly coloured. When you are married, of course, it is quite a different thing, but it is of the first importance that you do not appear fast!'

Florence pouted.

'But I like my things to be pretty! And you told me yourself that the Queen wore very ornate clothes before she was married, and she was hardly older than me.'

'Than I,' Lady Winterbourne corrected absently. 'So she did, but she was Queen of England, and you are not. Besides, I said that she did so, but not that she should have done so. Her family never did have any taste. Look at her uncle, when he was Regent! I remember visiting Carlton House once, and I have never been so shocked in my life!'

'Really, Grandmama? Oh, *do* tell me!'

Lady Winterbourne recollected herself.

'It was a long time ago, and quite unsuitable for your ears. Suffice it to say that so vulgar a display is quite unacceptable nowadays.'

With these wise words in mind, Patience found it easier to steer her niece into choosing clothes fit for her age, rather than the ornate creations she longed for, but which Charles, when consulted, said rudely made her look like an opera-girl. Florence forgave him, for every afternoon brought carriages to the door, and the tray of cards left by callers overflowed more and more every day. An exhausting round of return calls had to be made, and Patience was relieved to find that Florence's claim to acting ability had been more than an idle boast. More than once Patience had to bite her lip when, in the sympathetic presence of other débutantes, Florence shyly confessed that Lord Deverham was very strict, oh, yes, quite fierce with her. She was able to convey, without words, that pressure from her grandmother had encouraged her to accept him, and while Patience could not like to hear it, there was enough truth in the story to keep her silent.

Such formal calls, timed to exactly fifteen minutes, were only the beginning. Before three days were out the morning post was full of invitations, and it became increasingly difficult to decide how many could be accepted.

'What do you think, Aunt Patience? The ball, or the opera? It is very flattering to be invited by the Duchess, of course, but still——'

'The ball,' said Patience decidedly. She herself would have preferred Covent Garden, where Grisi, Persiani, Alboni and Pauline Viardot were performing at the Royal Italian Opera House, but Florence was not musical, and there would be many more men for her to meet at the ball.

It was to be a masquerade. Deverham, arriving with his sternest expression to take Florence for a drive in the Row at the fashionable hour of five o'clock, seized the opportunity for a few quiet words with Patience.

'I suppose this means that I shall have to rig myself out in some inane costume. Isn't it enough that I must act the fool, that I have to look one, also?'

She was stricken.

'Shall you dislike it very much? I am sorry, but I thought it would be better than the opera. There are several young men who will be there, and she will be able to dance with them.'

Charles was immediately contrite.

'I was not blaming you, darling. I know you are doing your best. But if you knew how I hate it, to be in your company, and scarcely able to exchange two words with you! I dare not even look at you, for fear I should forget myself.'

'Oh, I know, Charles. The worst thing is, when someone says something funny, and I long to be able to share a smile with you! But at least I can see you. That is my one pleasure.'

His immediate response was to take her into a crushing embrace. Since they were alone in the small morning-room, she did not resist, and returned his kisses with enthusiasm.

'Dearest girl,' he murmured into her hair. 'I cannot bear to go on with this much longer.'

She was silent. The strength of his arms, the passion of his kisses, brought both elation and sadness that they were not free to admit their love.

'We have the rest of our lives together,' she said softly. In answer he kissed her again, with something akin to desperation.

'Life is uncertain, and I want you for myself, now.' He was not, thought Patience, used to waiting for what he wanted.

'Would it be better if I went away?'

'No! Unthinkable. Little love, you must teach *me* patience. Forgive me, I know this is as hard for you as it is for me. Will you dance with me at the ball?'

'Certainly not. I attend as Florence's chaperon, in place of Mama. I shall not be in costume.'

'So you will pass your evening among the old tabbies? Don't be ridiculous. You will go in costume, and you will dance with me at least once, or I shall not go myself.'

She smiled at him tenderly.

'Anyone who heard you would believe all Florence's tales of your fierceness at once!'

'Does it well, does she? I thought I had received a few odd looks here and there.'

'I am surprised it was no more than looks! Oh, it is all done in the most delicate way possible, the lowered eyelids, the phrases begun but not finished, the speaking silences. I wish you might hear it! If it were not so important, I should never be able to keep from laughing.'

'Little minx.'

They had not heard the door open behind them, and sprang apart at the sound of its closing again. Florence, becomingly arrayed in rose-pink, with an exquisitely embroidered shawl and elegant bonnet, surveyed them with annoyance.

'Really, Deverham, you are most indiscreet! Anyone could have come in and found you embracing my aunt! What would people say?'

Deverham eyed her with disfavour.

'Nothing worse than they are saying already, by all accounts.'

She was pleased.

'Well, I do think I have been doing it rather well. Under different circumstances, I could have been a great success as an actress, I believe.'

'No doubt about it. What part do you take for the ball?'

'I haven't decided. Something classical, perhaps, like Helen of Troy.'

'The most beautiful woman in the world. Of course. Or what about Narcissus?'

'Who was she?' enquired Florence innocently. Patience choked on a giggle.

'You should know by now that Florence is quite impervious to such darts. Never mind him, dear. Narcissus was not a female.'

'Oh, then I expect he was saying something disagreeable,' said Florence. 'If we are going to drive, Charles, it is time we left.' She wafted out of the room on a wave of attar of roses, and Deverham had time to do no more than plant a firm kiss on Patience's lips before following her. Rather disconsolately, Patience trailed back upstairs to her mother.

It was difficult to know whether or not their plan was working. Florence, as they had foreseen, had been an instant success, and at any function was liable to be surrounded by men, eligible and otherwise. Charles played his part by frowning from a distance, dancing with her once or twice and then withdrawing, apparently in an ill humour, to some other part of the building. The trouble was that Florence, while she was enjoying herself immensely, seemed completely unmoved by any one individual in the throng that made up her court. She danced and flirted happily with whomever might be there, but when discreetly questioned afterwards showed a distressing inability to remember the names of her partners.

On the night of the Masquerade, Patience and her niece waited for Deverham, who was to escort them to the ball. Florence, having changed her mind a dozen times, had finally settled on appearing as Juliet, demure in shimmering white silk with Italian sleeves, sewn with seed pearls, as was her little silk cap, below which her hair, unbound, floated in a dark cloud. She looked enchanting. Patience, suppressing the impulse to array herself in homespuns and appear as her Nurse, or in rags as Cinderella before the transformation scene, had decided finally on the Queen of Hearts of the nursery rhyme. Her gown, in the Tudor style, was of stiff white satin, the hem of the skirt and of the hanging sleeves ornamented with red silk hearts, interspersed on the skirt with tarts cunningly created with beige silk and red satin. The little lace ruff that stood up from the back of the square-cut neckline was sparkling with little heart-shaped red spangles, as was the coif with one little tart set in the middle, like a jewel. Her hair was contained in a gold net, and she carried a round fan on a slender stick, made to resemble a plateful of the same delicacies.

Deverham, his own costume hidden by a cloak, smiled when he saw Patience.

'Queen of my heart,' he murmured, for her ears alone, as he put her cloak round her shoulders, and escorted her to the carriage. On their arrival they donned their masks, Deverham's being a full-face one, held before the face on a long stick, and lavishly decked with whiskers and beard in deep blackish blue. Patience made her way to the side of the room, and found a seat with the other chaperons. Rather to her surprise she was almost at once invited to dance, by a stout gallant dressed as Henry VIII. She was thus in a good position to observe the edifying spectacle of her niece, every line of head and body speaking of misery, dancing with her fiancé.

Deverham's face, unhidden by the mask which he was not bothering to hold up, was cold and angry. He appeared to speak little to Florence, but it was clear to any observer that he was merely restraining his annoyance for some more private place. Patience bit her lip to keep back a smile, and her partner, following her gaze, interrupted his flow of small talk.

'That is one little *affaire* that does not seem to be prospering,' he remarked. 'I hear that the lady is rich as well as beautiful, so it is not surprising that Deverham is anxious not to lose her, but, even so, I wonder at him.'

'Why?' Patience kept her voice innocent. Her partner obviously had not recognised her beneath her mask, and in any case her retiring ways meant that in general she was not very well known.

'Your Majesty has not been in London for long?'

'No, and never before.'

'Then you may not know that his lordship has a certain reputation for philandering. One would have thought he would have known better than to treat her so heavy-handedly.'

'He does not seem very happy with her,' offered Patience.

'No, and it's not like him to show it. A pretty little filly like that, she's not likely to stand for it for long.'

Indeed, as they watched it could be seen that the little Juliet's eyes were straying round the room, as if looking for escape. Suddenly she stiffened, and faltered in the dance.

'She's not paying much attention to him,' Henry VIII said with the relish of one who anticipates some excitement. 'He won't like that.'

He was right. Before Patience's bemused gaze, Deverham spoke a few curt words, but almost before he had finished speaking Florence had torn herself from his arms and was running, pushing between other astonished couples without a word of apology, from the ballroom. Her partner, taken by surprise, was left standing alone and foolish in the middle of the floor.

A little whispering hush came over the room as other dancers, interrupted in their gyrations, paused to inform those near them what had happened. Several heads turn to stare. Most, however, returned to their dancing with well-bred indifference, only the brightness of their eyes and the renewed chatter of conversation showing that the event had been marked.

His face like thunder, Deverham strode in the wake of his erstwhile partner. Then, realising that he could scarcely make a spectacle of himself by hunting through the crowded rooms for her, he took himself off to find a glass of something stronger than champagne to soothe his battered self-esteem. Not long after, Patience, returned to her chair by her own partner and left alone while he fetched her a glass of lemonade, found the empty chair beside her taken by a familiar figure, his mask now in place. No one was near them, and the sound of the orchestra effectively masked their voices.

'Well done,' she said with warm approval. 'I saw it all.'

'I know you did, I saw you dancing. Who was that fellow?'

'My partner? I have not the least idea. Come now, Charles, you are not going to let your acting spill over on to me, are you?'

'No, but you have almost always refused to dance with me.'

'Of course I have, with Florence there. More than the occasional courtesy dance would have been a great mistake, and generally speaking I have been firmly among the chaperons, and no one else has asked me. This time, however, I am in costume, and no one is likely to recognise me.'

'So you will dance with me? More than once? Splendid. I needed something for my wounded pride.'

'You cannot tell me you are that sensitive,' laughed Patience. 'After all, you know she is only pretending.'

'I do, but she does it so dashed well! And I think she might have warned me of her intentions, before running off like that and making it look as though I had been bullying her unmercifully. I felt a complete ass.'

'Well, you did not look it, merely rather angry. I did not know she had such a plan, I must admit. I will have a word with her tonight. Of course, it was very effective. Maybe she was right not to warn you.'

'So you don't have faith in my acting? Come and dance with me, and I will give a command performance of a man doing his duty by dancing with one girl, while simmering with anger over another.' He rose and bowed with antique courtesy, his eyes sparkling through the holes in his mask. Patience rose, curtsied, and placed the tips of her fingers on his outstretched hand.

'By the way, I quite forgot to ask you,' she murmured, as he led her into the dance, his clasp round her waist outwardly correct, actually rather tighter than was discreet. 'Who are you dressed as this evening?' He gave a little laugh.

'Had you not guessed? Bluebeard, of course!'

CHAPTER FOURTEEN

IT WAS an unexpectedly happy evening. Patience, dancing blissfully in Deverham's arms, caught one fleeting glimpse of her niece, in close huddled conversation with another young girl, and dismissed her from her mind, content to enjoy her moment of happiness. Deverham took her into supper, saying that as long as they did not look as if they were enjoying themselves too much, it could scarcely matter.

In the midst of a crowded ballroom it was possible to be surprisingly private. Deverham, who was familiar with all the great houses, had no difficulty in locating a quiet corner of a conservatory where, screened by palms and other foliage, they were able to converse in low tones in the damp, sweetly scented gloom.

'I wish I knew what she is playing at,' said Deverham gloomily. 'I know we have a part to act, but this evening was beyond a joke.'

'She has several gentlemen paying court to her,' said Patience thoughtfully. 'Maybe she is satisfied with her success, and will bring the engagement to an end. No one would be surprised, and as long as we did not announce our engagement too quickly, it would be all right. I know that she does not favour any of them particularly.'

'Are they eligible?'

'Several of them. Of course, there are a few fortune-hunters, but that is only to be expected, and she is too clever to be caught like that. She is not likely to be enticed into a runaway match, the world well lost for love, and that sort of thing. She is far too level-headed.'

'Yes, I know. We have had some conversation on the subject. Is she really as heartless as she seems?'

Patience sighed.

'I hope not. There was a man, once, when she was at school, the brother of one of her friends and a sea captain. He was lost at sea, with his ship, and she was certainly very unhappy. I think her heart was truly touched, but since then she does not seem to care very much for anyone. Oh, Charles, she is so very young, and her life has not been as it should. Do not blame her if she seems selfish.'

'I admit that I was shocked when I first saw her as she really is, but recently I have learned—well, to respect her in a way. She is very self-centred, of course, but she has some courage, and I think that the right man might be able to teach her, and make her into a person of some worth.'

'But who is the right man? I cannot see that any of those paying court to her would do. It would be disastrous, for both of them, and I cannot allow her to ruin herself.'

'Wretched girl! Here we are, alone for once in the most romantic of circumstances, and all we can find to talk about is Florence! Let us instead consider ourselves. Forgetting all the problems that litter our path to happiness, where do you wish to live when we are married? Shall I take a house in town?'

Patience had not put aside her white satin mask, and he reached up to undo the thin ribbons that held it in place. Her eyes gleamed in the near darkness, her face shadowed and mysterious.

'You must know, Charles, that as long as I am with you I do not much care where I live.'

His fingers caressed her face with a soft touch, running from temple to cheek and along the line of her jaw to lift her face to his kiss.

'Manchester?' he murmured, his kisses feather-light against her lips.

'If you like,' she replied equably, leaning into his embrace and twining an arm round his neck.

'O most biddable one! We shall have a house in town, and you will be the hostess that Florence would have liked to be, but cannot, because she is not clever enough. But I know that you like the country best, and our home shall be my country house. You will like it, Patience. And so will our children.'

'Counting your bridges?'

'Before they are hatched? Yes, but it will come true for us. I know it.'

Lost in a world of their own, kissing and being kissed, they lost all count of time. At last Charles, with Patience lying quiet on his breast, her head divested of its coif nestling confidingly beneath his chin, stirred. Looking down, he saw that her eyelids were heavy, almost closed, and she was nearly asleep.

'My poor love! You are worn out, and I must get you home.'

'Oh, do not move, it is so comfortable like this,' murmured Patience. He dropped a light kiss on her nose.

'Come, we shall be remarked if we stay hidden like this. As it is, Florence must be wondering where we are. Here, put on our crown, or whatever it is, and go to rejoin the throng. I will join you in a few minutes. It would never do for us to be seen coming out of here together.'

Obediently Patience resumed her coif, but not her mask, since the time for revealing the guests' identities had certainly passed, and walked with what dignity she could muster back to the ballroom. The crowd had perceptibly thinned, though many of the younger set were still dancing enthusiastically, and several of the older chaperons were unashamedly asleep. Patience glanced round for her niece, not much perturbed when she did not immediately see her, and went hunting through the ante-chambers and other rooms.

By the time she had looked everywhere she was annoyed, but unworried. It was quite possible that Florence had hidden herself away, as she and Deverham had done, for a little flirtation. Patience looked again, more carefully this time, and visited also the ladies' retiring-room. Florence was nowhere to be found.

Still more irritated than anxious, Patience returned to the ballroom. Deverham was now lounging by the wall, exchanging a few words with an acquaintance. Seeing Patience alone, he excused himself and came towards her.

'What is the matter? Where is Florence?'

'I cannot find her anywhere. I have looked all through the rooms, twice over, and she is nowhere to be seen.'

'Well, she must be somewhere. Sit down with these comatose ladies, my dear, and let me look. I know all the hiding places.'

'I'm sure you do,' she said archly.

'And isn't it lucky that I do?' he retorted, walking off with unhurried pace. It was not long before he returned, and one look at his face told Patience that he had not been successful.

'Where can she be? Oh, Charles, what can have happened to her? Does nobody know?'

'It is a little difficult to ask. The last thing we want to do is to start people gossiping about her. The most obvious explanation is that she became bored, or unwell, was unable to find either of us, and went home by herself. Not very sensible, of course, but nothing to worry about. She has plenty of friends here, who would have seen her home. She is hardly likely to have attempted the journey on her own.'

'I did see her talking to a young lady, when we were dancing after your... little disagreement. Maybe she went with her party,' said Patience hopefully.

'Maybe. Anyway, if that is the case, our hostess will know of it. I suggest we say our farewells, and if she does she is sure to mention it.'

Such proved not to be the case. Their hostess, a fashionable countess, bade them farewell with the greatest cordiality, her glance travelling beyond them.

'But where is your charming fiancée, Deverham? Surely she arrived with you?'

Her arch glance revealed that she was completely *au fait* with the tale of their disagreement. Charles gave a small bow.

'I regret, Lady Auburn, that she is a little indisposed. She was obliged to leave earlier, and requested me to give you her thanks and her apologies, as she did not want to make any disturbance.'

'Poor child,' purred Lady Auburn. 'I expect she had a headache? I thought she was not looking quite herself.' Her eyes surveyed them greedily, hoping for a titbit of scandal.

'Not exactly, ma'am. I think she was taken unwell after supper. Of course, I am sure it could not have been anything she ate...' With a small smile and another polite inclination, Deverham left this small shaft to do its work and escorted Patience to the carriage.

'Really, Charles,' she said in some amusement when they were moving, 'you cannot go about saying that Lady Auburn served bad food at her ball!'

'It's no more than she deserved,' he said callously. 'I shan't mention it to anyone else, anyway, but she doesn't know that. Maybe she'll keep her mouth shut about Florence. In the meantime, we must pray that we find her safe and sound at home.'

Their prayers were not answered. Admitted by a sleepy butler, they at once saw that no one had returned from the ball. Patience ran swiftly upstairs to Florence's room, where her yawning maid awaited her return. Everything was as it should be, and the maid quite obviously knew nothing. Deverham waited impatiently in the morning-room, and when Patience returned, white-faced, he promptly sent the butler away on the pretext of requiring some warm milk for Miss Winterbourne.

'Charles, she has vanished! What are we to do? Can she have been kidnapped, do you think?'

'From the middle of a crowded ballroom? Unlikely, I think. I pity anyone who tried to abduct Florence, she would make mincemeat of them. No, she must have gone willingly, but where? Someone must have seen something. I'll have to go back. Wait here, and don't worry. You'll have to think of some story for the butler.'

This proved to be a task almost beyond Patience's ability. She was aware that her stammering recital of the sudden illness of a relative, of Miss Florence's instant errand of succour, did not ring very true. The butler said nothing, but his look expressed his opinion of the idea that he should believe that the young lady should go in the middle of the night, in a masquerade gown, without so much as a change of clothing, and without sending for her maid. He withdrew with dignity, every line of his body expressing his opinion of such goings-on in a respectable household.

Deverham was not long in returning. With the pretext of a lost watch, he had been able to engage the servants on duty at the Countess's door in conversation. A small gift of money had been enough to ascertain that a young lady, all in white, had left alone some hours earlier, requesting that a hansom be summoned for her. The servants had thought it odd, certainly, but she had paid well, and it was not their place to ask questions. As to the destination of the cab, they had no idea.

Patience sat silent, her hands clasped so tightly that her knuckles stood out white. She was pale to her lips, and Charles came to sit beside her, laying one hand comfortingly over hers, and putting the other arm round her.

'Do not despair. We know that she went of her own accord, and also that it was not planned. Surely she would have found some way of taking something with her, a few clothes, and her jewels, for instance, if she had intended to do this? She is not a fool, my dear.'

'But so young, and in my care,' whispered Patience through trembling lips. 'If I had been there, in the ballroom, as I should have been... Oh, Charles, I cannot but blame myself.'

'Then you must blame me too, and I know you will not.'

'What shall we do?'

'I do not know.' She looked at him, stricken. 'Do not look at me like that! This is something quite new to my experience. I do not know how to find one seventeen-year-old girl who has vanished, in the middle of the night, from a society ball.'

'Do you think... the police, perhaps?'

'Not unless you want the whole thing reported in the newspapers, tomorrow or the next day. That is what makes it so difficult. If she were a servant, or a child... but a young girl, with a reputation to lose... our hands are tied.'

Patience closed her eyes for a moment to press back the tears that welled in them. He saw the movement.

'Nevertheless, we cannot just sit here! At least, I cannot. I must go out and look for her, at least.'

'But where?'

He groaned.

'Anywhere. Everywhere. I hardly know. I will start at the Countess's house, and go from there. If I know Florence, she will not have gone anywhere unpleasant, or unfashionable, if she can help it.'

'If she can help it,' echoed Patience dully. Then she sat up straight, her eyes wide. 'Hush! What was that?'

'I heard nothing,' Charles began, when the sound came again, louder this time. Knocking, at the front door. Patience jumped up and flew to the door of the morning-room, reaching the hall just as the butler, long-suffering mingled with curiosity on his face, opened the front door. Florence, radiant and immaculate, danced indoors.

'Oh, hello, Aunt Patience! Did you wait up for me? There was no need! Oh, you are there too, Deverham.'

'As you see,' he responded sternly, his gaze moving from her to the figure that had followed her indoors. A large gentleman, neatly but unfashionably attired, with a pair of bright blue eyes in a deeply suntanned face, he bowed with much correctness to Patience and Deverham.

'That's very good, because I wanted to talk to you,' said Florence cheerfully.

'Not half so much as I want to talk to you,' he replied grimly. Patience, with a start, caught the butler's fascinated eye and with a few low words dismissed him, to his great and obvious regret.

'Well, you will have to wait, because I have something very important to tell you. You will never guess what has happened!'

'Florence!' interrupted Patience, unable to bear it any longer. 'Where have you been? We have been very worried about you!'

'Really? I can't think why. Anyway, I'm back now, and what do you think?'

'I think,' said Deverham through his teeth, 'that you are about to get that hiding I once promised you, but with interest!'

The stranger, who, unintroduced, had till now stayed modestly in the background, stepped forward and interposed his bulk between Florence and Deverham.

'You will forgive my interfering,' he said in a deep, calm voice, 'but I cannot allow you to lay a finger on this lady.'

'And who the hell are you?' Deverham was in no mood for the niceties.

'I have the honour to be, sir, or at least I hope to be, this young lady's intended husband.'

'Are you, by God? Well, so am I, and I believe I have the prior claim. You may beat her afterwards, and welcome.'

'Sir! To offer violence to a lady—any lady—cannot be called the conduct of a gentleman. But one so young, so fair, so delicate...' Words seemed to fail him.

'Young, and fair, maybe, but as for delicate! My advice to you is, to tame her like the shrew she is!'

A brick-coloured flush of anger could be seen below that deep tan. Florence, quite unmoved, was watching with bright-eyed interest, clearly enchanted to have two men fighting over her. Patience, who had been thinking, decided that it was time she intervened.

'Charles,' she said in a gentle voice. At once the look of anger left his face, to be replaced by a reluctant grin.

'Well, it was good advice, you know,' he said. She ignored him, going up to the stranger.

'We have not been introduced, I think. I am Florence's aunt. And you are, you must be, though I can scarcely believe it, Captain Curbridge?'

'Yes, Miss Winterbourne, and honoured to make your acquaintance.'

She gave him her hand, liking what she saw, and turned. 'I must make you known, sir, to Lord Deverham, my fiancé.'

'Yours? But he said just now he was engaged to Florence!'

Florence came to his side, hanging on his arm and scolding him fondly.

'Oh, Anthony! I explained all that to you, before! You cannot have been attending. That was all a pretence, I am not really engaged to him.'

Charles stepped forward, his hand outstretched.

'Forgive me, my dear Captain. I am afraid I was a little hasty with you, but if you knew how worried Florence's aunt has been ... she was with you all the time, I suppose?'

Rather bemused, Captain Curbridge shook the proffered hand.

'Yes, of course, and perfectly safe. I am afraid that I, too, reacted too swiftly. The fact is, everything has happened so suddenly, I hardly know whether I am on my head or my heels!'

'I think you speak for all of us,' agreed Deverham. 'Late though it is, I think we must have our explanations at once. Perhaps in a less public place?' He raised an eyebrow at Patience, who rang the bell. The butler appeared with suspicious alacrity.

'Is there a fire in the small drawing-room? Good. Then please bring some brandy for the gentlemen, and tea for Miss Florence and myself. Then you may go to bed. The gentlemen will see themselves out, and I shall lock the door myself.'

'Very good, miss.' Somehow the butler packed a wealth of meaning into his expressionless tones. When they were comfortably seated, and he had finally withdrawn, Patience turned to Captain Curbridge.

'Perhaps the story will come more comprehensibly from you. The story of your death was obviously mistaken?'

'Yes. The ship went down, and I and three of the crew reached the shore of Africa. It was a benighted place, and it was many weeks before we reached a place where we might take a ship for home. My letter warning my family was lost, and I arrived in Bristol to find that they were all in London, so I followed them here.'

'And I did not even know that my dear Lavinia was in London! She had not been here more than two days, and her letter to me had gone to Manchester!'

'And you saw her at the ball?'

'Yes! At least, I would not have recognised her, because she was masked, and I did not expect to see her, but I saw Anthony! I could not be mistaken in him!'

'You were at the ball, then?' Patience, familiar with Florence's haphazard style of storytelling, was eager to have it told by Captain Curbridge.

'Yes. Arriving in London yesterday, and after a joyful reunion with my family, my first concern was to ask for news of Florence. Only to learn, to my sorrow, that she was promised to Another.' He looked down, pausing, and Deverham tightened his lips on a smile as he met Patience's glinting look. 'I knew, of course, that I had no claim, no claim at all, on her.' He looked earnestly at Deverham. 'Even now, my lord, you have only to speak——'

'Not at all, not at all, dear fellow,' said Deverham quickly. 'You are entirely welcome to her. I mean,' he added, seeing the other's clouded look, 'I would not dream of coming between two hearts so miraculously rejoined. Yours, after all, was the prior claim.'

'Not really,' pursued Captain Curbridge, doggedly. 'I was never in a position to propose to Florence, before. I would not have presumed.'

'Oh, Anthony, don't be so stuffy!' begged Florence.

'Pray continue with your tale, Captain Curbridge. I do so want to hear what happened. How did you come to be at the ball?'

'As I said, I heard of her engagement—with what feelings, you may imagine—from my sister. She had an invitation to the masquerade, as did my younger brother and my parents, and she guessed that Florence would be there. All I wanted, all I ever hoped for, was to see her one last time. I did not expect to speak to her, and certainly I did not mean to reproach her. I just wished to look at her, and be sure that she was happy. So, with my sister's connivance, I took my brother's place.'

'But I saw him immediately!' put in Florence. 'When we were dancing. I couldn't believe my eyes, at first, but even with a mask on I recognised him straight away. It was so wonderful! Of course, I had to go to him at once!'

'Of course,' said Deverham, with another smile for Patience.

'Well, so I did, but when I got to him, he was gone!'

'My courage failed me,' the Captain said with manly simplicity. 'I had come prepared to see her, a happy bride, but when I saw her! So sad, so frightened! It was more than I could bear. I knew that if I stayed another moment, I might make an unseemly fracas, my lord, so I left in haste.'

'Well, thank heaven for that!' exclaimed Deverham. 'It was bad enough being abandoned in the middle of the floor, but to be set upon by a complete stranger, newly returned from the dead . . . I should never have lived it down!'

'I know, and Florence has explained it all to me . . . I think. But need you have been quite so severe with her, my lord? To see her made so unhappy was a dreadful sight.'

Deverham cast a fulminating glance at Florence, who was giggling delightedly.

'I am a *very* good actress, am I not? Never mind, Charles, I shall make him understand in the end. He wasn't really so cruel to me, Anthony. At least, only when he threatened to spank me, and he hasn't done it.'

'Yet, my girl. I'm not promising that my wedding gift to the Captain will not be a dozen well-seasoned birches.'

'So, of course, I went after him,' continued Florence blithely. 'That is, I spoke to Lavinia first, naturally, to find out their address. Only, when I got there, Anthony had not come home! Wasn't it a pity!'

'I did not feel I could go back to the house, feeling as I did. I went for a walk.'

'How very abstemious,' murmured Deverham. The two men's eyes met, and for the first time they exchanged a look of smiling complicity.

'Yes, well, fortunately. And equally fortunately, I returned before the rest of my family, and found Florence waiting for me.'

'It did not occur to you, Florence, to ask your young friend to accompany you back to her house?' suggested Deverham.

'Oh, no. I did not want anyone else there, to spoil things! Besides,' added Florence severely, 'Lavinia was so enjoying the ball, and I would not dream of depriving her of her pleasure.'

'If you had only let me know,' pleaded Patience. 'I was very worried, you know, and had it not been for Charles's good sense I might have called out the police to search for you.'

'That would have been silly, Aunt Patience. You know I can take care of myself. Besides, you were nowhere to be seen, and I thought Deverham had probably taken you off to make more pretty speeches to you. I would not have liked to interrupt you.' She observed her aunt's expression, and laughed. 'I was right, then! Then you must forgive me. You had your pretty speeches, and I so wanted to have mine! You are not cross with me, are you, Aunt?'

'Not now that I know that you are safe. I only hope that Captain Curbridge will be able to take better care of you than I have done.'

'I am afraid that I have been rather premature,' said the Captain in some gloom. 'I should not have spoken to Florence without her grandmother's consent.'

'I should be prepared to hazard a tidy sum that she did most of the speaking for herself,' said Deverham drily. The other man gave a quiet smile.

'She has such an open, confiding nature,' he said.

'Yes, hasn't she?' agreed Patience. 'Of course, if tonight's episode ever became known, there would be nothing for it but for the two of you to marry, anyway.' A happy smile from Florence showed that this had not escaped her. 'Nevertheless, I cannot speak for my mother, nor for Florence's trustees.'

'In other circumstances I should hesitate to mention it, but my situation in life has recently improved.'

'He found a diamond mine!' put in the irrepressible Florence. 'Isn't it lovely!'

'Hush, dear.' The tone was gentle, the look mild, but to her amazement Patience saw her wilful niece fold her hands quietly in her lap, her eyes fixed on the Captain's sunburned features, the picture of obedience.

'I was fortunate enough, while in Africa, to make a discovery of some significance,' he admitted modestly. 'I think I may say that I shall be able to give Florence every luxury she might desire. My birth, though I am not noble, may be said to be equal to hers, and I shall resign my captaincy.'

'Will you not mind that?' asked Patience.

'Mind? If I can have Florence for a wife, how could I think of going off on long voyages?'

'Then it's all right, then? Oh, Anthony, how happy I am!' Florence cast herself into her beloved's arms, and with some embarrassment he returned her kisses before informing her firmly that it was long past her bedtime, and he would see her to the foot of the stairs, and call on Lady Winterbourne first thing in the morning. Patience watched with a fascinated eye as once again Florence obeyed without demur. At the doorway Captain Curbridge turned.

'She's a good little thing really,' he confided. 'It's just a question of knowing how to handle her.' With a shy smile and a courteous bow, he was gone, closing the door with careful consideration behind him. Patience and Charles looked at one another.

'A good little thing...!'

'Knowing how to handle her...!'

Their eyes met in an ecstasy of laughter. Later, wiping her brimming eyes on a handkerchief, Patience said:

'What will Mama say, do you think?'

'About Florence? Nothing, she will be too busy saying things about us.'

'Yes, she will be a little ... surprised.'

He stood up and pulled her to her feet in front of him. She would have gone into his arms, but he held her off, his hands on her shoulders, and looked down into her eyes.

'You will not let her talk you out of this? She may try, you know.'

'Of course she will, but I shall not take any notice. I have never really needed to stand up to her before, but it does not mean to say that I cannot. I am afraid she will try every trick in the book: tears, the vapours, threats of a relapse, but, as the gallant Captain said, it's just knowing how to handle her, and heaven knows I have had plenty of practice at that!'

'Do you want her to live with us?'

'No. Does that shock you? But it would not do. Of course, she is always welcome to visit, but she should have her own home, with a paid companion. It should not be too difficult to arrange.'

His hands slid down her arms, and lifted her hands to his lips, one after the other, kissing first the backs, then the palms. As he released them she slid them from his lips to his cheeks, and round his neck.

'Queen of my heart,' he whispered, for the third time, as his lips met hers.

ROMANCING
THE PHONE

Win the romantic holiday of a lifetime for two at the exclusive Couples Hotel in Ocho Rios on Jamaica's north coast with the Mills & Boon and British Telecom's novel competition, 'Romancing the Phone'.

This exciting competition looks at the importance the telephone call plays in romance. All you have to do is write a story or extract about a romance involving the phone which lasts approximately two minutes when read aloud.

The winner will not only receive the holiday in Jamaica, but the entry will also be heard by millions of people when it is included in a selection of extracts from a short list of entries on British Telecom's 'Romance Line'. Regional winners and runners up will receive British Telecom telephones, answer machines and Mills & Boon books.

For an entry leaflet and further details all you have to do is call 01 400 5359, or write to 'Romancing the Phone', 22 Endell Street, London WC2H 9AD.

You may be mailed with other offers as a result of this application.

Unwrap romance this Christmas

A Love Affair
LINDSAY ARMSTRONG

Valentine's Night
PENNY JORDAN

Man on the Make
ROBERTA LEIGH

Rendezvous in Rio
ELIZABETH OLDFIELD

Put some more romance into your Christmas, with four brand new titles from Mills & Boon in this stylish gift pack.

They make great holiday reading, and for only £5.40, it makes an ideal gift.

The special gift pack is available from 6th October. Look out for it at Boots, Martins, John Menzies, W.H. Smith, Woolworths and other paperback stockists.